MW00474916

IRON CHAMBER OF MEMORY

Books by John C. Wright

IRON CHAMBER OF MEMORY

JOHN C. WRIGHT

Iron Chamber of Memory

John C. Wright

Published by Castalia House
Kouvola, Finland
www.castaliahouse.com

Editor: Vox Day
Cover Art: RGUS

Acknowledgements

The author thanks David Lindsay and Tim Powers for their inspiration, Jeffrey Nowland for his generosity, and Saul and Justin and one other whose name I do not write, for their protection, and guidance, and above all, hope.

I STILL keep open Memory's chamber: still
Drink from the fount of Youth's perennial stream.
It may be in old age an idle dream
Of those dear children; but beyond my will
They come again, and dead affections thrill
My pulseless heart, for now once more they seem
To be alive, and wayward fancies teem
In my fond brain, and all my senses fill.

...

—Lord Rosslyn (1833–1890)

Contents

Prologue: The White Boneyard

Standing and frowning in the New York snow, Hal Landfall realized he did not recall the name of the woman pushing his mother's wheelchair toward his father's grave.

He had been overseas for the last four years, studying. It now seemed all too long since he had last been home. He remembered how his sister Elaine had insisted he go abroad, that he take advantage of the rare opportunity being afforded him. In less than a year, their father's health declined like a rapid childhood in reverse: there was a day when his last tooth fell out, a day when he took his last upright step, a day when he spoke his last word.

When he offered to abandon his studies and come home, Elaine talked him out of it. She vowed that she could shoulder all duties their father had so carefully performed in watching and tending their mother. Hal could not recall, even among his simplest, earliest memories, a day when his mother had been entirely well.

Elaine said she recalled the brighter days of their childhood, when their mother could play with her children, sit on the nursery floor and roll a ball, clap and sing rhymes, and hold them as they repeated their bedtime prayers.

But he remembered little more than the bedroom door, looming in the darkness. He had to reach over his head to touch the knob. Shouts and screams of different voices—but voices he always knew were his mother's too—would come from the door. Young Hal was forbidden to touch the door, even when nightmares woke him at midnight, and he needed a gentle voice or loving hand. Dad told him to be nice to the woman with the wild and empty eyes, be nice and not upset her. He never told Hal what upset her or why. Hal tried not to complain when she bit him.

Elaine said she recalled custard they once had shared, something actually made by their mother in the kitchen, not bought from a store, not take out. Father never cooked.

As his eyes got bad and his hands shook, Father still prepared the needle for Mom's injections. He carried her upstairs and downstairs. There was a wheelchair on every floor. He spoon-fed her. He carried her to the bathroom. He said she had no weight.

Hal had been in England when it happened. It happened suddenly. He talked to them both. Elaine had passed the telephone to their mother, but Mrs. Landfall did not remember who Hal was.

Instead she kept talking about a black dog. "I hate the black dog," she said, in the voice one might use when confiding a secret to a stranger met by chance. "Sometimes I see him stand upright on the road, under the streetlight outside the window. The black dog howled when Henry went. I think he was laughing at me. I'll get up in a moment, as soon as I've rested. I have to remember how to walk. I don't remember what it feels like."

Elaine was not at the funeral. His sister was snowed in, trapped in some Midwestern airport until further notice, and, with Hal returning to the British Isles that same day, it had seemed impossible to cancel or delay.

Mounts of white snow were on all the gravestones. The angels wore caps and cloaks of white, as did the spears of the fence. Beyond the fence, Hal could see the East River, and the traffic moving slowly through the gray weather. It seemed unfair that so many people would have so many places to go, families and friends unmarred by tragedy. Hal felt a bitterness in his heart; it was as if the world could tolerate to continue only because it forgot the tortures of the world.

After the priest was done saying the words, Hal tucked the hawk-headed walking stick he always carried under one arm, stooped, and reached down to take his mother's ungloved hand. There was neither a cap on her head nor a scarf at her neck, and the sweater was old enough that he remembered it from his youth, a favorite of hers to be worn in all weathers, but now festooned with holes. There was no one left to patch them.

"Who are you?" she said.

"I am your son. I am Hal," he told her. He gave his mother a warm smile, but there was ice behind his eyes as he glared at the nurse standing behind the wheelchair with a bored look on her face. The woman was dumpy and potato-shaped. "You don't seem dressed warmly enough!"

"Henry will take care of me," said Mom. "He always takes care of me. Did you hear Father O'Brien just now? I don't know why they made me come out here on a day like this. I might miss my programs!" She looked cross. "What is going on? Who died? Was it someone I know? I want to ask Henry about it. He said he would come to see me!"

Hal did not realize at first what she meant. When her rambling words finally sank into his soul, he felt as if they left burn marks there. He patted her hand, unable to speak. She looked at him benevolently in the way one might look at a kindly stranger.

She was shivering now. She wore no hat over her grey and thinning hair. Snowflakes were landing on her head, and she did not even raise a hand to brush them away.

"If I could remember where I put the door key, I would let years flow in. Rose and silver-white and iron! And gold beyond that! Old years, green years, and the good ones would wear all white. Oh!

How I adored the crowns and the trumpets! So pretty! Henry knows where I put it. He always takes care of me. Where is he? Where did he go? I was talking to him just now."

Hal straightened up and looked around. There had been other mourners, two veterans from Mr. Landfall's old unit, his partner and one loyal customer from his days running a bookstore, a student he had tutored, and a neighbor. All had said their farewells earlier, and were drifting away, silent, down the paths out of the little churchyard and back into crowded streets where tall buildings loomed, indifferent. Hal glanced left and right, looking to find his sister, even though he knew that she was not coming, that she could not come.

He glared again at the nurse. Elaine had told him her name, but it escaped him now. "Where is this place you keep her? Who are you?"

The nurse gave her name and the name of the sanitarium. Saint something or other. Hal asked her to take his mother inside, into someplace better, and into a warmer outfit.

The fat nurse shrugged, wearing the same serene expression as a cow chewing a cud, and said indifferently, "We all want some place better, honey. Don't mind me. I just do what I'm told. They say take her out, I take her out. You say take her back in, I'll take her back in. No problem."

Hal's hand tightened on his walking stick, as if it had a mind of its own that was toying with the idea of bludgeoning the nurse with it. Was no one actually taking care of his mother?

Mrs. Landfall must have been following part of the conversation, for her trembling voice broke in, querulous: "When can I go home? Henry will take me home."

The casket had been closed the whole time. Hal insisted on that point when Elaine had been making arrangements. Seeing their father lying motionless inside it would have been terrible for his poor senile mother, a punishment worse than anything she deserved.

The priest, a bent-backed, bald, short man with an odd, sad smile, and eyebrows of astounding size and color that looked like two albino caterpillars on his forehead, came over to them. He spoke in a soft, kind voice to Mrs. Landfall. Hal did not hear what the priest said, but his mother's reply was sharp and clear in the cold air: "I'll have Henry leave it for you in the black iron moly chamber in the church, so you'll remember."

The old priest turned to Hal, put out his hand, "So this is Little Henry?" The priest had to crane his head to look up at Hal, who towered over him. "Father O'Brien, Henry. Your mother has often spoken of you. We hope for great things, heroic things, in the struggles ahead. Keep your sword always by you, and your prayers ready at hand, eh? These sorrows, these present sorrows, will melt when this world melts, eh! The last enemy to be conquered is death, but there are others before it. You are deployed to England, I understand?"

Hal was puzzled by the little man's odd behavior, "Did Mother tell you I was a soldier or something?"

The little priest raised his oversized eyebrows. "Well, she said, ah…"

Hal smiled mirthlessly. "I am in England working on my master's degree. At Saint Magdalene College. Elaine arranged the funeral so I could come during Christmas holiday. Did she think I was in the army? My mother, I mean. Not Elaine."

The little priest smiled back, albeit enigmatically. "We serve in the hosts of the light, and you are born of a great warrior. For *we* wrestle *not against flesh and blood*, but against principalities, against *powers*, against the rulers of the darkness of this world."

Hal was unsure he was hearing the priest properly. The words were strange, unearthly. He vaguely thought he had heard something like this before, but the memory eluded him. He shook his head sharply, and said, "My father served in the Navy for five years before I was born. She does not remember me. That must be what she is thinking of, his military career. She does not know me."

"No, she speaks of you often."

"We are both named Henry. I am Henry, Junior. I go by Hal."

"But if you are not kept away by your official duties, then why weren't you here earlier, when your mother needed help?"

Later, Hal did not recall what he answered, or even if he answered. They were interrupted by a commotion. In the distance, through the snow, beyond the belt of trees and the low fence of wrought iron surrounding the churchyard, was a city street filled with gray snow and honking cars. Some stray dog, a big, black mutt, was motionless in the intersection, barking at a truck, and the cars had stopped.

At that point, mother became hysterical, and the nurse took her back into the church. The little priest took out a small stoppered bottle of liquid and his prayer beads, and walked toward the fence, toward the noise of the barking. Hal was alone. Only the two gravediggers were left, stony-faced foreign-looking young men, who were cranking the geared wheels to lower the casket into the ground.

Hal stood in the snow. He wanted to follow his mother and comfort her, but he did not move. He shifted his soaked feet in the snow uneasily, his best shoes wetted, a fierce look on his square and simple face, as if he wanted to strike someone or break something.

He wanted an explanation from his sister about this sanitarium where his mother had been abandoned. Why was she not staying at Elaine's apartment, as they had so often discussed? What sort of institution could it be, what sort of venal fools ran it that would so negligently send old ladies out to funerals in the snow without a coat?

He wanted to yell at his sister, but her absence robbed him of that release.

And more than that, he wanted an explanation from the priest about this world where his mother had been abandoned. Had Heaven forgotten mankind? What kind of world was it that so negligently, so cruelly, allowed a helpless woman's husband to decline so swiftly, and die so suddenly, when he was so needed?

But Hal had a taxi to catch, holiday crowds with whom to wrestle, and an airplane to board, and a sea to cross. He stalked away from the cemetery with none of his questions answered.

Chapter 1

The Island Untouched by Time

Green-Eyed Girl

"Should it be horribly *improper* were we to break in?"

From behind him in the wooded twilight, the voice of the green-eyed girl was dry and arch, a slow music in her throat. She was the fiancée of his best friend, Manfred Hathaway, who had been his roommate during their undergraduate years at Oxford. He had just inherited this island. He had been Hal's only friend at school, and the only one to share his dreams and his solemn oath. When she came along, at first he resented her as an intruder, but soon she grew into a dear friend and the third member of their circle. Her name was Laurel du Lac.

He came free of the last trees of the forest path. Hal Landfall wondered why a thrill of disquiet ran through him as he beheld, through the stone pillars of the ancient gate, tall and angular on the crest above him, gigantic in the gloom, the High House of Wronger-wood. He had been so eager to come, to see the survivals from the period of late antiquity that he studied and so loved. In the dialect spoken by the islanders, the house was also called *La Seigneurie*, the Master-house.

This was the fastness and the residence of the Seigneur of the Island of Sark. Queen Elizabeth the First had granted letters patent to one Helier de Carteret, Seigneur of St. Ouen in Jersey, granting him and his heirs Sark as a fief in perpetuity, provided he kept the island free of pirates, and occupied by at least forty of her subjects.

All the windows were dark. The chimneys were unlit, free of smoke. Four towers, each of different shape and height, rose against the stars like the horns of a beast.

Hal Landfall felt that strange sensation called *déjà vu*, as if he had been here before, standing in a spot like this, staring uphill at the dark and oddly eclectic mansion, with a girl one half-step behind him.

Her voice was as gentle as the rustle of the young leaves beneath the caress of the scented wind of the early spring night, or the murmur of the waves caressing the beach. "I've never felt so very *felonious* before!"

The Unmet Visitor

Hal had waited nearly until sunset for Manfred Hathaway to keep his promise, and meet him with a horse cart, and show him the house and island he had unexpectedly inherited last year. The island was charming, and Hal felt strangely at home surrounded by this glimpse of living history, as he never felt in the streets of New York or London. Hal's impatience grew unbearable. He wanted Manfred to come and introduce to him the treasures of this small island. Who knew what quaint and forgotten things, the flotsam of time, were here?

Neither the constable nor the seneschal, nor any of the villagers in shouting distance, seemed to know what could have become of Manfred, their new Seigneur.

Hal therefore left his luggage at the dock, under a tarp, with no one to watch it and no fear whatever that anyone would molest it.

A dozen times he drew out his little black appointment book (where he also jotted down notes and questions, as the thought struck him, for his dissertation), and checked the date. It was February, two months after his father's funeral. The college was not in session, and this was one of the few trips he had been able to afford. The December flight to New York had wiped out nearly all of his stipend for the current semester, and only the urgency of the request from his friend had sufficed to summon him from his books.

In his appointment book he had jotted down the address of the manor house. *Le Seigneurie. Sark, Guernsey. Rade Street.*

It was not hard to navigate. As he strolled through the tiny town, with its stone houses and clay chimney pots and horse-drawn carriages, Hal saw rustic men doff their caps to their womenfolk, or greet with a bow the parish priest. That worthy raised his hand in a gesture of blessing Hal had ere now seen only in images in tapestries or stained glass. From the sight of things, these folk were closer in their works and ways to the days of yore than any recent generation. It was as if the common people from the time period of his studies had been preserved, but not the knights and ladies, holy hermits, wise men nor sacred kings. What was knighthood now in England, save an honor paid successful rock stars for being filthy rich?

Here, the jeering vulgarity of the modern age seemed absent. The timelessness was enchanting to him. The forgotten world seemed but a step or two away. He wished he knew in what direction that step lay! He resolved to stay here, rather than in Oxford town, while doing the onerous work on his dissertation; he hoped the surroundings would inspire him when his willpower flagged.

The island's one inn, a refurbished sixteenth-century farmhouse owned by the Stocks family, was within view of the dock at Port du Moulin, and there was only one main road from which every other path branched, running over steep green hills, tall standing stones, past sheep pastures, apple orchards, and farms, running south to north along the spine of the island. The north end of the island was rougher ground, unsuitable for farming, and covered with a few acres of wild trees as old as the last Ice Age.

All the coastline to the north was interrupted by looming rocks, narrow coves, and booming caves. The south was crisscrossed under the earth with mining tunnels. It would have been a smuggler's paradise here, and Hal wondered how the first seigneur had kept his promise to clear the pirates away.

It was remarkably dark under the trees. The path as it climbed grew tricky and rocky, in places like a staircase, with stones and ruts harder to see as the sun failed. Hal was unnerved when he thought he heard soft, light footsteps padding after him in the deepening gloom.

He waited, gripping his walking stick, wondering at his sudden, unexpected sense of fear. There was nothing dangerous on this small and rustic island, surely. But why were the footsteps so quiet, and so stealthy? And what had happened to Manfred?

So he hid himself behind the bole of an ancient oak by the side of the path, waiting. When the sound of the stealthy, half-inaudible footfalls passed him by, he stepped out suddenly behind his pursuer.

She gave a yelp of surprise, and then burst into a merry laugh, seizing him around the waist. Hal found himself suddenly in the strangely familiar embrace of a girl in black silk. Reflexively, his arms closed around her, tightening as if to protect her. She clung to him, as if in fear, even though she had been the one pursuing him. She buried her face in his chest, as if she was a woman crying, but his shirt remained dry. The movement knocked the wide straw hat she had been wearing from her head and it fell silently to the ground. As the evening breeze blew over her hair, a burst of well-known fragrance, like honeysuckle after a spring rain, assailed his nostrils.

Suddenly remembering himself, Hal released her. With a lingering squeeze, Laurel let go of him as well, and she stepped back, breathless.

Her hair was dark as a thundercloud. She currently wore it up, but Hal knew that when it was unbound, it fell well past her hips, brushing the curve of her calves. Her eyes were green as glass, and glinted in the dark like the eyes of a she-wolf, large and expressive. Her skin was the fairest he had ever seen, free from moles or freckles, eerie in its porcelain whiteness. She was not an outdoorsy girl, though she had the vivid, high-cheekboned features that spoke of Spanish or Italian blood, or perhaps of a long-lost ancestor from Araby. Her lips were wide and full, and her smile was full of mischief.

Like Hal himself, she preferred to dress in a modest and old-fashioned style. Her wanton masses of hair were pinned up high in a Gibson, a coiffeur so large it made her head seem small in comparison and exposed a graceful neck. She wore a high, starched collar, a blue bow tie, a dark blouse of silk with opal studs, a dark sash nearly as wide as a man's cummerbund, and a long skirt that brushed her black-leather, high-topped buttoned shoes. The vintage, narrow-waisted style she affected could have been designed with her in mind, so elegantly did it frame her timeless charms.

Her motions and gestures were poised and graceful, as if she were a ballerina. The footfalls that had pursued him had been light, not due to any deliberate stealth, but rather to a naturally fawnlike gait.

"You so startled me." In the deepening twilight, her voice sounded unexpectedly close and low, almost a whisper.

She explained that she had been waiting in the inn for Manfred since yesterday. "He was supposed to meet me, to show me the new house he inherited. But he forgot. When I saw you from the window walking up the Rue de Sermon, I called out, but you did not hear me. I trotted after you this whole way, waving, but you never turned to look. And once you were in the woods, the path bent and twisted, so you were never in sight. But I am not one to give up so easily!"

"My apologies," he said gallantly, inclining his head.

He was extremely glad to see her. In part because a familiar face was always a comfort when one was alone in a strange place, but mainly because, upon seeing her, he was struck by the cheering thought that while Manfred might conceivably forget one of them or the other, he was hardly likely to forget them both!

Hal had known her over the last two years, as she and Manfred had been seeing each other steadily. The two of them had put off their wedding until after Manfred's dissertation was due at the end of the spring term. Hal had been selected as best man, and he took his duties seriously. He determined to be as fiercely loyal to Laurel as he was to Manfred. When at the University, he made it his mission in life to keep other students and professors from coming between Manfred and Laurel.

They spent a few moments looking for her dropped hat, gradually circling out from the path as they searched, but the did not find it. It seemed the wind had taken it away and hidden it somewhere among the trees. He found the size of them oddly disquieting, rather like seeing a cow taller than a man. They were giants; it was an old-growth forest. It was amazing to him that in all the years back before the reach of history, despite all the boats and ships that sailed forth from France and from England, no mariner ever cut down these mighty boles for ships, no crofter for planks, no shepherd for firewood.

He called off the search, saying the two would have to come back in daylight. She took his hand playfully.

"Now you have to lead me there. I don't know this path. I've never been here, not at night, I mean. Small wonder they call it Wrongerwood! Everything about it is wrong."

He said, "Is that really the reason for the name?"

"No, *Wronger* is a corruption of the French. Like most things English, I suppose. It comes from *Rongeur d'Os*. It means Wood of the Gnawer-of-Bones. Lovely name, don't you think? After the ghastly hound which supposedly haunts this forest. But perhaps we can we talk of something more pleasant?"

He agreed to change the subject, and they walked under the trees together as the world grew darker.

He asked her about the house and the island, and she told him what she knew.

The Unlit Isle

The island of Sark rose sharply from the sea eighty miles south of England, between Jersey and Guernsey. It was small, inhabited by less than a thousand souls all told. Magdalen College, where Hal and Manfred first met, was more populous. He tried to recall how many people lived in his dormitory; it was entirely possible that there were more people living there than were now present on the island.

There was one abandoned silver mine on the south spur of the island, called Little Sark, and one manor house to the north, on Greater Sark, perched on a promontory rising three hundred feet above the sea. The two segments of Little Sark and Greater Sark were connected by an isthmus called *La Coupée*, a bridge of rock as tall and narrow as a wall. It was three hundred feet long, with a dizzying drop of two hundred sixty feet or more to either side. Before railings were put up, children were wont to crawl across on hands and knees, fearful of being thrown over the side by the powerful winds that often rushed out to sea.

The island's single village held exactly one inn with rooms to let for travelers, whose lower story, which had once been a livery stable, was the public alehouse fronting the road. This macadam road, the only one on the island, had been paved by German prisoners of war. The post office was in back, where the postman, who was also the volunteer constable, and something of a local hero as well, kept his bicycle.

Sark was not just an island in the Channel, it was also apparently an island in the stream of history, stubbornly unchanging. It was the last feudal government in Europe. The seigneur held it as a fief directly from the Crown, and the island landowners held their parcels from him in return for their ceremonial vows of service, duly and properly sworn. The parliament of the isle, called the Chief Pleas, consisted of the Seigneur, the Seneschal, the forty Tenants and the twelve Deputies.

The fiefdom had passed through many hands since the first seigneur. In the nineteenth century, the island had been mortgaged to a privateer named John Allaire in order to keep the mines in operation. The fiefdom was sold thereafter to a family called Collings, whose descendants were the ancestors of the Hathaways.

During World War II, the island, along with the other Channel Islands, was occupied by the Nazis, and ruled by one Kommandant Major Albrecht Lanz in the name of the Third Reich.

In the autumn of 1990, an unemployed nuclear scientist named Andre Gardes, armed with a single semi-automatic weapon, posted notices all around the island proclaiming himself to be the rightful seigneur, and announced his intended invasion, which was scheduled to take place the next day. He arrived as promised in the morning, seated himself in the tiny brick building housing the Court of the Chief Pleas, and declared himself the conqueror of the island.

His reign lasted less than a day: when Dr. Gardes was sitting on a bench after lunch, changing the gun's magazine, Perrée, the volunteer constable, complimented him on his choice of gun and convinced Gardes to remove the magazine and let him admire the weapon. When Dr. Gardes, nuclear scientist, did so, Constable Perrée confiscated the firearm and punched the would-be conqueror in the nose. The weapon now sat in the island's small museum next to old naval bric-a-brack.

By ancient law, the Seigneur of the Island was the only one allowed to keep an unspayed hound, or keep pigeons. All the flotsam and jetsam thrown up by the sea to the beach belonged to him.

In the twenty-first century, Sark was designated by the International Dark Sky Astronomy Association as the first Dark Sky Island in the world, which is to say that Sark was so devoid of any urban light pollution that naked-eye astronomy was possible there.

There was only one ship that regularly made port; she traveled to the island of Guernsey twice a day, on the morning and evening tide, and she did not sail at night.

No automobiles nor motorcycles were permitted on the road and horsepaths, all of which were unlit.

The Unlit House

When he finally saw the house for the first time, dark and tall by the light of the dying day, he was so overtaken by the feeling of lost memory, that, for a moment, he did not hear what the green-eyed girl was telling him.

The architecture was a strange eclectic collection, built over many periods, a graceful jumble that adhered to no coherent plan.

Midmost was a tall circular stone building beneath a squat dome, the remnant of the Priory of Saint Magloire of Dol, built by sixth-century monks. The bottom floor was stone, and the upper stories, built in a later era, were thick wood panels fantastically carved, pierced with small arched windows set with stained glass.

To the east sprang a curving wing built in the seventeenth century, the main hall and living quarters, roofed in slate, with a servant's dorm attached at an angle. The main hall was of dark stone and had a distinctly military look to it, with narrow archers' slits for windows on the bottom story, but broader windows above that were framed by decorative patterns of thick gray rock.

A gold lion, as lithe as a leopard, was inscribed over the main doors of the east wing. Its face was turned toward him, terrible in the deepening dusk. It stood on three paws and raised the fourth, claws extended, while above its back a sinuous tail curved in seeming anticipation.

Behind, to the north, peering over the shoulder of the main hall, was a square tower built in an overwrought Victorian style, fantastic with gables and peaks and tiny black obelisks. Originally these had been two separate structures, but the tower and the north wing were now connected by crenellated gallery, which ran from north to west behind the Priory, enclosing a bed of weeds and hedges in a semicircle. In the middle stood a stone pot the size of a birdbath; it was a quern that had once been used for grinding grain.

To the west was the *colombier*, connected to the gallery by the kitchens and pantry and dining hall, originally separate buildings, now one interconnected pile of corridors, colonnades, and porticos. The *colombier*, or dovecote, was the exuberant exclamation point of the meandering architectural sentence. It was a pale tower with a steep conical roof like a witch's cap, punctured by rows of curiously carven miniature hatches for the birds.

Hal imagined that somewhere, amongst all the various ancient and peculiar laws on the island, there was probably one about doves.

In the foreground was an Edwardian chapel with an octagonal

belltower or carillon at one end, and at the other, past the vestry, a round signal tower, built of stone shipped from Spain. From the roof of the signal tower the mouth of a bronze cannon peered, a remnant of days when privateers ruled this isle.

At the foot of the signal tower was a thing Hal could not quite fathom in the dusk: it was a circular stone track about two yards in diameter, in which a great stone wheel on a wooden arm was contrived to turn and turn again. To one side was a spigot carved like an open-mouthed gargoyle. It looked like some barbaric torture machine. Then he remembered Manfred mentioning a nineteenth-century cider mill, turned by a horse, whose stone wheel could crush the gathered apples.

The house was at the crest of the hill. Beyond the hilltop, Hal could dimly see the crowns and upper branches of the woods that fell like a great, uneven staircase to a beach of shells and pebbles far below. This was steep and tumbling terrain that even the most desperate forester had never tried to log. From the gigantic height and girth of those massive trunks, it was apparent that those serene and ancient trees had never felt the axe of man. This was Wronger Wood, for which Wrongerwood House was named. Beyond were the waters of the Channel. The gray line on the horizon before them might have been a low cloudbank, or the coast of France.

The sun was sinking into the Atlantic, and the red light glanced from square windows and arched windows, and glinted from one round window like a giant's eye peering from beneath the dark eaves.

Then a cloud smothered the dying sun. The windows were black. There were no lights visible either near at hand or far away.

He caught the scent of her perfume as she stepped closer. Hal felt an unexpected tingle as she softly touched his arm.

"Did you not hear me, Hal?"

"I beg your pardon, I was not listening."

No Way In

Laurel said, "I say! You are taking your sweet time to ponder this, Hal. He left us no choice!"

The words were light with gaiety, but there was another and more urgent note beneath. Hal Landfall felt fascinated by her voice, and wondered what that other note meant.

"He and I will be duly wed—Manfred and wife, as it were—in two months, and I will be mistress here. This will be my house, too. At that time, I will remember to retroactively give myself permission to enter here now. That should suffice, should it not?"

Like a small drop in a still pool, insight came to Hal. He knew what the deeper note in her voice meant. It was as if she held the world and herself to be opposing players in a game, a charming game to be played seriously, but not taken seriously. It was a game she meant to win. She must have some personal reason to get into the manor house that she had not mentioned aloud, something more than a mere desire to escape the cold.

Hal had known many women, most of whom were either stoic and hard, or shallow and soft. Laurel was neither. She glided through life with a droll aloofness that was distinctly at odds with the inner *joi de vivre* that he could occasionally glimpse shining through her outer coolness, like a candle seen through a frosted window. Manfred had found himself the perfect woman, an ideal, even. Hal wryly acknowledged the ripple of envy as it ran through his heart.

Hal spoke. "It was not the legality, but the practicality I was pondering, Miss du Lac. You are sure the house is locked? All the doors? Is there no groundskeeper, no parlor maids, or whatever you Englishmen have?"

She smiled. Her teeth were bright and even in the gloom. "You are so formal and old-fashioned! We've known each other for ages!

But of course the Best Man is allowed to call the Bride by her first name. Laurel, please."

"Laurel," he replied obediently, slightly dismayed at how good it felt to say her name.

She said, "And I was here with the Seneschal of the Island yesterday night, and he could not find a way in. I have the key to one of the inside doors. I don't know what happened to Mrs. Levrier. She and her boys are supposed to be looking after things."

"This island is smaller than some golf links I've been on. How can a man disappear? A whole man? Well, let's look under the welcome mat. Maybe he left a note."

He turned his back to the enchanting woman, and shook his head wryly, half-ashamed and half-amused at himself. They had been friends for years. It was not the least bit improper for them to spend time together. But then the two of them had never been alone before, not for any length of time, not in the dark, not on a timeless island that seemed unexpectedly glamorous. He reminded himself not to get carried away with her.

Hal trudged up the slope to the house. The stars here were so bright and so many, that he wondered if there were some strange atmospheric condition over the island to magnify them.

He had no flashlight, and the moon was not up, so Hal was soon reduced to groping, running his hand along the cold gray stone of the walls, searching for a doorway.

The back lawn came into view. In the near distance, in the starlight, he could see ghostly rectilinear outlines of outbuildings, perhaps a stables, or an icehouse, a pumphouse, or servant's quarters. Beyond the outbuildings were boxes that once might have held beehives, solitary walls, and archways standing alone, tall and strange, which once might have opened up on formal gardens. Farther away and down the slope was the fishpond dug by medieval monks to provide for their Friday meals.

The doors of the main hall were some wood too thick and heavy to return an echo when he pounded on them, and were bound in iron. He doubted a battering ram would have dented them.

The golden figure above the door, *lion passant-guardant or*, was bright in the starlight. He could not shake the strange sensation that the yellow beast was a living being, holding still, pretending to be a carving. He was happy to back away from it and circle the house.

The same stone face, with bristling mane, fang bared in silent roar, was carved into each cornerstone of the arched window slits. The eyes were yellow chips of topaz, and pointed at him, no matter where he moved. He told himself it was a trick of his imagination.

Groping, by touch, he walked around the many bays and inlets of the house.

He stumbled across bootscrapers, or hitching rings, set in the lawn, and odd protuberances of stone, gutters carved as gargoyles.

It was futile. He found six doors and one hatch. All of them were locked.

No Way Back

The windows of the main hall were set six feet off the ground. With great difficulty, he clung to the rough stones and pulled himself up. With one hand he fumbled at the casement and the glass, discovering that the windows were small, thick panes set in iron frameworks, with no way to swing open. They were more like the windows of a church than a house, and no wider than eighteen inches. Even if he broke the glass, he could never force his body through the narrow opening.

He was climbing down. As he turned to dismount from the

wall, he misjudged the distance to the ground and stumbled. She, hearing him fall, put out her hands to catch him. For the second time that evening, he found the fragrant warmth of her silken body in his arms.

"Sorry about that," he murmured into her ear. He wondered if the perfumed warmth coming from her masses of hair was a scent, or heat, or both. Perhaps it was an electric aura, for it seemed to tingle and dance. "It is so dark. No one will see us."

No, that was not what he had meant to say. "I– I didn't see you."

She disengaged from him slowly, moving perhaps an inch away, perhaps half an inch. He could feel her breath from her lips on his neck and chin.

"I am a little turned around, I must say," she said, her voice unexpectedly husky. "It was not supposed to be this way. Where is Manfred? Did he forget us?"

She took another step away, and his arms ached to seize her again. The thought that it would serve Manfred right for forgetting them here, leaving them locked out, in the dark, on his half-uncivilized island, in the chill of winter, buzzed in the back of Hal's mind like a fly he could not find and swat.

He sternly dismissed the notion as unworthy of him.

"Who locks their doors in the country, anyway?" he said.

He was slightly out of wind from his climb and stumble. His voice was breathless, rough, and his heart was racing.

"It's the wild beasts. Such savage creatures!" she drawled mockingly.

"Actually, no one is allowed to own dogs on the island, except for Manfred's great-aunt twice removed or whoever. The Seigneur can keep pigeons, but cannot get cell phone coverage."

She said, "Remember he has to keep the island clear of pirates, or else it reverts to the Crown. The English love their queer old laws. Did you know Her Majesty the Queen, personally, owns all the swans that swim the Thames? Counts them once a year in a grand ceremony. There is also a ceremony, the day before Good Friday, where she gives out tupence and thruppence to beggars to sell to coin collectors. I think there is one where the Prime Minister tramples on the face of an Irishman every leap year on Saint Matthew's festival, but the UN Commission on Irish Faces put a stop to that as a condition for letting us out of the European Union."

"I cannot tell when you are joking."

"Always, otherwise life is dour and dull. Getting the manor house wired for electricity is one of the things Manfred was talking about with that dreadful lawyer fellow, Mr. Twokes. There are rules about how many lights can be lit here on Sark... well, speak of the Devil! Look! A light! Someone is here!"

So she spoke as the two came around a corner and saw a lit window. It gleamed in the angle between the north wing and the dovecote like a spark between cupped hands. Halfway up the ancient curving wall of the central priory, twenty or thirty feet off the ground, was a small arched window burning a pale red light. It was dim, furtive, flickering, like a pink star.

Closer, they could see an arch of glass was decorated with the image of a rose in bloom, and a figure of a helmed knight embracing a fish-tailed woman.

Hal shouted up at the window. Silence answered. He shouted again, and then threw pebbles.

"You're making a good deal of racket," said Laurel in a dry, half-mocking voice.

"From the look of it, that is not an electric light. Someone lit a fire, or a lamp," Hal said. "They don't burn forever. I wonder if Manfred is up there."

"No doubt he fell asleep reading some massive, dusty volume on native mesmeric cures for insomnia found among Patagonian Hottentots, or some other such nonsense. Or perhaps he is watching us fumble at his doors as one of his psychological experiments, timing us with his pocketwatch to see how long it takes us to get frustrated."

"Well, I am frustrated now." He glared at the tiny red light, seemingly bright in the great darkness all about him. "I suppose we should go back to the inn?"

She said, "Which way is that?"

Hal turned away from the lit window. The night somehow seemed darker and larger than it had been a moment ago. He could hear the wind moving like some massive beast prowling among the treetops. The rustling noise receded into the distance as the wind passed, mingling with the murmur of the sea caves, the lapping of the shore. Hal thought that if the village had been showing lights, they surely would have been visible from this manor house on the hill.

The starlight was not bright enough to show where the stone gate was. No doubt he could have found it by walking until he saw—or more likely struck—the wall surrounding the manor house lawn, but after that it would be more difficult. Hal imagined trying to follow the twisting dirt path of this automobile-free island through the rocky and uneven ground of the ancient forest in this moonless night, and decided it would be foolish.

He said, "I think one of the things I barked my shin on was a cellar door. That cannot be locked, or how would Manfred get his coal? Or his bottles of wine. Or whatever it is that you Englishmen keep in their cellars."

"British."

"What?"

"I am Cornish. From Cornwall. Not English."

"Isn't that part of England?"

"Just like Canada is part of America, yes. And I don't know whence the *Sercquiais* get their coal. Brought in by boat from Guernsey, I suppose."

She laid her hand on his shoulder. He gave it a comforting pat. They walked through the starlit gloom. He found the slanted wooden trapdoor leading into the cellar as he had before, by barking his shins on it. He stooped and tugged on the handles. The door rattled loudly and loosely in the frame, but did not open.

"This is illegal, you know," he said.

She said airily, "Manfred has no one to blame but himself. Am I supposed to sleep on the wet grass all night? Let's go in together and find a couch. I wouldn't mind a hot bath, or something to eat. We are entitled to some comfort, are we not?"

Hal hesitated, startled. In the gloom, he could not see her expression. He realized that he must be imagining something in her words that was not actually there.

He tugged against the doors, listening to the loose, metallic rattle. The doors could be pulled apart enough for him to thrust his fingers inside, but not his hand. He felt along the doorframe, but could not find whatever latch or chain was holding it shut.

"This does not seem very secure. If I had a crowbar, I might be able...."

She handed him his walking stick that she had been carrying for him. He hefted it.

She said, "You don't think it will snap, do you? The stick, I mean. It's quite heavy."

He absentmindedly fingered the streamlined hawk head of the handle. "My grandfather's. Took it off a German officer he'd killed in the French Alps during the war. The center was bored out and filled with some wonder alloy made by Nazi science. Whatever it is, it never sets off metal detectors in airports."

"I don't want to see an antique suffer damage."

"Things were built more solid in the old days."

"And they spoke more correct as well," she said dryly. "But seriously, one of these buildings behind must be the woodshed. Wouldn't it be more prudent to find an axe, instead?"

"Grampa told me it would never break as long as my heart was pure." And he jammed the heel of the cane between the loose-fitting door leaf and the stone lip, then shoved mightily with both hands.

There was an alarming snap, sounding, to his ears, almost like a thunderclap. A bright flash of lightning dazzled him. The door flew up suddenly, and violently, and the cane handle came loose in his hands. He fell backward, surprised by the sudden lack of resistance, and landed heavily onto the grass.

Chapter 2

The Unremembered Mansion

The Broken Door

"Well, I guess my thoughts were not pure after all," he said, chagrined. "My cane snapped in two."

Laurel approached rapidly in a rustle of silk. She knelt and leaned over him. Her hands felt soft and warm against his chest. Her hair was slightly mussed, for several long, black locks now escaped their futile pins, and when she stooped over him, the stray locks formed a temporary tent between her face and his. For a wild moment he thought she was going to kiss him, and he almost began to lift his face toward hers. But then he realized she was only straining to see him in the gloom.

She straightened up, throwing her loose strands of hair back impatiently. "Are you all right? What happened?"

He stood up, avoiding her eyes as he brushed off his trousers, blushing with the embarrassment of a disaster narrowly avoided. He reminded himself how great a friend, how loyal and devoted, Manfred had been for years, how Laurel trusted him, relying upon him to be the gentleman. He was glad for the darkness, happy that Laurel could not see his face and, thus, could suspect nothing of his shame.

It had been too close a thing. Over the years, he had become accustomed to the wittily dismissive put-downs she delivered to any gentleman with the gall to favor her with unwanted attention. He shuddered at the thought that, but for the accident of the lateness of the hour, he might have been her next target.

"I broke my...."

But the walking stick was whole and hale in his hand, and as he ran his hand over it in the dark, he could feel no scratch or break in its surface.

He gave a low whistle of surprise. "Grampa was right. Remind me to listen to my elders, eh?" Hal turned to her. "What was that flash of light? I thought maybe the metal core of the cane struck against a chain or latch, or... no, that was no spark! It was like a flashbulb going off."

"I did not see any light," Laurel said, surprisingly. She was already going down the stone steps, her knees and hips vanishing under ground.

In the starlight, he could see very little of her, aside from her slender silhouette, and the mass of hair that was escaping its confinement.

"Coming...?" she called lightly. "I don't want to start my life of crime all alone."

"You must have seen it! It was like an explosion!"

"Perhaps you hit your head," she said over her shoulder, as she descended. "I could use a light right about now. This coal cellar at night is as black as a... well, dear me, I am not sure I can think of an apt metaphor at the moment."

She disappeared from view. He walked down the stairs after her, tapping with his walking stick like a blind man's cane.

"Mind your head!" she called back to him. "I think people were shorter back when this was built. Or perhaps the lord of the manor liked seeing his serfs with bruised scalps."

The roof beams were evenly spaced, so he learned to duck them after three or four brain-rattling collisions.

In the pitch darkness, he was acutely aware of what his other senses told him: he felt the warmth in the air, heard the click of her heels, the sigh of her breath, and breathed in the scent of her hair. His collar seemed suddenly tight. As he loosened it, he found himself wondering if perhaps it would have been wiser to dare the darkness and return to the inn.

After a surprisingly long period of groping over dusty boards, bumping into knee-high obstacles, tripping over bulky objects that smelled of rusted iron and cobweb, Hal heard Laurel cry, "I've found the stairs!"

"You are sure they are not the ones we just came down?"

"No." He heard a hollow knocking noise. "These are wood."

And he heard the rattle of a doorknob. He stepped closer, bumping his nose into something feminine, round, and silken. At the same moment, she cried, "No Dens!" and fell backward onto him. He staggered but caught her, just as she was turning to grab at him for support. The stairs must have been as steep as a ladder, and she must have been very high on them, because when she turned to grab for him, her arms went over his head.

He caught her awkwardly, with his hands high on her thighs, as she flopped over onto him, nearly toppling him over. Absurdly, ridiculously, appallingly, he found himself carrying her Tarzan-style, her backside in the air, her stomach resting on his shoulder, and her head hanging down his back. His walking stick clattered to the cellar floor. He heard it roll across the stone slabs, lost somewhere in the utter darkness.

He let her down quickly, stammering an apology. But there was no way to put her feet on the floor that did not involve a very close embrace. The softness of her curves pressed against the hard planes of his body as she slid down him. His hands still encircled her slender waist.

"Sorry," he murmured, taking a rapid step away from her. "You startled me!"

"We do seem to keep bumping into each other!" She laughed in her throat, "Maybe it is animal magnetism. Are you North, or South? In any case, you can try the stairs next. There is some sort of net or booby trap over the door. Be careful. It is locked, but," her voice became a mocking purr, "a great brute like you should be able to force it open."

Her hands pushed him gently forward. They were so small and light-of-touch that he doubted she could have budged him had she shoved with her full strength. Still, he allowed himself to be pushed where she wanted him to go. His foot found the walking stick, almost tripping him as it rolled under his heel. He stooped and took it up. He used the stick to tap on the stairs and then on the door. Waving his hand in the air, he felt the wooden panels and then the knob. It turned easily under his hand. The door opened with a creak. The air beyond was dusty and cool, but free of mold; somehow he could sense it was a larger area than the cellar.

He waved the walking stick before him, encountering air. "What did you bump into? There is nothing here."

"Something shoved me back. It felt like a mattress. Maybe it fell. Don't look at me like you don't believe me!"

He said, "You can't even see my face."

"Women's intuition. I can feel your dubiousness."

"Is that even a word?"

"Perhaps not in America. Don't they instruct you in the English language at Oxford?"

There was no light in this room either. They encountered no furnishings, but Hal's stick clanged loudly onto the box-like metal surface of what might have been a stove, and Laurel said she found hooks in the ceiling, as well as bins and shelves. She said it must be the kitchens.

He heard her opening and shutting drawers. He touched the wall, found the door, and opened it. Beyond was a room whose narrow and high window slits held stars, but the starlight was too weak to find its way to the floor. They were still in the dark.

She came and stood behind him, her hand soft on his shoulder.

Hal automatically put his hand on the wall next to the door, as if expecting to find a lightswitch there, and his fingers fumbled long enough that Laurel, hearing his nails scrape the surface, said, "This house was built before Mr. Edison's lightbulb, remember? Or I should say Mr. Swan's. Did you know he invented the lightbulb before your American Edison? And yet, we Brits get none of the credit."

He uttered a small laugh. "Well, I remember, but my fingers don't. Which way shall we go? The air here is stuffy. I'd like to find a window. None of the first floor windows look like they can be opened. This place was built for a siege."

She said, "Well, the first Seigneur was supposed to drive out pirates, so I suppose he needed a strong house. And we will need a lamp. I found nothing in the kitchen drawers at all, no candles, no silverware, no convenient box of matches. We should find the chamber with the lit window we saw."

He said, "That was an upper floor of the North Wing."

"Manfred told me once there are no less than sixteen staircases here, not counting the ones in the towers. We should be able to stumble across one."

He turned left and walked. He took four steps, put his hand out, and just so happened to find the doorknob immediately.

"Huhn!" he said. "That's funny. I found the door."

The silken rustle followed him. It struck him as sad that modern women in modern dress, wearing trousers or dungarees, were not accompanied by that seductive, almost dangerous, whisper of silk when they moved. In the darkness with the dark-haired beauty, the mere sound seemed unbearably sensual.

"What's funny about it?" she asked.

"My fingers knew where it was. The door, I mean."

"Maybe they have déjà vu," she said in her mocking, slow drawl. "Or you have a psychic power, but it does not reach up past the wrist."

He said, "I don't know. I had the feeling, earlier, as if I had seen this house before."

"Manfred must have described it to you in a letter."

"No, his letters were mostly about the legal difficulties of moving in, getting the place ready, the reading of the Will, that sort of thing. He told me this house has 'great character' and he's been bewildered each time he enters. You can start from anywhere and get to any room two or three ways. Manfred says he gets lost in here even in the daylight. And he never gets lost, and never forgets an appointment."

"Well," she said, with a dulcet note of scorn in her melodious voice, "I do not know how Manfred managed to forget inviting his Bride To Be and Best Man to this old pile on the same day. It is not as if wild beasts got him."

"Maybe he was detained?"

"Manny in jail? Well, that would be delicious. But, no, he would have had his barrister or someone tell Mr. Stocks at the Inn what had happened, to tell me. He forgot."

Hal marched through the darkness, footsteps booming on the uncarpeted wooden floor, turned left, took a step, turned right, took five steps, found and threw the latch, and pushed open the two leaves of the great front door.

Now the fresh air met him. Enough starlight fell in through the open door, that his eyes could make out the dim shape of the main staircase when he turned. There was nothing else in the main hall. Hal had been expecting tapestries and suits of armor or some other decoration; he saw a square shadow that may have been a coffin, or may have been an empty crate.

The Open Door

The slender girl came up next to him. From here, the great front lawn was visible, the pale stones of the wall, and the dark murmuring shadows of the ancient wood. Beyond that the shadows implied the textures of pasture and farms, outcroppings of tall rock, and the glint of starlight on the sea. The moon was not up.

He said thoughtfully, "I have been wondering, ever since last Christmas, actually, how anyone forgets anything. I mean, why would evolution or providence design our brains to have our memories be like words written in the dust, that any footstep or wind can wipe away, instead of making our brains like a stone with the marks of memory engraved forever?"

She said, "I think it would be unbearable if we remembered too much."

He felt her shiver. She said, "I'm cold." He doffed his coat and draped it over her shoulders, and then put his arm around her.

He did not bother to remove his hand, even though a small voice inside him told him it might be wise. After all, the night was cold, and it would be rude to keep his warmth to himself.

Laurel pressed herself closer to him, eager for warmth. "My nurse told me once that if we saw the bright powers and the dark at war in the earth and sea and sky, struggling over every soul, we'd be petrified. If we saw the spirits of evil that hunt men like famished wolves, like leopards and lionesses with shining eyes in the dark, hungry not for mere flesh that rots, but for our immortal souls, hungry with a terrible hunger, we would go blind. I used to have such terrible nightmares about drowning, about seeing a palace at the bottom of the sea, I was glad to forget."

Still standing in the doorway, Hal felt as if eyes were in that dark forest watching him. He could not shake the sensation. It was unnerving. He reached out and hooked the handle of the door with the hawk-beak of his cane, and yanked one leaf shut, and then the other. Again, with the cane, blindly, he smartly struck the upper bar of the latch and shoved it home, and then, with his boot, the lower. The thick iron bars fell to with a loud sound in the close darkness.

"I say! I think we rather need all the light we can get," the girl objected.

"I think I can find that lamp we saw," he said, and with the girl his best friend intended to marry still cuddled tightly in one arm, her body pressed against his side, he walked slowly up the staircase to the upper floors. His footsteps were sure, and he did not stumble on the top step when he crossed it.

The Empty Attic

The pair kept their arms about each other. Hal assured himself that any man would be duty-bound to place a brotherly arm about any cold girl in the dark. With the door closed, it was a little warmer but he could still feel the shivers that caused her body to tremble from time to time.

It was strange, he thought, how they had been drawn close to each other so many times during this evening, after years of contact no more intimate than brushing shoulders. He could count on one hand the number of times it had happened before and still have two fingers left over.

There was the time he helped her out of the boat at Brighton, and the tide moved the vessel away from the dock as she disembarked, causing her to fall against his shoulder. There was that time they were running up a flight of stairs, for what purpose, he could no longer remember. Those absurd high-heeled shoes she always insisted on wearing had slipped, causing her to stumble, and he reached out a hand to steady her back. He still recalled the jolt he had felt when he had perceived, through the silk of her blouse, the soft slenderness of her body. And then there was the time at The Golden Lion Inn, in Cornwall, when he had uttered some foolish drollery, and she had laughingly pinched his ear. Caught up in the grips of mirth, she had leaned forward and rested her forehead for a moment upon his back, unwittingly filling his nostrils with the sweet perfume that seemed to cling to her hair.

Other that those three incidents, however, it had been Manfred whose ear she pinched, Manfred whose back she leaned upon, Manfred whose hand she took.

Today, on the other hand, he and Laurel seemed to be falling against each other and clinging to one another at every turn. It was almost as if she were...

No. He forced himself to abandon that treacherous line of thought.

Returning his attention to their surroundings, he tapped about the room with his cane again, finding doors to one side that boomed hollowly, and square openings to the other. The first two doors he tried were locked. The openings to the other side at first he thought were niches or alcoves, but there was no glass, no shutters. Hal stuck his head out one: the world beyond was utterly dark, and the air was still and close. Hal shouted, listening to the echo. He realized these must be interior windows overlooking a central nave of the Priory, a large multistory space, like a roofed-in courtyard, with the dome overhead.

She slid from under his shoulder, leaving a place along his side that tingled in the sudden, unexpected cold now that the warmth of her had departed. Taking his hand, she pulled him forward. "Let's not stop to shout at things in the dark, shall we? I don't want to hear the answer."

The corridor turned after a dozen steps. He felt around the corner where wall met wall. It was wider than a right angle. He said, "I bet this corridor goes all the way around the Priory."

He closed his eyes and tried to imagine the shape it would make. Was it a pentagram? No, surely not!

She said, "I think I see a light."

It was true. Up ahead was a thin line of silver touching the floor. It was light escaping under the door crack. Hal rattled the knob. The door was locked. He smashed his shoulder against it once, twice, and heard the wood frame crack. He stepped back and kicked with his boot. The door flew open with a bang.

She made a little noise of exasperation in her throat.

"What?" he asked.

"You are hurting my future home, Hal. I already love it. These old things have no one to defend them. Usually you are so gallant."

"You told me to break into the cellar."

"Well, don't be stupid. Nobody loves a cellar."

The broken door hung suspended from its hinges. But there was no candle in the room beyond. The light had come from the newly-risen Moon, which was visible in a dormer window, that had neither blinds nor shades. The window was open and Hal could smell the night wind. Two walls were white and empty except for a few nails and a crooked scrap of wire. The far wall was white-painted wood planks slanting sharply, pierced by the gabled frame of the dormer window. This was an attic room. There was a cot sitting foursquare in the center of the room, on the uncarpeted boards.

Hal stepped forward, and felt something roll under his boot toe. He stooped, groping, and picked up what felt like a cylinder smaller than his thumb. He held it to his nose and smelled a familiar smell. It was the spent shell of a large-caliber bullet.

"Jackpot!" exclaimed the girl. "I've found a torch!" There was a dazzling cone of electric light. All the objects in the room snapped into sharpness and solidity. Hal blinked, momentarily blinded. Laurel pointed the flashlight down. The cot was a folding wooden frame of green fabric, like something that would have been found in an Army surplus store forty years ago.

She said, "Oh, this is odd." And for once, the note of dry humor that floated through the music of her voice was absent. The flashlight shined on two neatly stacked pyramids of aluminum cans. The first was canned goods, pears in syrup, hash, baked beans, pasta, meat. The second was the empty cans, stained and crusted, lids bent up at identical angles. There was a can opener, a fork, and knife, laying carefully on a handkerchief on the floorboards. The circle of the flashlight darted over to the small fireplace in the corner. The grate was clean, free of ashes but dull with dust. It had not been used recently.

She said, "What sort of beast eats canned ravioli cold from the can?"

"Manfred does," said Hal. "I remember he used to eat it like that when our hot plate broke."

"How long has he been living here?" She looked at the tall pyramid of empty cans. "He must have been here for a month! Did you realize he'd been away from school so long?"

Hal said, "No. I have not seen him lately. I moved out of the dorm last year, remember? I live above a smokeshop in town, these days."

In the light reflected from the walls, he saw two upright lengths propped up near the window. He stepped over and picked one of them up. It felt comfortable and familiar in his hands. A hunting rifle.

"Now this is strange," he said.

"Two months," she said. "Because he moved here the day after Christmas. The Feast of Stephen." She shined the light at Hal, blinding him.

He blinked and shielded his eyes. "Do you mind?"

"What have you there?" she asked.

"A large-bore Winchester 70," he said. "It's a hunting rifle."

"For hunting what?"

"Anything, really. It could shoot a .308 or a .270."

"I don't know what that means. I'm British. We don't speak in numbers."

"You could hunt anything from vermin all the way up to pronghorn antelope or deer. Or a black bear. Not a grizzly, though."

"There are no bears in England."

"It is also good for target shooting. It shoots flat, it's very accurate."

Hal felt something roll under his boot, and go tinkling away. "Shine the light at my feet, please." When she did, he saw dozens and dozens of other expended shells on the floor, over a hundred, in a pool of brass to the right of the hunting rifles, just where the ejector would throw them each time the bolt action was worked. "He was doing a lot of target practice out that window. Is that even legal in England? I thought you guys have all kinds of regulations about these sorts of things."

She stepped over and shined the flashlight beam out the window, sweeping the circle of light back and forth over the grass, the well house, the overgrown bushes near the dovecote.

Hal stepped near. Without thinking, he put his hand around her waist.

"There!" she whispered. He jerked his hand away from her, remembering himself. But she was not paying attention to him, she was staring out the window. He looked where she was looking.

The shadows near the foot of the dovecote flickered and swayed as the girl's hand trembled. Wedged between two unclipped bushes, with its pierced skull resting on flagstones that were cracked and marred with bullet holes, was the corpse of a large, black dog.

The Rosy Light

Some of the gaiety was gone from her voice. "Why was Manfred here alone in a house without lights or heat during the last two months of winter, sleeping on a cot and shooting at dogs? He is the only one on the island allowed to keep a dog."

Hal said, "I did not hear any cooing of any doves in the dove tower either. If Manfred were bringing animals here, one would think he would put his dove in the dove tower first, before bringing a dog."

Laurel made a delicate noise in her nose. "If he purchased a dog just to blast its head off with a firearm while eating cold beans, there are more aspect to his multifaceted character than I had previously suspected. And I used to think his interest in reports of mesmeric influence among non-European peoples was his most eccentric idiosyncrasy. I do hope he does not expect me to take up the sport of shooting game puppies once we're married. But I will try to be supportive."

Leaving the room, they tried the doors along the corridor. She pointed the flashlight at one door after another, and he rattled one knob after another. All doors were locked. She shined the beam into the small arched openings to the other side. The width of the nave defeated the strength of the light. There was a dark floor down below, a set of concentric roof beams above, but no sign of an altar stone or lofts or whatever had originally been in this round empty space.

Every dozen paces or so, another corridor branched off from this one, leading to a short stair or a long one, a straight flight or a crook spiral. In one place, was a ladder that led to a trap door. In another, an archway led to a ramp that reached down and down beyond the reach of the flashlight, a narrow flagstone passage with no turns and no openings, serving no imaginable architectural purpose. All was uncarpeted, undecorated. In one place an empty bookshelf stood. The walls were bare.

As they walked, they talked about ordinary trivialities to keep the darkness at bay. Laurel asked Hal about his mother and his sister.

Hal said, "I can only do so much by telephone. It is as if I am fighting some monster at a distance that is trying to swallow up my mother. Elaine's new husband is the one causing all the domestic confusion. I would fly home and take care of it myself, except I can't afford the flight. It's funny, but my strongest ally is that little old priest I met at the funeral. And I cannot even remember his name."

He changed the subject. "How is the acting career going? Are you going to stick with it after you get hitched?"

She snorted. "I have not made up my mind."

"You know Manfred expects you to quit once you are married."

Laurel's voice grew soft and thoughtful. "When I was a little girl, I discovered that my life was pointless and powerless. The real world is safe and gray and too confining. So I thought that if I could not have adventures, I would pretend in plays and such. I have a natural talent for deceiving people, which is all actresses really do, after all. But looks only last so long. There is no future in it. The state of the British theater is atrocious. No one can make a living at it, except by means well-brought-up girls do not mention, let alone consider. It is a dirty business, really. I rather hope for something better."

"The world is not as safe as all that," Hal observed. "There are still dangerous deeds that need to be done, and God knows there are people who need to be protected."

She laughed deep in her throat and laid a hand on his arm. "That is what is so charming about you, Hal. You always see the nobility in things! You really lost your true calling when they shut down the Round Table."

Hal chuckled as if this had been a joke, but he was warmed in his heart. Laurel had a talent for saying exactly what men wanted to hear. "You are an insightful woman, Laurel. Manfred is a lucky fellow."

He smiled at her in the dark, glad that, ever since they had found the torch, the unexpected intimacy in which they had found them-selves earlier in the evening was gone, vanished as mysteriously as it had come, and they were back to their customary ways, easy and companionable.

As they turned a corner, a window at the end of a hallway showed a glimpse of the sharp cliffs and the moonlit sea.

"This island is an angler's dream," Laurel told him. "Do you know that this island is fishable from any water's edge? In most cases, you need to climb a bit, though. Competing for fishing records is one of the tourist attractions here. If you catch anything you think might make the cut, you can bring it round the tackle and bait shop in town to be weighed and measured. The owner is a member of the Bailiwick of Guernsey Record Rod-Caught Fish Committee."

Then she laughed. "Look at me, and my useless array of knowledge. Which just goes to show, you can take the girl out of the fishing town, but you can't take the fishing town out of the girl. No matter how desperately the girl might want it.

"Hang on!" She stopped abruptly. "We've gone in a circle. There is the door you kicked in."

Hal said, "This house is insane, or maybe we are. We must be near the window we saw before, the one with the lights."

"We should have seen the light we saw, leaking under a door or something. Do you think the candle went out? If it were a candle."

"Douse the flashlight. Perhaps if our eyes adjust we'll spot it."

Darkness closed in like a tomb. The wind could be heard moaning softly in the distance, and taps and creaks, such as old houses are wont to make, began creeping near to them. She stepped near to him nervously, and he put his arm around her before he realized he had done so. He told himself this was not an embrace. It was like putting one's arm around one's little sister, really.

In the darkness, he said, "Is there any madness in your family?"

Her voice was close in the dark, her breath scented and warm on his cheek. "I don't get along with my mother very well. Our mother-daughter love is expressed by shouting, as it were. I have an uncle who collects Spanish coins and believes in ghosts, if that is what you mean."

"Dementia runs in my family. I've always been worried that—well, when things seem odd, I need to know it is not just me. Haven't you been in this house before?"

She said, "I wish I could say I have, to put your mind at ease. But no, never. Manfred just inherited it from his great-aunt or something. Dame Hathaway. She lived in London, where it is civilized. Not here. No one lived here. Manfred was thinking of reopening the old house to save on expenses, because he could not afford to live anywhere else. He is just a penniless student, like you." He felt her shrug beneath his arm. "Like nearly everyone we know."

"Other houses on this island have electric power. Why would the Seigneurie House not?"

"Rank hath its restrictions, you know. Maybe some queer law dating from the reign of Alfred the Great forbids lighting lamps here during Lent. Or a Masonic rule reaching back to Solomon the Wise. Maybe Dame Hathaway never filed the proper tax receipt in triplicate from the Inland Revenue to show the Utility ministry. I have no idea. The International Dark Sky Astronomy Association might have forbidden it. Sounds like a gloomy organization if you ask me; like something from a spy novel."

"So you don't think all this is odd?"

"Very odd, but I think Manfred knows what is behind it all. The dead dog, the bare room where he's been living for two months without telling us. Him telling us to meet on this date at the dock, and then skipping off who knows where…"

"And my feeling that I know this place? It looks so familiar."

"There is a simple explanation. Must be! This place just reminds you of what you see every day at Magdalen and Oxford. The College dates back to Henry the Sixth, and the University to Henry the Second. Manfred has a knack for ending up in creepy old buildings. They all start to look the same after a while."

"There was an empty bookshelf we walked past. It is coming back to me. It was filled with books with red leather bindings. There was a steeplechase scene hung above it. I remember because the horses were drawn to look as if they were jumping like frogs, with their forelegs and hindlegs spread in opposite directions. The stone corridor slopes down to a tunnel built by the Nazis when they were here during the war. It leads through an old silver mine shaft to a sea cave. How do I know that? And don't tell me Manfred wrote me a letter. You know he hadn't."

She was silent a long while. Laurel said, "You know he does tricks with mesmerism, altered state of consciousness? Research for his Master's Dissertation."

"You think he hypnotized me? That's absurd."

"I think he is a magician."

He said, "I have seen him on No Talent Night in our fraternity pull a dove out of his sleeve. It was a good trick. But it is the same one he did last year. My act was juggling bowling balls. Harder than it looks."

"No, I mean an occultist."

"You must be joking."

"Hal, have you never seen that little green book he always carries with him, the one that he keeps locked with a key? It is filled with all sorts of diagrams and recipes and morbid little pictures."

"His diary, no doubt. He hates the occult. He even hates the astrology page in the newspaper. It is rather extraordinary. He does believe in ghosts, though. Did you know? Fancy that, in this day and age."

"My mother says he must have hypnotized me; she still cannot believe I am marrying him. I suppose she'll change her tune once she sees the house and realizes that I am to be the lady of the manor and mistress of the whole island."

"And allowed to keep pigeons, too, don't forget that!"

By now, their eyes had adjusted to the dark. There were lines of moonlight seen beneath the cracks of the doors facing toward what must be the east. But one line was pink, not silver, and farther away than the others.

"There," he said. This knob turned. Hal said, "I know we checked every doorknob. This is impossible."

She flicked on the flashlight, and shined the beam towards either side, surveying the passage. This corridor passed under an archway and led away without turning from the many-angled corridor ringing the central nave. Anyone approaching as they had just now would find himself in a new wing of the house merely by going straight. Anyone coming down the ring corridor the other direction might not see the archway behind him in the dark. "I don't think we were up this wing before. I think we are above the cook's quarters."

"I feel like I am in a dream or something."

She opened the door. Beyond was a narrow stair leading sharply down. The passage was lavishly decorated. The oak railing was hand-carved with floral patterns and impish faces of children. The stairs were carpeted with a design of fishes. The barrel-vaulted ceiling was painted with birds of fantastic shapes trailing long tail feathers. The stairway passage was set with silver-backed niches to both sides. In the niches were ivory or brass statuettes, each about one foot tall, of crowned and haloed figures bearing wands or swords, or holding babes, or books, or longbows.

Hal stopped and peered at a statuette of an armored knight spearing a writhing serpent. It was not brass after all, but gold, or at least, gilded.

"This is getting odder and odder."

At the bottom of the stair was an alcove containing an arched door. The door was painted and enameled in pink, beneath a stone carving of a rose in bloom.

"Turn off the light a sec," he told her.

She complied. To either side of the red door were glass panels of translucent quartz, that allowed a flickering light to escape, but no view of the chamber beyond.

He pulled on the large glass knob, which was just above a brass keyhole fashioned to look like a rose. "Locked. Who locks all their inside doors? Does Manfred carry a keyring with five dozen keys on it?"

She said airily, "Don't break anything."

Laurel handed him the flashlight, which was still off. In the dim illumination from the tiny windows to each side of the red door, he could see her untie her silk bowtie with a slither of noise, unbutton her high collar and undo the top two buttons of her blouse.

He saw her draw out the fine gold chain that had lain around her neck, along with a glimpse of a lacy black brassiere. Around the chain was a large and old-fashioned key. The bow of the key was carved like the rose above the door.

Where had she gotten that, he wondered. But he did not ask.

She inserted the key. To his surprise, the door unlocked with a metallic chime. Laurel pulled the door open. He smelled the scent of lavender from the chamber beyond. Hal could not see inside the chamber at first, because he only saw the rosy light that spilled out of it to surround Laurel.

For a long, lingering moment, she stood staring at the room he could not see. She fidgeted, but did not speak.

In the soft half-light her profile, her lowered eyelids with luscious lashes, seemed mystical and dreamlike.

"I've been here before," she whispered, more to herself than him. "But when? When?"

She put out her hand. Perhaps she merely wanted the flashlight, but he put his hand into hers, astonished at the smallness and fineness of her fingers.

The Chamber from Without

He pulled the door further open, and looked within, expecting to see more barren boards and empty walls.

Instead, the chamber was a phantasmagoria of coral, pink, scarlet and lavender. It was larger than it had seemed from without. Slender white-painted posts held up a silvery dome, each decorated with a different floral design. The ceiling was pink and white. The curving walls were covered with tapestries and Japanese rice paper screens; there were women with foxes' tails playing with burning, floating pearls; and women singing to a Greek sailor tied to a mast; and a young woman seated beneath a tree, luring an unwary unicorn to lay its head in her lap. The walls themselves were hidden behind drapes of colored silk, giving the chamber more of the aspect of an Arabian pavilion than the sort of room one expected to find in an English manor house. On one wall, the drapes parted to reveal a massive fireplace made of pink-veined marble.

Beneath the dome, suspended by chains, was a pink-glassed lantern made of silver metal and ruby-hued leaded glass, sculpted to look like the petals of a rose. From this rose, pale red beams illuminated the chamber. Directly opposite them was the arched window looking out to the northwest they had seen from without. Next to it, at a slight angle, stood a full-length looking glass in a heavy wood frame next to the window. The mirror showed the reflection of the space of the floor behind them to their left. A second arched window was to the other side, facing north. The stained glass showed a knight, raising his sword against a menacing wolf.

There were couches and divans draped in silk. There was a brass table to one side, an unlit candlestick to the other, a brass image of a deer on a pedestal, and flowerpots.

The chamber was not round, but was shaped more like the heart of a nautilus spiral. In the mirror, they could see that the stairwell was near the center of the chamber, and the wall behind them curved away out of sight, passing behind the rear wall without meeting it.

They took a footstep together. There was a mild sensation of an electric tingle, almost like a bubble popping, as they stepped over the threshold. Now they were in position to see themselves in the reflection. The first was a tall, blond man with the broad shoulders of an athlete and strange scars on his arm.

He held hands with a dark-haired beauty with an hourglass figure, pale of skin and red of lip, her teeth perfectly white, her eyes half-lidded as if she thought droll, dark, sultry thoughts.

In the mirror, her engagement ring seemed to be on the wrong hand, and the stone was missing, the tines to hold it bent and twisted.

The green-eyed girl's eyes grew wide as she screamed.

Chapter 3

The Rose Crystal Chamber

The Chamber from Within

No, not a scream. A shout of joy.

The green-eyed girl spun around and grabbed him, her hands seizing his arms, her eyes urgent and giddy and wild.

"What is my name?" she whispered.

His answer was to kiss her so passionately that her supple form swayed against him, held close in his strong right arm. He recognized her now. He knew her.

"Laureline," he whispered back, "Laureline du Lac. Not Laurel. *Laureline*. And it will be Laureline Landfall soon enough."

Then there was neither breath nor time for speech.

In his arms was his true love, whose wit and high spirits he adored. She was a fairy creature from the Arthurian myths that for all his life fascinated him, the Matter of Britain that would win him his master's degree. With her, he could see a rich, strange, unimaginable future that held all the glories and honor of that lost past, and find something as fine as the Holy Grail for himself. He could not see what it would be, not yet, but he knew it was coming.

And yet, he could imagine no possible future with her, because outside this chamber he could not recall himself, his love, or his soul. Nor could he imagine any future without her.

Two Lives

Here, in the Rose Crystal Chamber, he could recall his outside life, everything about it, his father's death, his coming to England to study, the master's dissertation on which he had been working for months: *Arthur's Great Wound: The Origin and Development of Substitutionary Atonement in The Matter Of Britain.* He had been pleased when his roommate and best friend, Manfred Hathaway, had met and fell in love with an alluring third cousin from Zennor, a village near Saint Ives. She was the great-great-granddaughter of the privateer John Allaire, the daughter of a minister, studying theater arts, a bit of a prankster and a bit of a flirt, eager to escape the smell of the fish cannery forever.

Henry was never sure what she saw in Manfred, who was ten years her senior, sober and intent, and seemingly nothing like her type. But the two of them had suddenly announced the date for a marriage and been planning it for months. It was delayed when the death of a remote relative allowed Manfred to inherit an ancient mansion on an island in the Channel. Henry had been shocked, a week or two later, when he learned Manfred had inherited not just the house, but a title, and the whole island as well. The letters from Manfred had grown few, and strange, and the last one had invited him here, to Sark, to the Seigneurie, to the House of Rongeur d'Os Wood.

Except it was false, all of it was false.

It was all there in his head, as clear as something from a favorite novel he'd read and re-read, the words and busy actions and the moods, passions and emotions of the characters. But not his.

It was not him.

He drew back, his hands on her white shoulders. "What do you remember?"

She rolled her enormous emerald eyes. "It always takes you longer than me. I remember everything. Just think, think back, and it will come back to you. How did we meet?"

Like a man shaking off the embers of dream, his true recollections returned to him....

True Memories

Dame Sibyl Hathaway was not some remote relative. Manfred visited her a dozen times in London during his school years, often bringing Henry with him. She was a gray-haired, sprightly old woman with a twinkle in her eyes.

The two old ladies, the thin and elfin Dame Sibyl and the sourfaced Countess Margaret, had explained the labyrinthine intricacies of the laws of the estates and peerages to them. It seemed a wealthy newspaper owner named Clayton, who lived a stone's throw from Sark on his own private island of Brecqhou, was agitating for a change in the form of government of Sark, on the grounds that it violated the European Convention on Human Rights. He wanted Sark changed from a direct Crown possession to some more democratic form of government, and joined politically with the neighboring island of Guernsey. But the marriage of two descendants of John Allaire, the 18th Seigneur of Sark, would make it more difficult for the Privy Council of the United Kingdom to enact the reforms.

Manfred had objected. Were there not three of his cousins in line for the title ahead of him? Countess Margaret dismissed his objection with a wave of her fan. "The fate of the uncooperative is not as certain as mortal men imagine," was her cryptic reply.

Manfred had come to Hal after a particularly long evening cloistered away with his aged relatives and explained that he was being offered up as a lamb to the slaughter. Either he had to marry some sharp-tongued minx, or the house and title—or the entire Sark Island, the last slice of living history—would be lost.

A month later, Henry accompanied Manfred to a New Year's Ball held by an association to which Dame Sybil belonged. It had been a formal party, white tie and tail. At first Henry was a bit awed, as the affair was far more elegant than any he had previously attended. Soon, however, he found himself looking through the glamour at the dreary reality. The wrappings might have been more stylish, but they clothed the same horse-faced girls who laughed too loudly and spoke too crudely with whom he rubbed shoulders every day at Oxford. The gloom of disillusionment fell over him.

As he stood nursing his second glass of champagne, Manfred strolled up to him, forbidding yet dapper in his black finery.

Inclining his head toward Henry, Manfred had murmured, "Don't look now, but the man-killing harpy to whom Dame Sibyl is trying to hitch me just walked in. Look at the door."

Henry looked.

Through the doorway glided a young woman, decked in her winter furs. She shrugged out of her long coat and drew off her gloves, carelessly tossing them to a footman who stood by the door without so much as a glance over her shoulder. Released from her outer garments, her curvaceous beauty put the pale and boyish charms of the other young ladies to shame. A few steps into the assembly hall, she had paused. Standing merrily aloof, with an arrow-like smile upon the bow of her lips, she surveyed the chamber like a queen reviewing her court. Something about her reminded him of the ladies of antiquity, a Nimue or Lynette, plotting how best to ensnare the wary Merlin or lead some hapless knight astray.

As she looked out at the gathered company, however, a weariness came over her face, as if she, too, had pierced the veil of the evening and discerned the banality hidden beneath the shining veneer of gaiety. The look passed over her for an instant, and then was gone. Then, she hid her ennui beneath a cloak of good cheer and sailed forth to join in the festivities.

However, in that moment, her eyes had locked with Henry's. In each other's eyes, they recognized the same discontent with the offerings of this modern world, the same longing for something finer, that they both felt in their own hearts.

Henry recalled very little about the rest of the event, except for her scent, her swaying grace, her smile, the way she had felt in his arms as they waltzed.

True Love

His mind still whirling from the sensation of stepping into the Rose Crystal Chamber, Henry smiled and spoke of what he recalled. "Sibyl invited Manfred to a swank party in London, and he took me along as moral support. Margaret, the Countess of Devon, introduced you to Manfred. You wore a blue shoulderless gown with a plunging neckline with a silver choker with an opal stone and matching opal earrings. You and Manfred had disliked each other at first sight. The marriage was suggested—strongly suggested, otherwise Manfred would be cut out of the family funds, and booted from school—in order to block some sort of political shenanigans. You never loved him."

"Yes on the plunging, no on the blue. I wore red," Laureline said, "And this house?"

Henry said, "I remember now. Manfred first invited me here four years ago. It was beautifully furnished and appointed. His cousins lived here while Sibyl was in London. Two years ago, you were here, with Manfred, with me... and..."

He dropped his hands from her shoulders, and pulled out his

little black memorandum book. There it was, written in his own handwriting, on the first page.

> *You are in love with Laureline du Lac, and have sworn to break the spell of forgetting that separates you, and promised to marry her.*
>
> *Every weekend for two years, you have tricked or lured yourself to come to the Rose Crystal Chamber in the North Wing.*
>
> *Only when you enter here, can you see and read these words.*
>
> *Only when you enter here, do you remember love.*

"I am yours," Laureline murmured softly, "not his."

Only When You Enter Here

"How is this possible?" Henry muttered furiously, rubbing his temples. "I mean, scientifically, how is it possible? Is there a gas in the air? Some hypnotic power in the lamp..."

She said, "Give it a moment. It will slowly come back to you. If we are careful, you and I, we can write ourselves notes to remind or trick or lure us into coming back in here. Leaving a book behind that you need for your research or something." She drew out a notebook smaller than the palm of her hand, bound in tooled pink leather. It had the slenderest possible little pencil tucked in the spine, with an equally dainty tassel.

"See?" She held her little book up, opened a page.

> *Friday: Unlock the Rose Door for H; he left his Mallory in the desk. V Important!*

She said, "But if I write any plain and open words, words of love, my eye cannot see them, not when I am in the Out-of-Doors World. Only here in the Inner World. We've experimented before, tried dozens of things. You forget the moment your heart passes over the threshold of the door or window. Yes, you tried climbing out the window once. You suddenly woke up, and found yourself clinging to the wall outside, with no memory of how you got there."

"No, I do remember that. I was helping one of the Levrier boys clean the gutters, and the wind gusted, and the ladder fell…"

"What color was the ladder? Wood or aluminium? What happened to the boys that they did not immediately lift the ladder again? There were no boys. There was no ladder."

He was silent.

Laureline said, "You see? The spell is very subtle. It not only sponges out memories, it covers them over with false ones. It explains away little inconsistencies. It made you forget this house entirely, this last time. Even though you have been coming here for years! Before, you were able to remember the house and the outside of the chamber. It is getting stronger, not weaker. It is an enemy, and a cunning one…"

Henry had rolled up his sleeve. He was staring in horror at the large and angular knife-scars which covered his left forearm from elbow to wrist. Two-year-old scars. The letters spelled out *I LOVE LdL.*

Henry said, "But it? It who? Some mind, some deliberate thing, must be doing this!"

"Must it? Does a deliberate mind send dreams, the little details in a dream, the color of a pair of shoes, or the words spoken by a figure we meet? Or do we do it to ourselves?"

"How can we fight this?" Henry asked angrily.

Laureline said, "We can influence ourselves subtly. The last time we were here, you wrote *The Memory Palace of Giordano Bruno* in your little memorandum book."

He nodded. "Yes. I became fascinated with the idea of picking up books about Bruno from the library. He died in 1600, burned as a heretic. Some say he was a warlock. He was famed for having the best memory in the world, the best in all history. He developed what he called the Ancient Art of Memory, mnemonics, based on the writings of the Greeks."

She was frowning, biting her thumbnail delicately, staring at the floor. "How does it work? How can that help us?"

"The idea was to build an imaginary house in your mind, a palace of memory, so that every room and bit of furniture is just so. You use rhymes and colors and figures from astrology or myth to help keep things in order. In each room, you fix an image to remind you of what you want to remember. For example, I can never remember the taxonomic classifications, so in the den, beneath the stuffed heads of a leopard, lion, and a she-wolf, I imagined a chessboard made of reddish-purple glass and I have a crowned king in an ermine-lined robe playing a game. I can remember *Kings Play Chess on Fuchsia Glass Surfaces.* Kingdom, phylum, class, order, family, genre, species."

"So?"

"These led to other books on memory and memory-binding. I came across the theory of state-related memory. You know drunks who wake sober on Monday, and forget the whole weekend of what they did. The surprising thing is next time they're plastered, the forgotten memories can return. The same with certain states of mind, drugs, hypnosis, altered states, or even returning to an old place. Memory retrieval is most efficient when a man is in the same state of consciousness as he was when the memory was formed."

"What does it mean?" she asked softly, searching his face with her eyes.

"Something in this chamber is changing our state of consciousness."

"And what does *that* mean?"

He looked bewildered. "I– but I don't know what it means. It is a start. If we can think of a solution, solve the puzzle…"

Laureline sighed scornfully. "You know we will forget the answer the moment we step out of this chamber, and the puzzle too. What is worse is that if I subconsciously influence myself, my out-of-doors self, to call off the wedding, then I will lose you too! Manfred owns the house and the Rose Crystal Chamber."

She pulled away from him now, and went and sat on a purple divan, and put her face in her hands.

"Only here, in this chamber, am I am alive. Out there, I am a sleepwalker." A broken sigh came from her. "I am so very weary of this! For two years we've been trying to make our Outer Selves remember, to let the truth out! But don't you see what's happened? What is happening to me? I've turned into a shameless flirt!"

Henry said gallantly, "I don't know what you mean!"

She raised her face from her hands, and her eyes were like two green rays boring into him scornfully. "So you did not notice how many times Outside Me contrived to press up against you this evening, to take your hand, to fall into your arms? I do not know which is more shameful: being a shameless hoyden or one who is so amateurish that the efforts go unnoticed!"

"No, Outside Me thinks you are very attractive indeed," said Henry. "He is just not going to hurt his friends by—wait a minute! Why am I apologizing for him? I mean, for me? In any case, you are not a flirt. All that was happening was that you subconsciously were aware of your true self. Your true heart. The real you was pushing you into my arms. You should be happy! It means we can beat this thing! Break it! My love, my darling, nothing can keep us apart!"

"But something is. The marriage is two months from now. Something, something we cannot understand, cannot put a name to, has kept us apart for two years. Six hundred days and counting we have been separated. Sixty days remain. The nothing that keeps us apart is amnesia. It is time for firmer steps."

Henry's face darkened. "Don't bring this up again."

"I tell you—there is only one way to break a spell in a fairy tale like this. Sleeping Beauty was not just kissed, you know. Prince Charming needed a deeper intimacy to wake his love. The Brothers Grimm just cleaned the story up. Here is a roomy purple couch. We can light a fire in the rose-red marble fireplace to warm us. Sit with me! Take me in your arms!"

She tugged on his hand, urging him to lower himself. Henry shook his head.

Laureline said, "But everyone does it these days!"

"Everyone can go to the devil. All we need do is bring a parson in here, have us perform the ceremony."

Her green eyes flashed scornfully. "And then what? After the Honeymoon, once the nuptials are over, and we've consummated the wedding, as soon as I walk downstairs, I will be unwed again, and marry Manfred, an adulteress in my own house? A different husband for every floor of the manor? I can go back and forth between this chamber and the master bedroom on cold nights, when one or the other of you grows tired. That will be a new scandal, even for England."

"Don't talk like that!" he snapped.

Laureline's eyes grew wide with dismay, and her lip trembled.

He knelt where she was kneeling before the divan, and took her hands in his, and kissed her. "Sorry—I don't mean to be sharp."

"No, it is my fault. I don't know what has come over me. I am so... so..."

"Darling, I know. Shush. I know. But maybe our wedding vows would break the spell. There is an odd power in those old sacraments. Then we can consummate our love, and we will be free."

She rolled her eyes in scorn yet again. "Fine! You write a note to yourself to invite a minister into this chamber when I am here. And somehow talk me into bringing a wedding dress. But I think those notes will be ones your eyes will never let you read, once you are out-of-doors. They are too close to the heart of the matter."

He glared at his scarred arm. "Maybe..."

Laureline said, "Do let me suggest a plan, for once. Let us try your new method. Write down in your little black book these words: *Buy diamond necklace.* Now in your memory palace, let us say in the swimming pool in the back, picture me wearing a black one-piece bathing suit, but with diamonds on a chain around my neck. See?"

He said, "What will that accomplish?"

"You are going to buy me a diamond necklace. When you see it on me, you will remember. Also, write down *Golf on Wednesday the 27th.*" She smiled, showing her dimples, her eyelids half-lowered, as she scribbled in her own little pink-leather notebook.

Henry said, "How is this going to work for us? There is no way Outside Me would buy a diamond necklace as a present for his best friend's fiancée. For one thing, how can I afford it?"

But Laureline said, "If I tell you the whole plan, that might drive the memory too close to the forbidden memory of love, and you will forget it. But if you don't know the details, well, you might recall just enough to do as I say. Trust me. We only have two months. I have written myself notes of very natural things for my Otherself to do, that will ensure you and I can meet here again."

Henry said, "How is it that this lamp was lit, just in this one room, and you have the key to it?"

Laureline said, "I arranged it. Last time we were here together, I wrote myself a reminder note to ask Manfred to let me see to moving the furniture out of this chamber."

"Out of the house?" asked Henry.

"The lawyers are forcing us to move materials left behind into storage until the ownership questions are cleared up. Naturally, every time I stepped into it intending to pack a box, I remembered myself, and left everything as it is. I was here earlier today, looking for Manfred. When I came in here, I remembered myself again, and lit the lamp, hoping it would lure us back in, once we found the house empty. I even arranged for this!"

And with a grin, she danced over to one of the hanging silk drapes, and pulled it aside. Here was an ice bucket and bottles of champagne. She smiled a most luxurious smile. "Why don't you pry open one of these stubborn corks, while I slip into something more comfortable? I tricked myself into bringing something for an overnight stay. Nice in a naughty way."

Like a man walking into the teeth of an arctic wind, Henry forced himself to turn away, and, step by leaden step, he walked toward the door behind which the upward stair waited.

She said, "Wait! What are you doing? There is no other place to sleep."

"But with you?" He hefted the flashlight in his hand. He would be able to find his way back to the one inn on the island, with that light.

Her lips trembled, but she said nothing.

Henry gritted his teeth and turned his face away, knowing one look at her would shatter his resolve. "My love, I adore you. Believe that. That means I love you too much to be selfish, to demean you."

She rushed up behind him, put her arms around him, put her cheek against his back. "I want to be demeaned, if it is by you. You may do what you'd like to me."

"Don't talk that way!"

"How else can I prove to you that nothing else matters, but us?"

Henry shook his head. "I will have you as an honest woman, or not at all. In the sunlight, not in the shadows. I will not betray Manfred."

"But what if his life outside is as meaningless to him as ours are to us? To whom are you *really* being loyal?"

He turned, and with some difficulty, disentangled himself from her. "One day the spell will break. We will be wed. I promise it! One day, your happiness and mine will be complete. You will belong to me and you will own me. On that day, I will not look back and regret that I did not love you strongly enough. You are worth the wait."

Her eyes narrowed. "You go out into that oblivion and you will forget your promise the moment your heart passes over that threshold. And I will stay here all night, alone, knowing that you walked away from me."

He kissed her roughly, intending it to be goodbye, but she pulled him with her small hands back toward the center of the chamber, toward the divan, toward the champagne. He took one step in that direction with her, then a second, and a third.

But then he firmly, but gently, put her aside, and turned, and walked out the door.

Chapter 4

Tales of Ancient Water Maidens

Old and Forgotten Woes

When Hal and Manfred met next, it was at a pub called the Old Granary in Dorset. They sat on a balcony with the River Frome chuckling and sliding on below, and beyond was the green view of the Purbeck Hills. Hal drank the Tanglefoot ale, brewed by a family of brewers who had been in business longer than his home country. Manfred drank the Kronenbourg Lager.

At first they spoke seriously, as friends do, about their progress and obstacles with their dissertations, but as the ale flowed freely and the afternoon progressed, the talk turned to more frivolous and exotic topics.

Hal looked at Manfred over the rim of his ale cup. Manfred was thirty years old, with a square brow hanging over deepset eyes. This gave his face an aspect of brooding and scowling which receded when he smiled, but never entirely vanished. His cheek bones were high and definite, his nose like the beak of a hawk. His jaw jutted, his lips were thick and red as those of an Assyrian. His hair was so dark as to seem almost blue. At all hours, even when he had just shaved with a close razor, his chin and jawline was shadowed with the hint of dark, coarse hair. He did not have the height of Hal, nor his wide shoulders, but he was thick through the chest, as stout as an old oak barrel, and his neck and arms were surprisingly muscular.

"I am surprised you drink a German brew, you being a lord now, and such," said Hal with an easy grin. "Surely love of Queen and Country demands otherwise? Surely there is some law from the time of Henry the Second, or something, demanding true Englishmen drink only their own true England beer?"

Manfred, as always, seemed to be glowering under his close-knit brows, but a slight smile touched his lip. "This lager is from France, and in the time of Henry the Second, we ruled France, or part of her. Brewed by a German family, of course. Trust the Huns with hops, the Gauls with grapes. Everything fine and good among the English came from the Continent. This was a haunt of giants before Brutus came, you know, and Caesar saw nothing but savages painted blue, Picts and cannibals, and druids burning slaves alive in wicker men on the moor. England is like a dark house of forgotten things, with basement, cellar, bunker and dungeon leading down to ever darker things no one remembers. Sometimes it is a mercy to forget."

"That is a glum attitude!" protested Hal.

"So says the Yank, whose country is hardly old enough to wipe its own bum. You Yanks still berate and bewail the bad deeds of yesterday, your one and only civil war, your slave-trade, driving off the Indians. When were those deeds done? Mere moments ago. We have had nine civil wars or more, and our slave trade since the time of John Hawkins swelled to encompass the world entire! Christendom was shipwrecked on this stony-hearted island in 1536, split in two, never to be whole again. All the subsequent wars in Europe spring from that, for without Henry and good queen Bess, the Reformation would have been suppressed like every other heresy before it. Without the divide between Catholic and Protestant kings, perhaps one contender would have eventually led the Holy Roman Empire from the Pillars of Hercules to the Ural Mountains, and world wars never been invented. Earlier, the troubles of Ireland started in 1192. Earlier still, Arthur in 518 fought the battle of Badon Hill, where he slew eightscore men singlehandedly: and the grief of that still haunts the Badbury Rings, through green turf covers the Roman stones. What are the ills of your measly two hundred years compared to that?"

"Haunts as in *haunting*?"

"Of course. The locals say the shades of Arthur and his knights appear there on moonless nights, fighting ghostly foes. In 1970 the spectral armies drove away an archeological expedition, who fled in panic from the clamor of an unseen battle in the air. And a ghost of a knight with a hideously scarred face was seen at night there, as recently as 1977."

"A real ghost?"

Manfred smiled again. "I am glad you did not say *a real, live ghost*."

Hal laughed with joy. Manfred was the only man he'd met in Oxford who took the older tales and yarns completely seriously. Even the other students of history and ancient literature seem to regard the past as dead, or, worse, as absurd. They almost seemed like amnesiacs, unaware of the true glory of their ancient and richly-fabled island even while they vivisected the records of it.

Not Manfred. He seemed to Hal to be a living relic of the days of yore, of the times of myth, like a wizard who had stepped out of an enchanted sleep into the modern world.

Manfred was by far the most open-minded man Hal had ever met. Hal could have an honest conversation with him without ever once having to worry about stepping onto the invisible landmines and pitfalls of forbidden topics and unspoken thoughts with which every other man he knew surrounded his conversation.

Best of all, he was as deeply interested in the topic of Hal's dissertation as Hal was in his. It was a joy to converse with someone who valued all the old, strong, beautiful things that Hal himself so cherished.

There was one other topic upon which they agreed, as well; they were the only two men either of them knew who still believed in the wisdom of chastity.

"Surely such things are just stories told by hysterics?" said Hal, returning to their conversation after emptying his ale.

"All of them?" Manfred looked skeptical. "Every story ever, even those told by sober men with nothing to gain by it? That may be more farfetched than believing in ghosts."

"What else could ghost stories be?"

"Something mankind has never seen before, or, far more likely, something our ancestors lived with daily, but which we forget. Perhaps a ghost is an echo from that time: a psychic residue. Perhaps it is the senility of the world trying to remember old and terrible tragedies and crimes, but not able to bring them clearly enough into focus to materialize them."

As if a small, inner voice were urging him, Hal said, "That reminds me! I just read a fascinating book on mnemonics. It is the art of building a memory mansion so that nothing is ever forgotten. You simply must read it."

"I am rather busy, between my schoolwork and my legal tribulations—"

"It is fascinating! It will help with your schoolwork—how could it not?" Hal was half surprised to see his hands had, as if without consulting him, unzipped his rucksack, and pulled the book out, proffering it across the table. "Please! For me! I insist!"

Manfred looked puzzled. "You seem rather keen on—"

"You must read it! It is that good!"

Manfred eventually agreed to take it, to make the time to read it. But he muttered, "I am not sure abolishing forgetfulness is a help. Perhaps we should be grateful that the world has amnesia."

"To the contrary! If the world could recollect Arthur in all his glory, manifest his ghost as a physical reality in broad daylight, surely he would set to rights all the wrongs of England of which you so complain. In any case, why list the victory of Arthur as an evil akin to the Invasion of Ireland?"

"I did not call it an evil, but said it was a cause for grief."

"Why would anyone be grief-stricken at the victory of Arthur?"

"Surely Mordred, for one." Manfred smiled again, and again it seemed to be an ironic smile, a mocking smile. "As for who else, you are the one writing the paper on Arthur. Who did he overthrow?"

"The pagan kings of Saxony."

"And did they practice polygamy, pederasty, slavery, and human sacrifice, and all the other delights of the true and honest pagans of yore?"

"Of course."

"Now, tell me this, who keeps a grudge longer? Good men who forgive and forget? Or wicked men who every day dream about returning to the sins and brutalities that civilization, sanity, and Holy Mother Church forbid? Which ghosts linger longer? Those of criminals and monsters, eager for blood, or those of kindly men, eager to escape this vale of woes for the paradise above all stars? I say that everything in England, when you dig down deeper, has a dark past, one that is best unrecalled. Our only escape is to forget!"

Hal turned and stared across the river. "You are in a grim mood. Let us forget the past for the moment and enjoy the day." He raised his walking stick and gestured like a stage magician sweeping aside a curtain to reveal his shapely assistant, uncut by any saw. As if at his signal, the sun peered through cloud, and scattered a dancing path of brilliance across the water.

Manfred nodded at the waters below their balcony. "Ah, the River Frome! You think it is fair and pleasant? I will tell you the tale."

Manfred leaned forward on the wood table, his eyes dark and piercing beneath their heavy brows, and he spoke in grim tones.

"Near Wool is the ruined Cistercian monastery of Bindon Abbey. A boy who once served the monks there would dawdle and frolic on his errands, and swim in this river. His name was Lubberlu. Well, once from between the bulrushes appeared a maiden whose eyes sparkled like sunlight on blue water, and whose silver hair was like a flowing waterfall. They dallied and kissed and laughed, and the boy day after day finding any excuse to be sent on errands, always found his way to the waterside as the summer days turned toward autumn, and the feast of all souls drew nigh. Lubberlu approached one of the monks of the abbey, and said he wished to marry the girl. But the monk knew she was no mortal maiden, and forbade it, warning him of the murderous ways of the daughters of the river water, the nix, the mermaids. In tears the boy fled, vowing to bring the girl to a proper Christian wedding, and turn her from her ways. The next day his drowned corpse was found floating face up in the river, tangled among the bulrushes."

Hal raised an eyebrow, and his laughter broke the dark spell the story had cast. "So *that* is what this is about!"

Manfred looked surprised.

Hal said, "A man on his way to wed a rare beauty, and he is murdered by her instead. Why would you tell me such a tale today? You are getting bridegroom jitters. Cold feet. Why else such downcast looks?"

New and Present Sorrows

Manfred now frowned in earnest, and his face was like that of a dark hawk glowering. "It is moving into the Seigneurie House. It is so bad, it is affecting my dreams! The legal troubles, the maneuverings, the Countess Margaret sticking her nose into everything. Well, my lawyer managed to get some of the red tape untangled, so that furnishings are out of escrow, and I am the undisputed owner of them. Who writes a will that passes title to land and house but not personal property? I am having workmen ship the whole lot over from Guernsey and be unpacked. Lord knows what I will do for carpeting and wallpaper. So much was destroyed by the court of escrow agents before they found me."

Hal waved his walking stick at the barmaid to bring another round of drinks, and soon the warmth and ease flowing in his blood began to loosen his tongue. "I don't know what Laurel sees in you, old man, if you don't mind my saying. Are you sure you have no bridegroom jitters?"

Manfred, after yet another drink, had also lost some of his usual stiffness of bearing. A melancholy look was in his deep-set eyes. "I am just not sure about her. Some times she and I—well, certain things are awkward…"

"You mean you don't like the same music? Or you mean something—more like a sexual incompatibility, ah–"

Manfred stiffened, and Hal wondered if he had spoken too freely. Manfred said, "You and I swore a solemn vow to stay celibate until we were married. We are the laughingstock at Magdalen. I assume you did it mostly for the old-fashioned romance of it."

Hal said, "It seems very straightforward to me. I hate how adultery killed Camelot, snared Merlin, marred King David, and made Abraham the father of Ishmael, whose sons vex his sons to this day, and so on. The Trojan War was started by the adultery of Helen, and the murder of Agamemnon was finished by the adultery of Clytemnestra."

Manfred nodded. "And the Gnostics say Eve committed adultery with the serpent, which would make that sin older and deeper than the murder of Abel, and stain the race more deeply. All very romantic and nostalgic reasons. You are a living eulogy for a world long lost! A world perhaps nobler than our own. My reasons are deeper." He looked down at his hands, and sighed. "I fear the damnation of Hell."

"Sorry, old man! I– I didn't mean to pry!"

Manfred spoke without looking up. "I think it is a real place, Hell. I saw it once in a dream, when I was a child, you know. Ten thousand faces of people drowning in boiling oil, all screaming, all biting and scratching and reviling each other, trying to push each other under, and climb up out of the sticky fires. And the worst, the worst thing, I cannot even tell you how this scared me when I was a little boy: I saw naked people diving in. Some were male and some female, but they had no age. Their faces were young and their eyes were old. They plunged in through a hole, like the mouth of the well, trying to get away from a beautiful clear azure sky filled with golden light. They could not tolerate the light, and hated it, and they dove into the pit to escape it, because they could not bear to see themselves. Dear God! What if such a thing were real?"

Hal felt embarrassed, as if he had accidentally read someone else's private diary.

Manfred smiled one of his rare smiles. "You think I am crazy."

Hal said, "Everyone at school thinks we are crazy. The two virgins. Even the professors jeer. We are out of step with the world."

"Good. Who the hell knows where the world is headed?"

"Something is really eating you, isn't it, Manny?"

"Hal, yes, damn it."

"And–"

"And, yes, damn it, you said it. I am not certain I want to marry her. It is as if I hear this tiny whisper in my heart, warning me. I am almost willing to postpone again."

"Until when?"

"Who knows? Forever. She is too damned interested in the house, in the title, in the island."

Hal felt a strange and disloyal leap of joy in his heart when he heard this. If Manfred broke up with Laurel, the beautiful, dark-haired Laurel, naturally she would need a shoulder to cry on, and late nights to soothe her woes in wine and…

Hal, shocked, smothered that tiny voice in him, hoping nothing of his secret thought had shown on his face.

But Manfred was staring down into the bottom of his empty mug, talking. "So much grief and tragedy! I visited the graves of my three cousins, and my great-aunt Sibyl. Horrible that they drowned. Islanders! They lived in boats! How could they lose control of such a large, fine yacht! And so close to shore. It does not make sense. I keep trying to form the picture in my head, and it does not add up. Why was there no radio call? Why did no one on shore see them? Were there no lifejackets aboard?

"And the report from the coast guard was that the boat had been scuttled, not holed. The valves were opened. Marie, and Pierre, and Earnest! My cousins were such handsome chaps, and Marie such a beauty, so kind, so good with horses. Willing to bend the rules to protect their tenants and servants, you know. Almost makes one forgive the aristocracy, to see old-fashioned loyalty like that. Without them—I don't know what to say. I don't believe in God any more, at least not in a kind and loving God. It is like having a leg ripped off. Like seeing the sun flicker, and go dark, and watch the final snow, the snow that will never lift, the cold that will never end, begin to drift down from the stars!"

"Manny, don't take it so hard—I mean, I thought you hardly knew them! You said you only visited them once or twice as a child."

"That is true. And yet somehow, in a way I cannot explain, my heart has grown cold. I suppose my visit to the family graveyard got me thinking about life and death. They are not happy thoughts."

Hal remembered burying his father. "I know the feeling. Believe me."

A small, inner voice told him not to say anything more. All he had to do was keep silent and let Laurel and Manfred drift apart. If Manfred were to decide not to marry her…

The possibilities were endless.

She was more beautiful than any woman he had ever seen. She had that imponderable aura called glamour, something only actresses and models had, women whose whole livelihood was in their looks. Hal had never met a woman as lovely, as lively, or with such impish sense of humor. Laurel was different from the other English girls. She had that wildness of spirit gypsy girls were said to have, or sultry Italians, or passionate Spaniards, or, perhaps, the silver-haired mermaid from the tale of the River Frome.

An image formed in his imagination. Laurel on Manfred's sailboat, or perhaps at the pool, with her glittering green eyes, lashes half-closed, a sultry smile playing about her lips. What would she look like in a bathing suit? It should be black, but not a bikini, a one-piece number. But she should be decked with jewels, wearing earrings and clashing anklets even while swimming, and a diamond necklace.

He could see it perfectly, a crisp and clear picture in his head.

If Laurel was his, each time he went swimming in his pool, she would be there, dressed like that. And every night, when he went to bed, and every morning, he would never be lonely again.

Hal, by an extreme effort of will, gagged his inner voice and blindfolded his inner eye. Lusting after your best friend's girl was atrocious. Doing so just months before his wedding was doubly atrocious. Slavering like a vulture at the news that your best friend was having the doubts all bridegrooms had? That was triple.

That was as low as anything Lancelot ever did.

The small, still voice was still trying to talk, to say something urgent, something about love and memory and the inner truths in life, but Hal would hear no more.

He reached out and clasped Manfred by the hand. "Manny, you have to listen to me! Laurel is a great girl, a wonderful girl, the best you will ever find! Tell her your doubts. Tell her about your cousins. Heck, tell her about your childhood nightmares. She is the one you have to pour your heart out to. Not me. Best friends are for bachelors. From now on, I am your best man. I have to move into an outer orbit in your life, and she has to be with you, one with you. It is like a bride who owns a cat on whom she dotes insufferably. Once she has a baby, she forgets the cat's name. I am the cat. Tell *her* your woes, not me. She can comfort you in ways even your best friend cannot, believe me."

Manfred smiled, and then laughed, and then roared and slapped his knee. "You are right about everything but that! Friendship is something no one talks about these days, but it used to be the very bedrock of life. You are not moving to an outer orbit. She likes you, too! I can see it in the way she looks at you. You cheer her up. So, here!"

And out from an inner pocket he drew a ring of seven large, old-fashioned keys. They were oddly and intricately made.

The Keyring

Each key was as long as a finger, and the bow of each was wrought and enameled to look like a different heraldic symbol: the golden head of a maned lion, a silver dove, a green apple, a Celtic cross in brass, a red rose, a white lotus, a black six-pointed flower.

"Each key opens a different door. This opens the main door; this the west wing, where the dovecote is; the apple key is for the north wing, where the cider mill is; and this unlocks the chapel doors. All the inner doors lock. My ancestors were suspicious a lot. Piracy will do that for you. Or living on an island with no lights."

"Privateers. And there are some lights. And, good heavens, why are you giving me the keys to your mansion?"

"Because you are not a damned cat. I am not going to forget you, although I will take my troubles to Laurel, as you said, and lay my head in her lap."

Hal smiled and hid his unexpected stab of jealousy.

Manfred said, "Besides, with these keys, you will not need to break in again. Ah, don't worry! Mr. Drillot saw you going up Rade Street into Wrongerwood near sunset, and old Mrs. Gascoigne, who is a better spy than anyone in MI6, she saw you as well. There is nothing else on that part of the island but my house. I am just wondering why you did it?"

"Well, it was pretty inconvenient of you to send me a message inviting me to come see your fine new house in its fine old condition, and then forget the date!"

Manfred shook his head, mystified. "I never sent you any message. In fact, I had plans that day. Laurel insisted, she practically twisted my arm, that I go meet her old man-eating harpy of a mother in Zennor village to try to get her blessing for the wedding. The woman lives in a gray shack on stilts that has two legs in the sea, like something out of a children's fairy tale where the children don't make it out alive. I nearly didn't. Good thing my dove saved me. So who sent you that message? I was not planning on showing you the place until this coming week. There is not a stick of furniture there. Just a cot."

"Why not stay in the inn? And why shoot at dogs from your window?"

Manfred looked blank. "Dogs? I have absolutely no idea what you are talking about."

"I found the room where you slept. It was filled with empty cans, as if you had been camping out there for months, eating baked beans cold, and the floor was covered with spent shells from your hunting rifles."

"I dragged in my old army cot for a night exactly once. It was part of the transfer of title that I had to spend the night in the house. One of the damn stipulations in the original charter dating back to before the Spanish Armada. Why would I stay in an empty house when Mrs. Stocks begs me to stay in the best room in the inn, free of charge? She feeds me rather better than cold beans straight from the can. I did that when I was a First Year, and I bloody well am never doing it again."

Hal Landfall felt himself suddenly more sober than he wanted to be. The sensation was the same as if a window in a warm room on a winter evening had opened behind him.

Hal said, "You are right about things not adding up. We need to get to the bottom of this. I need to know I am not going mad like my poor... never mind. But this feels darker than it looks. That old house is strange. I wonder if it is..."

"Hiding something?" asked Manfred.

"I was going to say *protecting* something. Like there is a treasure there, for me."

"For you?" Manfred raised both eyebrows. "It's my damn house."

"And somehow, I don't know how, I get the feeling that Laurel is also involved. It is just a feeling that I have. I can't explain it."

Manfred sighed and said, "If there is a mystery involved, or a conspiracy, then it is coming at the worst possible time. I am supposed to be finishing my dissertation, supposed to be planning my wedding, and supposed to be beating my way through a massive thicket of British law and English customs, all while keeping my name out of the papers. The conspirators picked the time in my life when everything is demanding I not look into any conspiracy theories..." He had started the sentence as if he were telling a joke, but by the time his voice trailed off, his tone was very serious indeed.

Hal Landfall said, "We can study the matter. Study hard! Things will clear up. We will get to the bottom of this. Together. As friends." His eyes crinkled in a smile.

Manfred said, "Well, you want to use any excuse not to work on your paper! I am glad. Let's toast the quest! How do we set about it, this new resolution?"

"With a smile in our hearts, a prayer on our lips, and a refill in our mug? You pay. You are the lord we are supposed to be getting drunk as."

"A pretty impoverished lord, as we all are these days. I can see to the smile and the refill."

"As to how exactly to start, I have no idea whatsoever," said Hal, with a sad smile. "How do you start unraveling a mystery that seems to revolve around a whole world losing its power to remember the past? As if reality itself were going senile?"

"Find reminders? Something to jog the world's memory? You are the one with the book on mnemonics." Manfred shrugged. "I am moving copies of my books and journals to the island, so that whether I am there or at Magdalen, I will still have my material."

"But I would like to spend as much time on your mansion as I can," said Hal. "Maybe some reminders are buried there."

And Manfred invited him to meet Saturday afternoon for a meal at the mansion, assuming the workmen, royal historian, and the officer from the royal commission on antiquities gave him no further troubles.

"And one more toast!" said Manfred smiling sardonically. "That I might find a cook, have the power turned on, and have a guest room furnished by then, or else it is the cold beans for you, and sleeping on that damned cot!"

Chapter 5

Worst Best Man

The Apparition

A storm rose over the channel, and adverse winds kept the ferry wallowing in the swells, like a cart tied to a mad horse running up gray hills and down, and the rain was a curtain. The tide changed, and the skipper was able to bring the ship to harbor just as the storm departed. Black clouds, as dark as locust swarms, crept slowly away from each other, an army retiring each man to his own tent. The first star shone, and the moon was a scimitar.

Manfred was not there to meet him at the dock yet again. Unsmiling and uneasy, Hal shouldered his rucksack, took up his hawk-headed cane, and walked.

A road that had never felt the tire of any motorcar ran straight through fields and pastures grown purple and blue in the dusk. There were no streetlamps in the half a dozen houses at the crossroads which formed the village, no floodlights, no lit signs. One small gas lamp was permitted to wink above the signboard of the Inn. Hal turned at the crossroad and continued.

Beyond the village, the ground rose and fell in domelike hills of green and sudden vales of shadow. Once or twice, he saw a cottage and a barn, windows shuttered, and no light showing. Then the farms and apple orchards were behind him, and pastures divided by hedgerows and low walls of mossy stones were before. In the distance, on a high peak, he saw the gaunt silhouette of the old windmill, called simply La Baton, its sails motionless.

The sound of his footfalls echoed oddly, and Hal was reminded of old myths of hollow hills under which inhuman creatures feasted in utter darkness and danced in perfect silence, to music inaudible to human ears. Then he recalled with a start that the hills of Sark were hollow indeed, or some of them: pirate coves carved out by the sea, or watery caves hidden at high tide, or shafts cut in the abandoned silver mines, or bunkers and tunnels burrowed out by diligent German soldiers during the war, some, perhaps, yet undiscovered.

"How like the mind of man this island is!" he thought. "Our daily worries and distractions walk through pleasant orchards of ideas, but the deep places are where our longings and obsessions hatch like eggs, or unspoken passions: all of that is below the roots of the landscape of the mind, where we can never meet them. Unless we fall into a pit."

And the walk grew steeper and more broken, until the path he trod was a stairway. Before him loomed the dark and breathing shadows of Wrongerwood, and the leafy mass against the twilight sky seemed to have been drawn by an artist using charcoal in feathery strokes.

As he feared, the great house was dark. The windows were blind. The dunce-cap peak of the dovecote rose silently to one side, empty of birds; the eight-sided belltower rose before him, empty of bells. Beyond was the crenellated silhouette of the northern wing, ancient and strange as the dreams of forgotten medieval sieges, melees, and massacres. In the gloom, he saw the silhouetted contour of the flattened dome of the central priory, the rectilinear shape of the northern tower, and round shape of the signal tower, its antique cannon protruding into the night air like the horn of a rearing unicorn. The image of the gold lion guarding the main doors of the East Wing glared at him with murderous fury.

Hal smiled apologetically at the imposing creature, fished the keyring out of his pocket, and held up the yellow key adorned with a lion's face at the bow.

"This time, I have permission!" he said.

Hal tucked his walking stick under his arm, grasped the massy brass door handle, and inserted the key. With a clang of noise, unexpectedly loud, the bolt drew back. With his boot toe he pushed open the right leaf of the huge front door. Wide darkness was beyond. His eyes could make out the hint of a stairway, a tall arch leading into larger and emptier rooms. He stepped inside, and was surprised when the wind caught the door behind him and slammed it shut. Now it was dark, save for the gray slits of narrow windows high above, lit by starlight. The windows seemed to hang in the blackness, since his eye could make out no features and no dimensions of the room in which he stood.

Hal felt suddenly foolish. He had not thought to bring a flashlight, since he assumed Manfred would have arranged for the power to be on by now, and would meet him. He doubted his ability to find his way through the twisting, unpaved, rutted and leaf-strewn path through Wrongerwood on a moonless night, which meant, as he had been before, he was trapped here unless he found a lamp or a candle.

The first time he had been here with Laurel, they had forced the cellar door, looking for a lamp seen through a stained-glass window. Instead they found an empty room furnished only with a cot, canned food, and hunting rifles. She had given him the flashlight found in the room and stayed to sleep on the cot, while he had made his way back to the village. In hindsight, it seemed more than a little odd that he had done that, left the girl alone in a deserted mansion. He could not recall the two of them discussing the plan, nor could he remember when and why he had agreed to it. He must have been more upset than he knew: upset because being alone with Laurel, even for a perfectly legitimate reason, kept luring his imagination down paths he did not want it to follow.

How had this happened to him now for the second time? It was as if something inside him were playing tricks on him, maneuvering him.

Hal shivered. "If it were my subconscious mind haunting me, bedeviling and bewitching me, this would not be so bad. I would only be going insane. Like mother. Science understands the subconscious mind. It is a real thing. It's real. But–" Even in his mind he dared not put the thought into words, lest the danger suddenly sound absurd, and his awareness of it pop like a bubble.

Wordlessly, then, he knew the danger was real. It was not the danger of madness he feared, or not that alone; rather he feared that he was being bewitched and bedeviled by something more like witchcraft and devilry than like mental breakdown. Something deliberate. Something aimed at him. But why him? Who was he but an impoverished student studying British literature?

He remembered being amused at Manfred's expense the day he discovered his roommate believed in demon possession and exorcism. "Surely it is just mania or hallucination," Hal had exclaimed.

Manfred had said most cases were mental illness, but some cases did not fit the pattern. If a man spoke strange languages, or knew things he could not know, or showed strength or powers beyond human norms while in the throes of a psychotic fit, there must be something more to it than mere psychosis. He had said, his deep eyes utterly serious and sober, that an unclean spirit could afflict a mentally ill victim as easily as a sane one.

"But science has proved that spooks don't exist!" Hal had objected. "Mental illness is not more supernatural than—than a broken clock ringing thirteen! It is just a matter of a bent gearwheel in the brain, or a loose mainspring."

When Manfred asked him to name the year when a scientist had proven this, to produce the research, the case studied, the experimental evidence, Hal had no answer at all.

So here Hal stood, in the darkness, gripping his cane in two cold hands, dwelling on dark thoughts, hearing the creaks and mutterings from the dark house, seeing nothing but the high, thin windows hovering so far above him in the dark and lofty hall.

"I don't believe in ghosts," he murmured.

A more logical but more horrible explanation occurred to him, sending a chill into the core of his soul. He dismissed it before it even took the form of words in his mind, unwilling to even consider a thought so disloyal.

A wan and uncertain light gleamed the air ten feet above him, thirty paces or more away. It flickered and fluttered like a live thing. He saw the gleam in what seemed to be an arched tunnel hanging in midair. Closer the light came, and now he saw it was held by a slender shape in white. The shape had a round face, and some flowing paleness beneath, but no legs were visible. From the grace of its motions, it was clearly female.

Closer she came.

Wrongerwood by Candlelight

Then he heard the clack and clatter of heeled shoes on floorboards behind him and realized what he was seeing. It was Laurel in a white nightgown carrying a candlestick. She was in a corridor one floor up, approaching him at a right angle. He was seeing her image in a full-length standing mirror on the wide landing of the double stairway. His eye had mistaken the arched frame of the mirror for the mouth of a tunnel. It was not a legless ghost, but Laurel wearing dark silk stockings that were invisible in the black background.

As her candlelight came closer, he saw more and more of the vast main hall around him. It was filled with boxes, crates, and the oblong shapes of chairs and divans crouched under white sheets. To one side was a porcelain bathtub with glass balls in its claws. To the other, a grand piano. A vast chandelier with twenty curving metal arms was hanging on its chains only four feet off the ground, all its sockets empty of bulbs.

Laurel came into view from his left and walked down from the balcony to the landing, moving with a doe-like grace. The unruly stormcloud of her hair was tied back with red ribbon, but certain wanton strands had escaped and now clung to her silk-clad body. The candlelight reflected in the mirror behind her turned the sheer fabric of her gown into a half-invisible cloud of white that caressed her half-visible curves as she moved.

The vision robbed Hal of any possible breath.

She paused on the landing long enough for her lashes to brush her cheeks. Then, she continued gliding down the staircase until she was two steps above the bottom, her eyes now level with his. Her face was serene, her gaze unblinking and hypnotic.

Her pale nightgown fell in silken loose folds to her knees but left her neck and arms bare. Lace decorated the top of its voluptuous décolletage, with a little red bow nestled deeply within her cleavage that rose and fell with her uneven breath.

Hal wet his lips, afraid that if he spoke, he would wake and she would vanish. Usually, one is not allowed merely to stare at a woman for more than a moment without speaking or looking away, even if she is an intimate friend.

He could not have looked away to save his soul.

She voiced no objection and pretended no coyness. Instead, she simply stood, basking in his gaze, her face hiding all her thoughts.

Finally he forced himself to speak. "Where is Manfred?"

When she spoke, her voice seemed so familiar, her tone half-playful, that it brought him back suddenly to himself. She was his best friend's fiancée. The two would be wedded and happy together, despite Manfred's current doubts, and Hal would toast his friend and rejoice, and that would be the end of it!

"...so was called away. I hope it is not anything too, too dreadful. The drama of meeting my mother nearly did him in. Poor fellow. But it does a girl's heart good to know her brave hero will pull on the harpy's whiskers for her, doesn't it? Come on. We can bed together." She turned with a graceful motion, the candlelight playing with the shadows of her voluptuous figure.

Hal blinked. "I am sorry, what did you say?"

The beauty paused with one foot on an upper stair, and half-turned to look over her naked shoulder down at him. Her skin glowed, luminous, in the golden candlelight. "I said we can find you a bed together. To sleep in. Some of the furniture is moved in, but the power will not be on until next week, due to a tax lien or some sort of late payment. I would have called you to warn you off, but there is no phone here. Hungry? I assume you want something to nibble on before turning in. Come along."

She started up the stairs, silk fabric rustling. He was three steps behind her, his eyes at the level of her hips, which swayed delightfully in that bewitching manner that no other movement can match. The outline of her figure was clearly visible through the candle-lit silk. He chivalrously forced his eyes upward, and found himself gazing the voluminous cascade of dark, shining hair that spilled down over her white shoulders.

Gritting his teeth, he intentionally stubbed his toe against the stairs, hoping the distraction would take his mind off its traitorous path.

Such as the question of why she was wearing high heels with a nightgown?

He barely heard what she was saying. "I found a chamber that is fully furnished, with a working light and wood in the fireplace, and, of all things, a wine bottle. Thirsty? It is sort of a weird, Arab-looking affair shaped like a spiral shell or something. I think Manny's ancestors must have been half-cracked, some of them, or hired a half-cracked architect. Whether it was the excesses of the Edwardian Age, or the prudery of the Victorian Age that drove them mad, I am sure I could not say."

He blurted out, "Why are you dressed that way?"

She glanced down at herself as if in surprise. "Well, I was on my way to bed."

"You wear heels to bed?"

"No, the floor is cold, and these were the only pair I brought." She stretched out one shapely leg and pointed her toe. "Like them? I thought I was coming to dine, and I wanted to look nice, more fool I. You were hours late, and so I assumed Manfred had phoned you in time, and you were not coming. The cook is long gone, I sent her home, and so are the Levrier boys who helped move in the furniture. Carried in on horse-drawn wagons from the dock, all throughout last week, so it was quite a sight."

"Shouldn't you put something on to answer the door?"

Her green eyes flashed, perhaps in anger, perhaps in amusement. "Bad enough when my mother tells me what to wear! I am mistress in my own house here, or it soon will be! And I was not coming to answer the door because you did not ring the bell. I heard a noise and I came to look. I did not know the door had opened. Imagine my surprise to see you standing inside my locked house where no one is supposed to come unless invited! Now I am sorry I tempted you to become a break-in artist. I did not think it would become your profession."

"I was invited!"

"To come at five o'clock! What ungodly hour is it now? There are no clocks here. Invited guests ring the bell, they don't break in!"

"I did not ring the bell because there were no lights on, and I thought no one was home because I assumed you had gone down to the inn!"

"Anyone who was a thoughtless boob, I suppose," she said coolly. "Manfred was called away, and he took the keys with him. So if I left before you came, I would have had to leave the front door hanging open, which would have been unwise. But how is it that you are not locked out?"

"I have the key."

Now she stopped and turned, looking down at him, and her eyes did flash with anger, with no playfulness in them. "That is *preposterous*. Why would he give the keys to you and not to me?"

"I– I don't know... He wanted my help to solve the mystery of this house."

"I would like to solve the mystery of why he does not trust me!" she blazed. "At times, he is a total stranger to me. He disappears, sometimes for days on end, and later says he does not remember where he went!" Her eyes sought his. She said, "You have a funny look on your face. What has Manfred said about me? Is he having second thoughts?"

A quiet inner voice told Hal to tell the truth, but instead he threw out his chest and forced a hearty grin to his features and said, "No, he is madly, head-over-heels in love with you! He just wants to get his dissertation out of the way, and clear up these legal matters, get his fine new house here up and running—it is hectic. He is under stress! You should not read into things, you know, Miss du Lac?"

She tossed her head to throw stray strands back from her face, and sighed, and said, "Well, that is nice to hear, even though I know you don't mean a word of it. Shall we go and eat the dinner Manny had the cook whip up for us?"

Laurel took a step, then two, and looked back again. Hal had not moved. She said archly, "Or are you going to run off, leaving me alone in a haunted house to sleep on a bare cot again? Well, there is actually a four-poster bed in the master bedroom now, and a battery-powered space heater. I appreciate that you don't want to cause a scandal by seeing me without a chaperone, but I will remind you that I am a woman of iron self-control, and your attempts to tempt my virtue have fallen considerably short of your sinister intentions."

"My attempts at what? Miss du Lac, I am not the one who came to the door half-naked!"

"No, merely the one who broke in on me when I was half-naked!" she said with a malicious smile. "But come! All will be forgiven once you sit and eat, and drink the wine I found. Wonderful vintage. And stop worrying about my attire! You should see what the girls on the beach wear in France."

"If you could put something on..."

"This is actually my wedding dress. I just left the veil in the hatbox," she purred, and she swayed with languid, swinging steps down the corridor, her heels clattering brightly, taking the candle with her.

Seeing no escape, and cursing himself for a fool under his breath, he followed.

The Silver Chain

They stepped again into the Rose Crystal Chamber, where Laureline, as she had said, indeed spread out a fine supper table. There was no shock this time as their true memories returned, they merely straightened, looked one another in the eye, saw the recognition there, the truth they shared, the burning passion.

Then they were in each other's arms.

They held hands while they ate, and slipped morsels into each other's mouths, each forcing the other to drink more than was wise. After the meal, he started nibbling on her. She pulled him down onto the rug.

The madness of longing drove him further this time than he had dared before, so that by the time he pulled himself back from where they lay intertwined on a tigerskin rug before the blazing fire in which their shattered wine glasses lay, she was naked from the waist up, wearing little more than her silk stockings. Oddly, her black shoes were still on her feet, as if, in the midst of their passion, she had forgotten to kick then off.

Panting, head pounding, he stepped back to help himself to more wine and paused to drink in the frankly erotic vision of her. She lay carelessly draped over the fur rug, displaying to best advantage the sensuous contour of her soft body—her lovely shoulder, her wasp-like waist, her curving hip, the smooth black lines of her stockinged legs, and her shoes glinting like onyx. He had seen such seductive poses ten thousand times in advertisements, films, paperback covers, calendars, but this was real. She arched her back and smiled her ensorcelling smile not for a camera, not for an anonymous audience, but for him and him alone.

A strange sensation ran through him then, a heated, animal energy that inflamed his body even as it seared his conscience. She was a blessing and a blasphemy; she was rare wine cast indifferently into the briny sea, the nectar of the gods poured into a sewer. And yet, he burned to slake his thirst and drain her to the very dregs.

Henry whispered, "This cannot go on. I will go mad."

"Mad with what?"

"We really should not be doing this…" without meaning to do so, he took a half-step towards her.

"Mm. A girl likes to know that she is wanted." Laureline made a soft noise in the back of her throat, half-sigh, half-moan. Rolling over, she writhed against the tigerskin, her shoulders and knees touching the luxurious fur, her hips high, her head low. Firelight caressed her, a red-gold dappling that danced over her porcelain skin. "You do want me, don't you, Henry?"

"You know I do." His throat was thick, his voice was oddly deep. "You know damn well I do. Why are you doing this to me? This is so wrong."

"It will feel right soon, very soon. Everything is all right. Kiss me, that will make it all better!"

"Do you even realize what you are doing? Are you doing all this on purpose? Do all girls practice in a mirror looking seductive?"

Laureline rolled onto her back and put her hands above her head, smiling at him. "You think too much, Henry. Live! Love! Feel! It is like dancing; let yourself go! If you are doing it deliberately, step after careful step, you are doing it wrong. Do all men practice in a mirror looking bold and masterful, so menacing and huge and hairy?"

He glowered down at her, his broad and hairy chest glistening in the firelight where she had torn all his buttons away, his face stern, his eyes like fire, his countenance like a pagan war god, or a lion towering over its helpless prey.

"Am I now?" he said in a low growl, as the fire cast his huge shadow across the ceiling behind him. "Is that what you want?"

"Of course. When the antlers of the king stag of the forest affright the other does, his royal consort can queen it over them."

"Outside you—is *she* marrying Manfred for his money, then? His title?"

Laureline shook her head. "I don't know. I can't psychoanalyze her. Maybe it is for the security, or the illusion of security. Or maybe not. It's even possible I want to marry him just to get closer to you, but I fear what my mother would say if I wed an penniless American nobody. Out there, in that outer world, I am a coward. Only here am I true."

He stared at her, bewildered. "But I *am* a nobody! I cannot even break us out of this chamber into the outside!"

"In here, you are my knight in shining armor, my champion, my demigod. You are strong and give me strength. Do you think I could fight this shapeless nightmare of amnesia without you?"

Henry plunged his hand into the ice bucket, pulled out a handful of dripping ice cubes, and wiped them angrily against his face and neck, hissing in shock. The pounding heartbeat left his face and released his groin. He stuffed the handful of ice under one armpit, then the other, which certainly drove away his erotic thoughts.

Laureline sat up on the rug, her arms behind her to either side, palms on the fur, black-clad legs stretched before her, crossed at the ankles. She watched his antics with both eyebrows raised. "Well, that must smart!"

Henry said, "You and I, we have to control ourselves. Things are spinning out of control."

She smiled archly and leaned back on her elbows. "It's not working. You still look huge, hairy and menacing to me. Damp, to be sure, but still desirable."

"I cannot imagine why you love me."

She smiled. "It is like dancing, if you look at your feet, you break the spell. Why do I love you? Look at me. What do you see?"

"The most attractive woman in the world."

"Beauty fades. Five years, or ten, or when I have your first son, and this will be gone. I am wasting my life studying theater and going to parties, hunting for eligible bachelors, hanging out with silly girls my own age even sillier than I am. I am never going to change the world. Do you understand why I love you now?"

He shook his head, as if trying to drive away the echo of her words from his brain. *When I have your first son.* She had said it so casually, as if, in her heart, they were already wed.

Laureline was saying, "All the little starlets and stage hands I know talk about power and empowerment, and how women must be strong. Strong, strong, strong is all their talk, all day. But I am frail, really. Like glass. My life could be shattered in an instant. Do you understand how opposites attract? I am sure all the beasts aboard Noah's Ark must have stared at the restless sea in awe. But after the waters receded, the fish learned to adore the land for its hardness and stillness, wondering why the mountains never break like curlers. You will not break either."

Since he felt as if he were already broken in two, he scowled and said nothing.

She smiled up at him, and saw his thought on his face. "Maybe you don't feel strong. That is because I have not been doing my job. It is the woman's job to put strength in her man. We are designed to need each other, man and mate. The cavegirl cannot kill a mastodon, but she can cheer up and cheer on the big hulking brute who can… and pan-sear a mastodon steak for him afterwards, in a light wine sauce with olive oil, butter and peppercorns."

"That *does* sound delicious," Henry said, "But it doesn't seem like a fair deal for the cavegirl."

"Do you think you men would kill mastodons without us, instead of lying about the cave all day, drinking cave-beer from a coconut shell?"

"On second thought, maybe the caveboy is the one with the wrong end of this deal."

"I'll say! You have to kill whole forests of birds and beasts for us, so we can have doeskin-leather bikinis and have necklaces of bearclaws thonging our cavegirl throats, and can adorn our cavegirl hair with prehistoric feathers. Speaking of adornment: Did you get it? Did you bring it?"

He had not taken off his shirt, pants, or boots, but his jacket had been flung across the chamber. He retrieved it and drew a long, flat box of black velvet from an inner pocket. He came and knelt.

She sat up straight and clapped her hands in delight.

He snapped open the box.

Inside, like a snake made of solid light, was a silver necklace with a tear-shaped diamond pendant. Tiny chips of ruby, garnet, and diamond dust circled the boss from which the pendant hung, and the boss was adorned with a pattern of waves and fishes. The links near the boss were tiny dolphins of silver, curling this way and that, each holding the tail of the one before it in its mouth. It was a cunning work, and Henry was sure the artisan must have used a microscope to see and work the fine detail, the drops of spray, the scales of the fish, the smiles of the bottle-noses.

Laureline made little noises of feminine joy and knelt at his feet. Holding up her outrageous masses of hair with both hands, she presented her graceful, swanlike neck. Her eyes were lowered demurely. The firelight gleamed against her naked breasts and the soft contours of her white belly.

Kneeling thus, Henry thought Laureline looked, in that light, in that pose, very much like the cavegirl she had described.

He snapped the silver chain around her neck. She put her hand to her bosom, looking down, to admire the glinting jewels.

She looked so lovely, there in the dancing light of the fire, that he could not take his eyes from her. She was so precious to him, so dear, far more so than a thousand such necklaces.

He imagined their future life, once this terrible curse had been broken, picturing them together, traveling, laughing. He pictured their future house, the children that they would have, sweet, dark-haired girls and stalwart, towheaded boys.

He recalled a time, soon after they had met, when he had come upon her bending over, talking to the granddaughter of the inn-keeper in town. She had looked so attentive, so intent, so patient, as she listened to the child. He had been entirely captivated.

He always pictured her speaking to their future children with exactly that same radiant expression.

Laureline spoke: "I was lost last time, and about to give up, and you were my strength. Now it is my turn to put your heart back in you! This proves your new system, your memory mansion, can help you recall more things more clearly. We have more control over our blind Out-of-Doors selves now! It was easy for me to lure us both back into the Rose Crystal Chamber this time! And this necklace—don't you see, it is a symbol! We are fighting our own subconscious minds, the minds that take over and make us forget our love when we step out that hateful rosy door! But symbols have great power in the subconscious mind!"

"I am still not sure what this will do."

"I will write a note telling myself to wear it Wednesday, and you write a reminder about meeting me for golf. You will see this glorious pendant on me, and you will remember. Here, now! Kiss me on the back of the neck where the clasp is! Kiss me where the teardrop rests! Look at the chain! Stare at it closely!"

"But I won't remember it is I who gave it to you."

"Why not? You bought it! You should be able to remember that. Put all the images of me you can into your new memory halls. Adorn the walls with them! Study me like a painter would a model. You will forget, but your lips and eyes will remember the necklace! When you see it, the impulse will break through, and you'll have to kiss me!"

"And then what? I kiss my best friend's wife-to-be? How will that change anything?"

She bit her lip. Still kneeling, she wrapped her white arms around his upper thighs. "Think of Sleeping Beauty! The kiss will break the spell!"

When he bent down, his mouth half an inch from hers, she put her slim fingers on his lips, and whispered. "No more tonight! Only if you are burning, aching, longing, will you remember. Your body and blood might remember, even if your mind does not."

He did step away from her again. This time, however, he had to put his whole head in the ice bucket to cool the rebellion in his flesh.

Laureline looked at him through heavily lidded eyes, her lips pursed. "You are going to have the locals start telling their old stories about ghosts and sea-witches, if they hear you howl like that."

Henry shook the ice water out of his eyes. "You slept in here that night. Why did you say you slept on the cot? Because that is what I remembered, too."

Her smile vanished.

She said sharply, "This means someone is coordinating the false memories. Do you think it is Manfred? You know he has all those books on hypnotism and the occult for his dissertation. He went to Rome last year, and got permission to study the books in the black library under the Vatican, where copies of the most blasphemous grimoires and manuals captured from warlocks and heretics are stored. Maybe including that Italian fellow you read, Giordano Bruno. Didn't you tell me he was burned at the stake in the Sixteenth Century?"

"It cannot be Manfred," said Henry curtly.

But his mind returned, against its will, to the suspicion that had touched his mind when he first entered the house. He and Laureline were bewitched by some manner of hypnotism that plagued them when they left this room. In all the world, he only knew one man who was studying mesmerism. And by some unlikely chance, it happened to be the very same man who owned this house.

Even he was forced to admit this seemed like a rather unexpected coincidence.

She looked up at him, and her eyes seemed deeper than he had ever seen them, like two emerald oceans, fathomless, bottomless. "He is descended from Arviragus and Anna, the Virgin's cousin, from Avallach and Eudelen, from whose heirs Helen of the Cross was born, who married Constantine the Great. From him King Athrwys son of Uthyr sprung."

Henry started. Some scholars thought Athrwys to be King Arthur, or, rather, the real name of the figure about whom the legends had gathered. He was struck by a sudden notion. Were not such gathered legends very much like the false memories that robbed him and Laureline of their true selves whenever they stepped into the air of the outer world?

He wondered uneasily what, if anything, Manfred might remember were he to enter this chamber? Would his friend remember the real version of events, where he had called Laureline a harpy and had not wished to wed her? Or had he changed his mind? And, if so, what lengths had he been willing to go to in order to win this emerald-eyed beauty?

Henry shivered and rejected this line of thought as absurd. Still, it was strange that Manfred, who had aided him in his studies, had never told him of any blood connection to the legendary King Arthur.

She said, "Owen Glendower the Magician comes from the same bloodline. Donne and De Vere families, who are the earls of Oxford, descend from the Magician, as does the Cavendish family—and the Hathaways. You know that what is happening to the two of us has no natural explanation. Who has the better motive, the stronger desire, to take me away from you? Why is this chamber, in his house, his very house, the only place where we are immune?"

Because were there any truth to it, the temptation to claim the willing girl as his own, to take her and have her before Manfred did, to consummate his passion not in love but as an act of preemptive retaliation, was simply too strong.

And because the accusation seemed so reasonable now that it came from her lips, so inevitable, Henry ran from the chamber, seeking the oblivion that would wash into forgetfulness the horrible thought that his best friend might be his betrayer.

There was no other way to forget it.

The Garret

Hal found himself in dark halls with his shirt buttons missing, dripping with icy water, and wondering for the life of him where Laurel and her candle had gone. Perhaps she went to change into something more decent, he hoped. He had bumped into a ladder in the dark, where a careless workman had left a bucket of water that had turned icy in the winter cold. Had she been doused as well? Oddly, he could not remember. She would have had no choice but to go change if she, too, had been caught in the icy drench. His imagination of what would have happened to her silky nightgown under such circumstances made him feel less chilled.

He stumbled around the lightless mansion for a time, barking his shins on unexpected crates the workmen had left behind, wondering where the dinner could be that she had promised him. Finally he found his way into a part of the mansion he recognized, despite the gloom, and found the cot in the spare attic room. It was equipped with a sleeping bag and an inflatable pillow. The hunting rifles were gone, and the pyramid of cans had been placed in a footlocker next to a cooler, and several car batteries were wired to a hotplate. There was also an electric teapot half-full of water and a propane lantern as well. His dinner consisted of a beer bottle from the cooler and a Styrofoam cup of instant noodles. He ate less than half, surprised to find himself not hungry at all.

The Chain and the Links

In Hampshire, Barton-on-Sea was between Highcliffe and Milford-on-Sea. The clubhouse was an imposing glass-walled structure with a peaked roof of brown slate like a tortoise shell. It was situated on a green hill commanding a splendid view across the Solent to the Needles on the Isle of Wight, along to Old Harry Rocks at Swanage. The golf course here dated back to 1879.

The day was blustery and unseasonably cold, with snarls of cloud promising rain that never came scudding swiftly against a deceptively bright blue-white sky. The lawn was as green and neat as only two centuries of maintenance could produce, surrounded by thickets of darker green rough and water traps like shining rugs.

Hal resisted the impulse to swat his golfball over the cliff into the sea. He could not remember why he had agreed to take Laurel golfing on Wednesday. A month ago, he would have thought nothing of it, but ever since the day that they broke into the High House of Wrongerwood, he had found himself entertaining distinctly unbestmanly thoughts. A private outing with her seemed a foolish move, especially with Manfred's doubts troubling him.

But agreed he had, and now he must make the best of it.

She was dressed smartly, obeying the strict dress code of the club, while managing to subvert it. Laurel wore white knee socks and very short shorts, her crisp white blouse tucked neatly into her wide black belt, buttons of her short-sleeved blouse straining wherever her bosom heaved in a laugh or indrawn breath. How she could breathe with her belt cinched so tightly was a mystery to him. She looked like a pouter pigeon.

She was dressed like someone set to walk a sandy summer beach. The other women golfing were wearing sweaters.

For some reason, she was wearing the expensive diamond pendant Hal had bought her as sort of a pre-wedding gift, and, against his will, his eyes were magnetized to it. The little silver dolphins nestled in the dell of her breasts, and seemed to mock him with their knowing smiles.

She was fairly good at the game, perhaps better than he was, at least at first. By the sixth hole, he was suspicious that she was deliberately missing shots to let him win, a habit he found very girlish and very annoying. Her normal gaiety was bubbling over, and she giggled at everything, funny or not.

The wind was coming from the cliffs, and the balls in flight during drives tended to hook north. Laurel wore her hair piled high atop her head in a Gibson, adorned by an absurd pin shaped like a golf ball, but even so the long unruly strands tended to escape the coiffeur, and fly and leap in the wind.

As they played, his eyes were repeatedly drawn to the back of her neck, naked with her hair pinned up as it was, with a few little stray wisps showing. The clasp of the chain rested there. He kept feeling this tingling in his lips and this unexpected urge to nuzzle her there, or to nip her ear right where her dangling earring swung: earrings which annoyed him because such jewelry was utterly inappropriate for a golf course!

It was clear she was flirting with her poor caddy as well, a freckled teenager with a thick Scottish brogue and thicker acne. She kept calling him "sweetie" and "dearie," no doubt because she had forgotten his name, and she touched his hand whenever he handed her a club, bathing him in lingering, warm looks from beneath her half-lidded lashes.

Why the devil was the woman wearing so much jewelry during a golf game? And why must she always contrive to be walking in front of him as they strolled from tee to tee? Between her parading herself before him and her incessant flirtations with the caddy, Hal found himself tempted to swat her across the backside with a fairway wood.

By the eighth hole, she was insisting that Hal give her tips on her stance and swing. So naturally, he had to put his arms around her to show her how to grip the putter, his breath warm on her ear. The playful wind tossed strands of her tickling hair that caught in his mouth or fluttered over his eyes and nose. It was nearly unendurable.

She exclaimed with equal enthusiasm over well-placed shots and abominable flops, shanks and whiffs. Whenever she did so, however, just as she turned, she would catch her breath. This tiny motion set the diamond bouncing and flashing at her cleavage, drawing his eyes and thoughts there. It was as if he could smell and taste her, as if his tongue and lips remembered the curving shape of her from some erotic dream of the night.

He knew he should have told her no.

On the ninth fairway, she teed off with her four iron, a picture-perfect swing. Her front leg was straight, her back leg a smooth arch of thigh and calf, with only one toe touching the grass; her torso twisted and gluteal muscles clenched, showing off the perfect lines of her legs, hips and wasp-thin waist. Her white and shapely arms were overhead. The club was over her shoulder with the shaft nearly parallel to her back leg. Her breasts jutted outward, and her swan-neck turned just so, betraying that delicate line which reaches from a woman's ear to her clavicle.

The wind gusted, plastering her blouse against her body, making her more naked than naked. Her wild hair strands snapped and soared like a dark pennant. Laurel froze in that pose for a moment—like a Greek goddess of white marble, contrived with emeralds for eyes and onyx locks—as the ball flew true in a smooth arc, over a hundred yards, bouncing and rolling to rest on the green within feet of the flag.

All at once, it was like the surface ice of a winter river broke in his mind, and the rushing thoughts flowing below were exposed. The sight of her in all her graceful beauty, her confidence, her high-hearted humor, her little stabs of sly wit, her luxurious sensuality, her film-actress glamour, everything about her shattered his heart at that moment.

She turned toward him, tossing her head in a mare-like motion to fling her hair away, her smile white and dazzling, her posture triumphant, the pendant blazing at her breast. "A stony! Well? Aren't you going to say *nice shot?*"

Hal could not speak, could not breathe.

This was no mere admiration for his best friend's wife-to-be. This was deep, erotic, raw passion, but, paradoxically, also tender, spiritual, and pure and selfless. He both wanted to cherish her like a saint in worship and to take her here and now on the grass in the blustery wind, and damnation to the caddy if he saw too much.

It was love.

He suddenly remembered why he had bought that necklace. He had not known why at the time. It was not in apology for some imagined wrong. No; it was a token of his love. The matter was as simple as that.

The only thing he wanted in life, the only thing that would make him truly happy, belonged to another man, a man whose friendship meant more than life to him. A man he could not betray nor even wound.

Manfred had everything. And that left him with nothing.

Simple.

In a black mood, his face dark, he drove his ball over the cliffs into the sea, threw his club into the grass, and stalked back toward the clubhouse without a word. The caddy stared in shock and silence at his retreating back, and Laurel called out to him, at first in confusion, then in wrath.

He left the keys to his sportscar with the manager, telling him to give them to Miss du Lac when she came in, and then he called a taxi.

Chapter 6

Wolfhound and Cunning Woman

Talk at the Inn

It was later that week. Hal was sitting at a table in the dark corner of the pub occupying what had once been the stable when the Stocks Inn had been a farmhouse, back before his nation was born. He was seated facing the fire, separated from the next table by a wall of stone that might once have been part of a stall. The half-melted candle on his table was unlit.

Hal had spent his days and nights before this leafing through volumes in libraries and, when he could get permission, private collections, gathering material for his paper. It astonished him how many records were still on microfiche, not digitized, or crumbling in the poorly preserved originals. It was depressing; it was a whole world of forgotten words.

He worked in a haze of distraction, wasting hours staring at a single document without reading it, chain-smoking enough to fill his rented room with ash and smog, and then taking long walks to clear his head. The room he was renting was from an old widower named Drake who ran a tobacco shop downstairs. Not only did the landlord not mind the smell, nor Hal ever run short of cigarettes, but the rich and delicious scent from downstairs would wake the craving in him at all hours. Not that the landlord approved of cigarettes. At the landlord's avuncular urging, Hal was developing a taste for fine cigars. One more expensive habit he could not afford.

Hal had blown out the candle on the table here, so that he would not be tempted to pull out a smoke and light up. And it was easier to brood when sitting here, staring at the leaping flames of the wide fireplace that occupied the rear of the tavern opposite the bar.

He loved Laurel. That was the simple and terrible thing.

It was fortunate that she had no idea. All her thoughts were absorbed in Manfred, whom she loved and whose love she deserved. She would never guess, she must never be permitted to guess, his true feelings.

This meant he had to act normal, act natural, and neither arrive too early nor too late at the weekly dinners he had arranged with Manfred. But, of course (so the frantic squirrel of his thought ran and ran, as if on a treadmill) he could not always arrive exactly on time, because that might seem suspicious, too.

Hal heard the clomping of boots, then the rustling and shuffling of a trio of local men gathered into the booth behind him, smelling of hay and sheep and honest sweat. Hal smiled in surprise to hear them toast the Queen with a clink of noggins, before seating themselves for some serious drinking. It seemed the sort of thing that real men with deep roots did.

Manfred had once told him that the islanders with stubborn loyalty still toasted to "Le Duc"—the Duke of Normandy—who ruled the Channel Islands until the Fall of Rouen in 1206. Perhaps these were modern, forward-looking youths, who had caught up to the Sixteenth Century. Hal smiled, now straining to listen for other amusing or time-defying oddities.

The Sarkmen spoke in a patois of French, called Sercquiais. Manfred had insisted it was not a dialect, but its own language, and claimed, (but for what reason, he did not say) that this language could never be written down. Be that as it may, it was close enough to French to let Hal puzzle out their meaning.

After a round of coarse jokes, complaints about the market and the health and safety regulations, or other idle matters, the three lads dropped their voices to murmurs.

The first voice was raspy. "...from a penniless student studying old books, to the Lord of the Manor in a single forenoon? It's not right..."

The second voice was sullen and thin, like that of an older man: "What old books, is my wondering. Who knows what the old heathens wrote down, back before the dark time?"

Hal froze, not daring to breathe. What was that? Had he heard that word correctly? The Sarks' patois added a *dr* sound to some of their word endings. Had the farmer said *noir ans* (dark years) or *n'ouidr un* (not a yes)?

The third voice was more melodic, but dripped with sarcasm, "Lord Manfred's not killed his aunts and cousins. He'd need to fear of the ghosts of the house."

Hal was flabbergasted. Were grown men of this day and age taking about ghosts? He must have misheard. The patois was throwing him off. The word for *spectacle* or *spectrum* was nearly the same as the word for specters. Perhaps the farmboy only meant Manfred would fear the *sight* of the house, or the *extent* of the house?

The sullen second voice said, "He's a studying one, reading the old ways from the old books. He knows the words to open and close. Coalblack dare not turn to the dogs..."

Hal was not sure what that meant. The word might have been a name: Colby rather than Coalblack. But what was that last part? Turn to the dogs? Turn away the dog? Turn into a dog?

The sullen voice: "...shots from the House on feast day of Joachim and Anne. Man's gun."

The raspy voice: "A bad day for our kind! The day of the Grandparents of the White Child is ill of star and stuck with frowning planets, for the older ghosts walk then."

Older sights? No. The word was definitely *ghosts* this time.

"And what has become of Nightenthrope?" This seemed to be a fourth voice than had spoken before, a deeper voice. "He has not been seen since.... The new lord killed him dead, killed young Nightenthrope, just as he killed the old Dame... the Countess said she was one of us."

But it was impossible. From the sounds, there had only been three who stepped into the booth, Hal was sure. Maybe one of the three men had simply lowered his pitch, or cleared his throat with a strong drink, or was doing a voice impersonation, or... or they were talking on a speakerphone, here on the island with no phone service! There had to be a reasonable explanation.

The smell from the booth seemed to be changing. Someone had brought in a big dog, perhaps. But there had been no sound of claws scrabbling on the floorboards. The stench of dog was unmistakable.

The fourth voice said, "Nightenthrope must have seen somewhat too much, or heard."

The sneering voice said, "He was always the peeking and prying sort. Peering here and there. Stuck his nose in too far this time, is all. Better off without him."

The fourth voice, the deep one, spoke. "I say the new Lord is a murderer and kinslayer. Killed his own blood, that's what. The thing is, what are we to do about it? No outsider will help us, no Englishmen."

What would Hal see if he stood up and peered over the partition separating the booths? A wild, irrational fear took hold of him, and he feared that he would see shapes no longer human slumped over their drinks, hairy-faced things, fanged things, with pointed ears poking out from under their caps.

The raspy voice said, "No. Wrong you are. The new one would not soil his hands. He is quality, he is. Too fine by half. The American did it. He has the killing look in his eye. I've seen those who come back from war. They have the look. Sure, there is a sword in his cane. Or a gun barrel. Why else carry it? Who carries a cane? He has no limp."

The fourth voice said, "We must deal with the American first. The empty cave will tell us how. We will heed the empty cave."

Hal felt cold sweat tickling him. Was he hearing men plan his own murder? It seemed impossible, something from a dark film with a sadistic director.

Empty caves? He must have heard wrong.

Cave was *grotte*. Maybe the thickly accented voice had said *grot* or *gueux*, which was slang for a wretch, a ragamuffin, or a beggar.

But that made less sense. Why would an empty beggar give them orders? On the other hand, *cruex* could also mean sunken, or gaunt, or vain. So these men who smelled like dog fur were getting advice from either a sunken cave, a gaunt wretch, or a vain ragamuffin.

Hal's thoughts rattled in his head like dice in a cup. What was real? Perhaps he was hallucinating. It ran in his family, after all.

The sneering voice uttered a breathing sort of wheezing laugh, "It's all in your bad dreaming, boys. Listen to your talk! Were the new Master a killer, why is he so openhanded with his money? Mother Dove to cook his meals he hired. Those damned and rowdy Wolfhounds, got work up at the Wrongerwood House weeding and planting. Open the old gardens. Why them?"

The other voices mumbled and grunted, but did not contradict the sneering voice.

The voice continued: "Burt and Liam Wolfhound are the worst farmhands on the island! The Wolfhounds? Eh, think of that? Why them?"

But no, he was not saying *Wolfhound*. Manfred had mentioned hiring a man named Liam Levrier to do gardening and keep the grounds. Hal realized his ears had misled him. *Levrier* meant "wolfhound" or "greyhound", but it was also a proper name. It was as if a non-English speaker were to have overheard talk about a man named *Smith* and think the conversation concerned shoeing horses or mending pots.

"The Levriers? Eh, think of that? Why them? 'Cause the folks is poor and wanting, what with their mother in hospital and all. Lord Hathaway is taking up here, on Sark, not away in London like the Dame."

At that moment, the barkeep came bustling up to refill drinks and swap gossip, and the talk turned to hat day at school, or the visiting historian from St Ouen in Jersey who was writing a book on Commandant Lanz during the war years.

There was a commotion at the door as two of the local women came in, one of them calling crossly for her husband. Hal heard the farmhands saunter to the door to expostulate, excuse, and explain. He was not sure if there were three or four sets of footsteps, and an inner voice warned him not to be seen. A few feet from him, with a wall between it and the rest of the room, was a side door. It led him past the larder, wine cabinet, and privy and then out into the bright late-afternoon sunshine.

Here his fears evaporated, suddenly revealed as irrational indeed. There were no hairy monsters plotting, but there clearly was trouble among the locals, and evil suspicions to be allayed. He would have to warn Manfred. He almost turned back to see who those farmhands were, discover their names, and see if they had been four or three. But then the need to arrive on time without being early or late pricked him, and he strode up Rade Street, twirling his walking stick.

Before he entered the forest, Hal took out his memorandum book and made a note to himself. His memory had been rather spotty, and he was afraid of forgetting even simple things.

Warn Wolfhounds about the Talking Animals! The Gaunt Man has landed on Sark. His stronghold is in the sunken caves.

He chuckled at his outlandish wording. Phrasing it that way would certainly fix it in memory.

Better yet, Hal took a moment to shut his eyes and picture the talking animals gathered at the doors and windows of his memory mansion, fangs bared and claws upraised, carrying torches and clubs. For some reason, there was also an image of Laurel diving into the fish pond behind the house. She was wearing a black one-piece bathing suit of sealskin leather, very dark and shiny, and did not seem worried about the talking animals gathered at the front. The diamond necklace like a circle of cold fire was around her kissable neck.

What had he meant that to remind him of?

Mnemonic devices did no good if you could not remember them.

Wrongerwood by Daylight

This was his first time seeing the Seigneurie House by day. Before going in, he took the opportunity to walk around the main house, retracing more or less his footsteps of the first visit, when he had broken in.

The great house looked smaller in the sunlight, but not any less impressive. The craftsmanship of architecture was astonishing, and the artistry of images in stone corbels or stained glass windows. Each detail was impregnated with the weight of time.

The simple and masculine lines of the South Wing with its chapel and signal tower betrayed an Edwardian influence; the romantic flourishes and eccentricities of ornament of the North Wing were Victorian; the classical portico of the West Wing and many brick chimneys betrayed Georgian tastes; the square and austere Main Wing to the East was Stuart; the uppermost dome was intricately Gothic, a phantasmagoric display of flying buttresses and leaning drainpipes shaped as gargoyles; the Cloister tower beneath it was Anglo-Saxon in its sparse stone dignity.

Thunderstruck, Hal realized that this house was the memory mansion of England. Each period of history back to the Battle of Hastings was represented here.

And who knew what earlier and older things might be buried beneath, from the age of Arthur, or Caesar, or the prehistoric Picts who raised massive monoliths and henges in high places or dark vales and danced and sacrificed and committed abominations to wild and maddened beast-masked gods whose names no scholar can unearth?

To the rear, he saw half a dozen men in work clothes hoeing and ditching in the barren brown square of what had once been the gardens. Two more lads, armed with ladders, were in the apple tree arbor. He wondered if these were the Levriers, whom he had heard called the worst gardeners on the island. He saw one of them digging with his hands rather than a shovel, and suspected it might be so.

Something winking and shining in the grass at the foot of an apple tree caught his eye.

Shells

Hal came closer, and saw the sunlight reflected off a small metal object as big as a man's finger. He stooped and plucked it from the grass. It was a spent shell from a heavy-caliber rifle.

He looked, and saw this tree was marred and scraped with claw marks. The bark was peeled away in long parallels, and the living wood beneath was scarred. Hal stepped under the tree, knelt down. Here were dozens of spent shells where the grass was trampled, and a broken twigs overhead. The number of shells was frightening to him. He was not sure why, but his heart was pounding madly.

Preoccupied, Hal jumped when a huge dog behind him spoke. "What've you got there, sir?"

Hal found himself on his feet, back to the tree, walking stick raised high like a weapon. A stalwart and scruffy-looking freckle-faced red-haired man in a full beard and a brown smock was reeling back, saying, "Hold on, hold on, sir! I meant no harm!"

Hal blinked, wondering what he had just seen. Was his mind playing tricks? The man was about his age, give or take a year, and burly like a linebacker. His hands were horny with hard work and looked like he could crack walnuts in his knuckles without resorting to a nutcracker. "Sorry! I was just thinking you were a—that is, I am startled. Are you Levrier?"

"Liam's my name, sir."

Hal pointed at the ground, then at the tree. "What do you make of this?"

"That's not my fault, sir."

"No one is blaming anyone for anything, Liam. You asked me what I have. Here." Hal tossed him the shell.

Liam sniffed the shell. "Fired not today, but not long past. No rust. A week or two."

"Fired by whom?"

"England has pretty strong laws about guns, but hunting is still allowed for some lords."

"Fired at what?"

"Hm. I don't know what you'd shoot with this. Maybe a yak. But ain't no yaks in these parts. There is Red Deer in the woods yonder." He gestured toward Wrongerwood. "But they belong to the Queen, and no one hunts them."

"Are there still Red Deer in England?" Hal asked, feeling a moment of delight. "But how could they be on this small island?"

"That I could not say, sir. Island is bigger than it seems. And your eyes would be big as saucers, if you knew what can come out of them woods."

Hal said, "How do you read these marks and prints?"

"Someone came from the house, seems like, with a long stride, wearing boots, firing every step he took at some beastie. Pretty large, seeing the size of those claws. Chased it into the tree, and then stood underneath, and fired rounds into the beast point blank."

"What happened to the body?"

Liam shrugged. "Dragged away by the hunter, most like."

"And who would that be?"

"Now, if I were a wagering man, I would have said yourself, sir."

Hal tried to hide his expression, but he felt that same sensation he remembered when he was a young boy in school, the day he learned the world was spinning at unimaginable speeds while whirling about the sun which was orbiting the core of the Milky Way, that was, in turn, rushing through intergalactic space in toward the core Virgo Cluster. It was too much motion at once, too dizzying.

"You're the American," said Liam. "You have the key to the house. You've gone sporting and hunting with Lord Manfred before, back when he was Mr. Hathaway."

"*How the devil do you know that?*"

Liam grinned sheepishly. "I was his Lordship's loader when you were shooting grouse in Scotland, sir. Dame Hathaway sent me to mind him, and I needed the work. I stood two feet from you, and heard all your talk with him about books and cars and some right scandalous talk about women, sir. You don't remember me, do you, not a wee bit? Not to worry! Folk never look at those who wait on them in the face, not even Americans."

"And about the keys?"

"You walked up here last week, in the night, and let yourself into the main house. You went up the only road, and you were not crawling in tall grass nor ducking your head, so everyone in the village saw you. You were alone with that Miss du Lac. On this island she has a name. We call her the Charming Girl."

Hal reached into his overcoat pocket, meaning to pull out his memorandum book and double-check the date. Something about Liam's story was not quite right. Manfred only knew of Dame Hathaway as a distant relative back two years ago. How could she have known he needed a servant for his sport shooting that weekend? But then he realized he had replaced the book into his other pocket after he had made a note earlier. What, then, was this? It was about the same size and shape as a small book, but much heavier.

He drew it out of his pocket. It was a flat black case with a silver clasp shaped like an ermine spot. Inside were a row of cartridges in loops. The case was mostly empty.

Liam silently held the spent cartridge up to the bullets in the case. The caliber and model was the same. "I say 'twas you, sir, that shot whatever it was."

Hal turned, trying to see which garret window was the one which contained that barren upper room with the cot. There were four garret windows peering from the slope of the roof.

"Why don't I remember it, then?"

"That I cannot say, sir."

Dining by Firelight

Burdened by thoughts, he did not see at first that the main door was answered before he knocked by a freckle-cheeked redhead in a white cap and lacy apron. "Hello?" he said, surprised. "And who are you?"

She curtseyed. "Brigit is my name, sir. You're the American?"

He put his hand out to shake, and she stared at it, and giggled, but before he could withdraw it, she seized it with both hands and shook it energetically. "How-dee!" she said, in an atrocious mimic of a Yank accent.

"I've just been engaged," she said. "I am Mrs. Columbine the Cook's daughter."

For a moment he wondered whom she was marrying, or how she could marry twice, so it took him a moment to unmistake her meaning.

She escorted him past empty rooms and unopened crates into the West Wing, and suddenly there was carpeting beneath, and wallpaper on the walls. The dining hall itself had tall and thin windows looking toward the west. The slender and level sunbeams passed overhead and struck the far wall, leaving the room below in shadow. There were candles in branched candlesticks on the white linen table cloth, but it served to emphasize rather than alleviate the thickness of the shadows lurking among the roof beams, or behind the pillars. The light came from a walk-in fireplace, large as a blacksmithy, roaring and whistling. On the chimney stones above was an image of the watchful lion of Sark wrought in pale metal.

Laurel was there, wearing a blue silk strapless floor-length gown with a sweetheart neckline that seemed to cling to her form by magnetism. She wore opera gloves, and opals in her coronet. Her black hair fell down around her like the mantilla of a Spanish bride, or the hood of a Blackfriar, and spilled over the arms of her chair. At her breast, shining, flickering with light that breathed when she breathed, was the diamond pendant.

The sight of her took away his power of speech.

Manfred wore a jacket and a dark expression.

The dinner seemed curiously formalized, a stageplay presented for no audience. Manfred and Laurel sat at opposite ends of a long table, and an old Welshman with a scarred and blackened face named Mr. Nodenson acted as butler and footman, and brought the dishes from the kitchen.

"I am having more security installed," said Manfred, after they were done with the soup and had toasted each other's health. He stood and ceremoniously carved the joint with a large knife. He pointed with his knife at the windows. "Some of the local boys came by last night for a bit of vandalism. I have a few smashed windows to replace, and some beer bottles tossed against the bricks to have picked up, but it is worrisome. I want grates on some of the windows and doors."

He sat and passed the plates to Mr. Nodenson, who carried them the long way down the absurdly long table to where Hal sat midmost, and, then, eventually, to Laurel at the far end.

"What is stopping you?" asked Hal.

He wanted to tell Manfred first thing about what he'd heard in the Pub, and seen in the back gardens, but he eyed the burned and blackened face of Mr. Nodenson warily, not knowing if he were a local, and decided to wait until he could speak to Manfred out of earshot.

Manfred said, "The National Trust for Places of Historic Interest or Natural Beauty has a veto over everything I do. One the one side, they are against my marriage, since they hope Wrongerwood House will be donated to them in lieu of death duties when I die. On the other, the Director-General is Dame Helen-Gosh, who used to play cards with Dame Hathaway, so I may have some influence there. Now, if I could afford to hire more lawyers, there is certainly more work to be done! Mr. Twokes is going mad."

Laurel smiled sweetly, "He has not far to go. Really, darling, if you'd taken my advice and gotten rid of that creaky old curmudgeon, and hired someone younger, and, well, *hungrier*, you might have had the lights on by now."

Manfred ignored her and continued, "Twokes got a preliminary injunction quashed, and so the undisputed fraction of the money from the trust and the estate is in my hands now, and it was enough to hire the gardeners, and the woman who comes up from the village at mealtimes to cook for me. It is not permanent staff, mind you!"

"If you had spent the money on a modern kitchen, you could do all the cooking yourself," Laurel said. "I don't know what you English have against comfort! If a microwave or electric stove is too continental and revolutionary for you, what about a gas stove?"

Hal took a bite of the meat, and found it so delicious and savory, he had to smother a full-mouthed mumble of pleasure. He wondered if this were because it was cooked over naked flames on a spit, the old-fashioned way?

Manfred said, "The power company man evidently hates me personally and is carrying out a weird vendetta by trying to annoy me to death rather than shoot me cleanly in the head. He says he cannot connect anyone with outstanding liens. And the man from the

Television Licenses Authority is mad as a hatter, for he insists I pay the damned tax into the Government Consolidated Fund before the lien is released on the property! And when I tell him I don't even own one of those damned idiot boxes, he insists that I give an inspector a tour of the house, unlocking every door and attic for him to confirm I don't have one. Does he think Edward the Confessor hid his telly on the Island of Sark, and picked this pile as the place to squirrel it away? What utter rot! The man actually thinks I can take time off from writing my dissertation to come down here and prove I am free from television. I should take another IQ test, and if it has not dropped sharply, that should suffice to prove I don't own one!" He stabbed his fork into the meat with a sharp motion, and grinned.

Hal said, "That is a bit harsh on him, Manny. Why can't you just take a few hours off from studying to come unlock the doors here?"

The grin vanished. "Listen, old man, you might think you have time to spare working on your dissertation, taking off long and lazy afternoons to go golfing and all that, but some of us want the grand and glorious title of Doctor of Philosophy!" Manfred shook his head dubiously. "I don't know what's gotten into you of late, but fortunately I have the library stocked with copies of my books and materials from school. Let us hurry the dinner, because reading by gaslight is something awful. We have about two hours before sunset."

Laurel said, "But Henry must come with me to see the house!" She turned and smiled at him, and Hal ached at the sight. He almost did not hear what she said. Something about furniture and goods from old Dame Hathaway being returned from storage, now that the law recognized Manfred as the heir. "And some of the paintings are priceless! The conservator had already collected bids from museums and such before Manfred popped up. You must come and see! There is this one chamber—no one seems to know when it was added to the house, and it is not on the floorplans or described in the Historical Trust documents."

But Manfred was scowling. "We need the time to work, and Hal much more than I. Do you know how much is riding on getting this Fellowship? They are not going to give you an extension, you know. It is time to crack the whip! I thought that was the whole point of us getting together today?"

Hal said, "No, not at all. You invited me here so that we could uncover the riddle of the house. We said. We were drinking at that place in Wareham or Worgret or wherever it was. The Grain-mill or something it was called. Don't you remember?"

Manfred said, "What riddle? I remember you said we would study and study hard. It was to be like a quest."

"No, that is not what we said at all! The quest was to discover what secret this old house is hiding, and why time and memory seem out of joint. Things not adding up, you said."

Manfred shook his head. "I said I was confused and saddened over the sudden death of my relations. That is what I said did not add up. But all that talk of reality out of joint—I thought you just meant you are muddled and confused. Which you are! I also wanted to get you out of that smoke-filled hole where you lodge. All that stench of tobacco from the shop below! Terrible for the concentration."

"But the house is more important!"

Manfred now scowled darkly. "Do you know how much tuition, how many hours, what sacrifices I have made? To fall short now— my career would be over! No, Henry, no! The mystery is merely that the both of us have not been getting enough sleep. I have been staying up late with this paper, and these legal matters. I have been working so hard and you—well, what in damnation have you been doing? You never seem to actually do any work on this paper of yours! Have you even started writing it?"

Hal took another sip from his wineglass. "Manny, I don't know what's come over you. I mean, I suppose it is like you to worry, but why are you so worried? There is plenty of time!"

Manfred stared at him in wordless astonishment. "Have you gone mad? Easter break is nearly upon us. After that it is but mere weeks until the end of the term. The paper was assigned last year. Have you forgotten the deadline?"

Laurel laughed, and her bright, silvery notes of mirth banished the sudden tension that had filled the air. "Oh, darling, don't fret so! Henry is a genius; you have always said so. He can pull off writing a paper without all this fuss. And besides, why do you need an academic career now? You are the Lord of the Manor and the Master of the Island! The last living feudal lord in all of Europe, in all the world, and the families owe you rents and duties and oaths of undying loyalty. Very romantic, don't you think so, Henry? Just like your King Arthur you are writing about, isn't it? But you must come with me and see what we've done to move the treasures of Wrongerwood back to their proper places. You must come with me, Henry. You must come, or I shall be very cross with you."

Hal stared at the diamond rising and falling. The hardness of the stone and the softness of the breasts between which it nestled fascinated him.

A silent inner voice told him not to go with this frivolous girl, and to stick to his books—it had been a while since he had done serious work on his paper, hadn't it been? But there was the necklace he had given her. He did not remember giving it to her, and yet, he must have done, mustn't he? He had certainly been the one who bought it for her.

Hal said, "Well, Manfred must come with us."

Manfred stood up, the anger like sparks in his eyes, despite his iron face showing no expression. "I am going to the library to study before I lose the light. Henry, do as you like!"

And, although Hal had not finished his plate, when the master of the house stood, the scar-faced old Welshman stepped forward diffidently to take his plate away.

The green-eyed girl skipped forward lightly and seized on Hal's arm. Her white and slender hands, of course, could not budge his arm an inch, but she tugged and smiled. "First we must see the Rose Crystal Chamber! The keyring Manfred gave me, I left it in there, and we need it to open some of the doors. He only gave me a few, not all. I wonder why? He is so strange at times…"

Hal was staring at her, realizing he could not refuse her anything. Even though it was wrong, even though he should study, even though the girl knew nothing of Hal's passion for her, and even though Manfred was having doubts—despite all, he had no strength to resist, because he wished to have none. What had Liam said the islanders called her? The charming girl. Of course, her name in their patois must have been like the French: *Le fille charmant*.

Of course, the word *charming* in French also meant *cunning*.

Chapter 7

Dreams in the Chamber

The Torn Dress

Memory struck. They were in each other's arms, kissing with mad ardor. But her eyes blazed; there was anger mingled with her passion.

Suddenly she twisted out of his embrace. Laureline fended Henry off, one slim arm against his broad chest. Her eyes were narrowed and gleamed with green fire. "You don't want me!"

"I don't?" Henry wiped the sweat from his eyes. "Why would you say that?"

He started to undo the back of her dress, but he moved his hand carefully, not wanting to tear the fragile silk loops holding the pearl buttons. She learned forward and bit his earlobe hard enough to make him yelp.

"Are you crazy?" He shouted at her and grabbed at his ear. It was bleeding.

Laureline's eyes were filled with wrath. "If you really wanted me, you would not be so hesitant and delicate. You would not carefully disassemble every fastening of my dress! You would be a caveman, and tear it off, and *take* what you wanted! Bite me! Bruise me! Leave your mark on me! That way, when I walked out of this chamber, with my dress ripped to bits, and my neck bruised, I could not forget, would not forget, because I would know!"

Henry looked at the scars on his own arm where he had written his words of love with a knife. "No, Laureline. It won't work."

She growled low in her throat like a hungry lioness. "You let *everything* stop you! You won't tear my dress, you won't bend the rules or taste the wild side of love, and you will not wound the fragile feelings of Manfred!" There was no longer anger in her eyes, but the contempt women hold for the men they despise as weak.

It was more than he could bear. He took her in his arms and threw her down to the tiger rug. She gasped, then laughed in triumph as he tore the bodice of her dress and sent pearl buttons scattering like hailstones across the floor. Underneath, she was wearing a black corset that barely covered her breasts.

He looked in surprise. "English girls really are rather racy!"

"Cornish," she said with a lift of her eyebrow. "And an off-the-shoulder dress would leave my bra strap showing. Don't you know anything about women?"

"I know they like *this*—"

Then, without warning, she pulled away from him. When he reached out for her, she slapped his hand away. Her face was frozen with alarm. She whispered, "What's that noise?"

Henry looked toward the door, surprised, and his hard grip on her wrists relaxed. She twisted like a snake, breaking his hold on her, and slid out from under him.

Laureline leaped to her feet and rushed over to the door. Her heels clattered on the floorboards. She glanced back, green eyes gleaming over the naked curve of her shoulder. "Aren't you coming? Or will you just sit there and watch me slip out of your hands."

Henry said, "No, wait!" He knew what she was about to try would not work. If he followed her out of the chamber, he would find himself with his best friend's fiancée, with her wearing nothing more than her underwear, and him wracked with false guilt. Their love, their reality, would be erased from both their minds.

Laureline said, "Oh, come on! The curse of the world outside cannot possibly make up an explanation for *this!* You *will* recall you love me! I'm going out!"

He shouted, "I did recall! I remembered I love you! It came back to me–"

She stepped through the doorway.

"–and it did not help at all. Nothing changed."

The Torn Heart

She had left the door open, so he could see her, taking a few, hesitant steps up the stairs. Her movements were tentative, fawnlike, bewildered. She looked down at herself, rubbed her neck, looked left and right.

"Laureline!" he said. She was less than four feet from him, and she should have heard him clearly. "Come back inside!"

Her eyes had a dreamy, unfocused look, as if she were trying to remember something. Or as if—a dread certainty gripped him— as if a dream were being poured into her brain by some invisible source, erasing and rewriting her conscious mind. Then she looked down and grasped the diamond pendant with her fingers, and her gaze grew sharper, more focused, like a sleepwalker about to wake.

He leaned out the door. His head passed over the threshold, but he did not lose his memory. He could feel a tension in the air like a bubble about to pop. He reached out with one hand while holding the doorframe with the other. She was only inches from his fingers. He shouted and waved. It was like shouting and waving at the moon. She simply did not see him.

He looked over his shoulder and rummaged in his pants, looking for something to throw. He pulled out the keyring. But a still, quiet voice inside him warned him not to throw her the keys to the house, not those keys.

That made him freeze for a moment, blinking in confusion. When he was out of doors, his true self, Henry, was able at times to speak out of the subconscious mind of Hal, and whisper warnings to him.

He remembered telling himself to study with Manfred this afternoon rather than return to the passion of the Rose Crystal Chamber. It would be unwise to let himself be alone with the ever-more-desperate Laureline. If Manfred's doubts grew, and Hal's love continued to grow as well, the mysterious triangle of amnesia torturing them would resolve itself naturally in time, but returning to the chamber would force matters to a head, and that might ruin all.

Buried under the layer of amnesia, the real Henry had been present, or partly so. He had felt then as he felt now: having forgotten her so often in the past, he was not willing to forget her again. So he could not leave the chamber. He was trapped.

So he himself had been the source of the warning not to go with Laurel on a tour of the house.

Who then was the source of the warning not to throw the keys?

He heard a voice. Manfred was at the top of the stairs, out of Henry's line of sight. Laurel tossed her head, straightened her hair, and put on an unreadable expression, and began walking slowly up the stairs, swaying her hips provocatively.

Seeing how artfully Laurel, when she thought no one was looking, had simply assumed her expression and body language, an actress playing a role, filled him with disgust.

He heard his friend and his lover talking, heard the tones of their voices, but could not make out the words. Manfred was sharp and impatient at first, and Laurel's voice was softer, nearly a whisper. Manfred's tone gradually grew warmer, reconciled, and then Laurel laughed. Henry heard the rapid clicking of Laurel's heels on the floorboard, followed by his friend's heavier tread.

Henry stepped back and closed the door, sinking to the divan, putting his head in hands. Had she gone to Manfred to claim what Henry would not give her? Henry hated her at the moment. He hated Manfred too.

And even more, he hated himself.

Because who was he to judge her, when outside this chamber, she acted in the same ignorance that he did? If women were vain and shallow, was it not men who made them so, by looking only at their most superficial beauty? If a woman had to put on an act to perform the mating dance, how was that different from any other animal on Earth? Love was not a contract, an agreement sealed with a handshake, but a divine madness, sealed with a kiss, and solemnized with closer, deeper, intimacies. Love was irrevocable, eternal, the only thing akin to heaven on earth. Why should it not have its rites and mysteries, its strange gestures and genuflections, and rituals performed for the sake of form, not because they were always and utterly true?

Henry knelt. He prostrated himself on the rug that still smelled of her scent, and lay facedown, weeping like a little boy. He was angry, and hurt, and ashamed of his own weakness. And yet here he was, helpless, trapped, unable to win the woman, or protect her, or even protect his own heart.

He burned with shame and anger at his failure. She had thrown herself at him, repeatedly, and by pushing her away, he had shamed her in her own eyes. He had cut her to the quick by rejecting her, by placing his self-regard over his regard for her. That was why she had run. That was why she had tried to force his hand, only to find herself back in the filthy clutches of her false fiancé. The caveman claims the cavegirl by chasing her, and the cavegirl by alluring the man to the chase. It was only by virtue of being claimed as the prize that a woman could consider herself prized. All the trappings of civilization were little more than confusions and gift-wrapping and safety belts meant to contain that essential truth about sex. But there was nothing that could change it. It could not be changed.

How could it be otherwise? And that meant Henry truly was trapped. If he left the room, he would recall that he loved her, but he would be deceived into thinking she neither knew it, nor returned his love. Betraying Manfred was out of the question: this was not merely a code of honor for Henry, it was his character. He could no more cheat his friend of marriage and life-long happiness than he could force his own elbow into his mouth and bite it off.

But would they be happy? Laureline was getting more impatient, more desperate, as the wedding date loomed. For her, for any woman, to be chained for life to the wrong man, to bear the wrong man's children, to be expected to love and give and sacrifice for the wrong family, was the deepest nightmare of the feminine mind. Laureline, too, was trapped.

And in her distress, she was taking greater risks, desperately trying to provoke Henry into assuming his proper manly role, into throwing everything aside, into proving his love by chasing her and not giving up the chase. For what woman wanted a man who would not throw everything aside for her, and trample every obstacle in his way, and slaughter all her foes?

A horrible thought struck Henry then, sharp as an arrow to the heart. He had not warned Manfred of the talk he had heard in town, the desperate mutterings, the suspicions that Manfred had murdered his aunt and cousins to acquire house, land, and title. He had held his tongue at dinner, not trusting the ears of the scar-faced butler, and then things had happened so quickly.

He sat up, wiped his eyes, and reminded himself that at least when he left this chamber, he would forget this shameful moment of childish weeping. At least he would be a man again, out there.

But a man in love with a woman promised to another.

And once he crossed that threshold, he would become a man who was an evildoer, a traitor, and a seducer, when in fact, in here, inside this small chamber of truth, he had behaved with utmost honesty, denying himself happiness for the sake of his friend. If he left, he would hate himself once more, but that self-hate would be false, an illusion planted in his mind by a curse.

Henry walked over and closed the door. He found a chair and placed it before a window he found hidden behind the silk drapery covering the walls. It was jammed, and he battered the latch with his walking stick until he could work the latch and swing it open. He found himself looking out at the sunlit lawns and gardens and outbuildings of the mansion grounds, at the forest and the cliffsides and the sea. This window was facing to the east, which should have been impossible, unless the Rose Crystal Chamber in the west wing curved like a snake all around the central tower holding the priory. But he was too weary to worry about one more impossibility, one more madness in a world filled with loss, and with memory loss.

What he knew was simple and clear. If he left this chamber, he would lose both love and self-love. It was a fair and large world outside. And there was nothing in it.

He watched the shadows of the house reaching out eastward as the sun set, never moving from the chair. After that he watched the stars rise.

Later, the large crystal lamp shaped like a rose began to flicker and sputter and die. He realized he did not know where the oil bottle was to refill it, or where the chain was to lower it. It gave one last flash of rose light and went dark.

Eventually his chin came to rest on his breast, his eyes without permission fell shut, and without knowing how it happened, he slept.

Slumber and Waking

He awoke. He recalled his dreams with a particular vividness he never had known before. The vivid dreams still gripped him.

He had seen mermaids singing to a half-sleeping sailor to open the stopcocks on the yacht, and flood the bilge.

He had heard the gaunt, gray man giving orders to a pack of talking animals, who crouched and whined like dogs within a sea cave that boomed like a drum with the waves. The cave walls were adorned with paintings of crowned and antlered god-kings, and leaping Irish elk or mastodons, and images to glorify the demon-gods that savage Man served in the neolithic ages.

In another part of the dream was a knight who wed a fairy maiden, and was given wealth, glory, and victory in war and tournament, if only he never boasted of his unearthly paramour; but gray-eyed Guinevere, seeking him as her lover, and in anger at his repulse of her, challenged him to name his lady; and he did so; and in an instant, with a single word, all his riches, honors, and worldly goods were forgotten.

In a fourth part of the dream, he saw King Arthur, golden of beard and crowned with gold, the mighty sword Excalibur in his hands, pointed downward in the ground, and the king leaning on it, panting, exhausted, smiling. The sword was covered with blood from tip to hilts, and so were the hands and forearms of the king, and his mail was broken in a score of places, and a dozen shallow wounds leaked, and his surcoat was so thick with blood that the Dragon of the West was mingled and unseen, red within red. Arthur spoke, too weary to raise his head, but not too weary to smile, and put heart into his men, "Sir Gawain and Gaheris, Sir Ywain and Sir Agravaine, Sir Caradoc and Sir Cai, Sir Lamorak and Sir Lanval! Father Sampson of York, wisest Merlin, and you, Sir Bedevere! We have by the grace of God slain the flower of Saxon chivalry this day, and routed the others, but you well know, ye Christian men, that to slay slays nothing, for men are as immortal as elves, although cloaked in the clay of Adam. Each night these wights will return, and fight again."

Someone asked the king how long the fighting would continue, and in the dream Henry was convinced it was his own voice.

"Forever!" was the answer. "But the mercy of the White Christ will raise a mist, that we shall no more recall the wars we must always fight and fight again, forever against undying foes, until doomsday and last judgment brings true peace.

"It is the mercy of God, for while they fight, it may be that one of these pagan souls will break faith with the demons, and flee to Christ, and be laved in the baptismal waters which alone can break their oaths to unclean spirits.

"As for us, the light of Rome departs now from our shores. Let the light of the Cup of Christ not fail, even if must now it be forgotten. We are all the blood of Aeneas that remains, and we shall build a third and newer Troy, a Troynovant, even as Rome was a second Troy. We next must pull down the high places, and overturn all altars and stone tables that ever tasted human blood, and unmake the evil designs written on the chalk hills—but mind you keep the horse well-tended and unmarred, for he is of our party now.

"Many are the elves and efts of England, and much you will forget, but your Pendragon will not forget, and when I blow the great horn of the Swan Knight, which shatters all witchcraft and wakes all sleeping knights, you will heed, and arise, and come, for England's hour of greatest tribulation will then be at hand.

"Until that time, delight you in all the diversions of the elfin dreams, and forget these endless wars, and rest. For the last battle of man grows near."

Henry blinked and stood up and the dreams faded in his mind. For there, across the courtyard from the Rose Chamber where he sat, he saw in the windows of the western wing, a light moving as it passed from window to window, soft as a will-o'-wisp. It entered the crenellated gallery. One window would grow light then dark, and then the next as it approached. He saw it was Laureline, more than naked in her transparent nightgown, candle in hand, pacing through the pools of moonlight, her hair like a great black hooded half-cape trailing in the night air behind her.

He stood, and walked around the curve of the Rose Crystal Chamber until he could see the rectangular pillar running from roof to floor, which contained the stairwell. The door opened. The candlestick fell from her startled hand as memory poured into her like wine filling a silver cup, but the flame expired as it fell, and the carpet was not burnt.

The Ultimatum

Henry rushed and seized her in his arms. It was a long while before he permitted her to breathe or speak.

Then he held her at arm's length, peering at her carefully for a long time. She laughed in her throat. "Do you think I turn pink when I get pregnant? It is not the kind of thing one can see just by looking."

He said, "You are lying! You wouldn't–"

Laureline said, "No, I would not, because I am in love, and I have a man. But she would, that other me, that outer me that is frightened and unloved and lost. Do you think I am a fool? She can see Manfred is slipping away, slipping out of her hands. But she does not have a true love to save her, because that boy outside in that outer world will not speak up for himself. So what better way to make sure Manfred knows the wedding is set in stone? Lovemaking is one chain. A baby on the way a stronger one."

"You cannot know if you are pregnant the same evening!"

"But I can fear that I am," she said with a slow, cold smile, narrowing her lovely eyes. "And the man will feel that fear threefold, especially an honor-bound man like Manfred. He always has to do the right thing. That is his weakness."

"You're disgusting!" But he did not turn away from her nor release her from his arms. She kissed him and drew him down to the tigerskin rug.

She smiled. "I know I am. But I just did something. I woke up at his side, still warm and flushed from the loveplay, and I got up, and thought I left something here, in this wing, in this chamber. You see? I remembered. I am breaking the spell. I did not know why I had to come back here, but I was able to do it. It was you, you, you I was searching for. You know and I know that I am bad for Manfred. You have to break up my marriage to him."

Henry said, "By warning him you are a manipulative vixen?"

She laughed again and put her head on his chest. "If he were the man who would heed that warning, and stop me, he would not be the man I need. Women are frail things. I do not have anyone I love out there, anyone to keep me on the straight and narrow. So I yearn for money and status and a fine house, yes, all those shallow things! Because the deep things are out of reach. I can give up a loveless marriage to Manfred for you. But I cannot give it up for nothing. Am I supposed to move back in with my mother? Men are so impractical."

She grabbed him by the shoulder and threw her body to the left. He let himself be turned over on his back, so that she was astraddle him, breasts and neck and face gleaming silhouettes and pale, curving shadows in the moonlight from the window, her hair mingled with the night sky. "You have to take me, here and now, Henry. I am peeling my heart with a paring knife to ask you this, because if a woman has to ask, the answer is always *no*. I cannot bear the thought of Manfred on top of me, inside me, his ugly lips on me, simply because I cannot recall in that outer world who I truly am!"

The image was too vivid. Henry turned his head away in disgust.

She said sharply, "Don't look away! The truth does not go away just because you don't look at it. Look! Look at me! Do you know what happened? Do you know how demeaning that was for me? Manfred saw me sneaking along in my nicest underthings, and he thought I was coming to lure him away from his books. It seems I have tried it before when he was studying, only to be turned down. But this time I was already all wound up. You see, your rough lovemaking had me more flustered and ready than I have ever been. It is not something Manfred could ever have done. You had already summoned the orchestra and the music was resounding all the way through my body!"

"You are the one who ran out on me!" he said furiously.

She bent down, a lovely scented shadow in the moonlight, and kissed him lightly on the lips. "And you are the one who ran out on me on the golf links. The caddy and the other players were all staring, laughing at me behind their hands. They knew what it meant."

"I don't believe you. Manfred is not the kind of guy who believes in pre-marital sex. He and I were the only ones at school who thought it was better to wait, and decided to be book-crazy instead of girl-crazy like our fraternity mates. He has been sleeping with you?"

"Sure," she said. He could not see her expression in the darkness. "Everyone does it."

"Not everyone."

"Just because I cannot get you, does not mean I cannot get him. I care about you, and that hinders my technique."

"What kind of woman has a technique?"

"All women have a technique. Why do you think we gossip and read trashy paperbacks? It is the talk of our trade. Like I said before, it is like dancing. It is not some evil manipulation of some poor victim if you know the steps and have natural rhythm and you find a man who also knows his steps and who is not afraid to lead! In a waltz, one partner leads, and the other follows. If the man does not—and Manfred has no sense of music when it comes to sex. He was born to be celibate!—I say if the man does not lead, then the woman must. The dance is less fun for her, but it is better than sitting in a corner of the ballroom with a cup of punch waiting in vain to be asked." Her voice turned bitter. "One of the few good bits of advice my mother ever gave me was this: Better to be racy than lonely. But if you would lead, if you would do your part, I would never be lonely again, and a wife is supposed to be hot and bothered and shameless with her husband in ways that racy girls cannot even imagine. I would not have to make that Hobson's choice, if only, if only—"

"If only we were both true to ourselves, outside this one chamber."

That seemed to anger her. "We? *We*? You mean *you*."

"And what is that supposed to mean?"

She was shaking now with cold fury. "You left me, abandoned and embarrassed with the other golfers watching…"

"What other golfers? I did not notice anyone."

"You thought I was a trollop, merely because I am trying, trying, to find some way to save our love from the curse of this chamber! What else was I supposed to do? If I act coldly toward you outside, how will we ever meet and fall in love? But if I grope, dimly, blindly, not knowing, never knowing, that my own true love is walking away from me, within hands' reach, it is too much to bear!"

"I left because I found out I was in love with you, you little idiot!"

She cried out with sheer joy and kissed him. "Then there is hope! Love is stronger!"

He said, "No, not so. For Outside Me does not remember me and us, even so. And what else could he do but leave you?"

"He could take me."

"And what about Manfred?"

"How dare you!" Her voice was venom.

"What did I say?" His voice was bewilderment.

"You have seen him with me? Do you think we will be happy together for the rest of our lives? No; he does not even like the things I like, or want to do the things I want to do. Name something he and I have in common?"

He could not.

She went on in a softer, sadder voice: "Do you realize that, at any moment, in the Out Of Doors, you might be called away, back to America? Unless you simply by accident or impulse wander into this chamber of this house, you will not even remember you found the perfect soul mate for yourself! The same little impulses and quiet voices in our hearts that are finding excuses to bring us together in the Out Of Doors, if I marry him, will make me do things to make my marriage unhappy, and *oh!* For the rest of my life! The whisper in my heart will tell me to hate my husband!"

He could feel her wiping tears on his chest.

"I have made my decision, Henry. It is too late. Your half-measures are no good. Either you make love to me, here and now, or it is over. The next time we wander into this room together, you will only remember that you had your chance at happiness, and lost it."

He was glad she had not seen his tears of weakness earlier. His mind was cold and clear. He said, "I can't live without you, but I cannot betray my friend, no, not even if my friend never finds out. My heart will break if it is over between us, but, at least, the memory will not torment me. I do not want you to love a dishonest man. It is that simple."

She sighed and laid her head on his chest. "Then you are saying it is over?"

He said, "No. I am saying I reject your ultimatum. We will not make love here and now, not until I marry you in a proper ceremony and make you mine. But you will not leave me nor betray me. I won't allow it. I will bite you on the neck if you disobey me. I am not asking you, Laureline. I am telling you."

She sighed again. "Me and my big mouth. I should never have told you about the dance. Now that you are taking the lead, I suppose I cannot complain about you stepping on my feet. But there is still nothing to do. There are no clues, nothing to investigate. I suppose Manfred could hire a team of scientists, or the kinds of kooks who look for ghosts in empty houses, but what would the kooks actually point their kook instruments at? Where are the ghosts? You won't know what to ask the kooks to look for. I don't know if any human mind can figure out something this strange. Unless, of course, Manfred is behind it."

"He is not," said Henry, but he wished he were more certain of his words.

"But if it is him?" she implored. "If it is Manfred keeping us apart?"

Henry gritted his teeth. "I shall certainly kill him."

Kissing her, he stood up, and pulled his memorandum book out of the pocket of his coat, which was thrown over a chair arm. "Do you have a light?"

She said, "For a man who smokes like a chimney, you would think you would have a box of matches in every pocket of every garment!"

"If I have to ask for a light, it reminds me not to smoke so much, and gives me an excuse to talk to strangers." He put the book under the open window, and found the moonlight was bright enough to make out the letters on the most recent page.

Get-well card for Mrs. Wolfhound.

And

Pick up crucifix at Brising Brothers.

He muttered, "What in the world is this?" He remembered that the Brising Brothers were the jewelers on the Parish of St. Ouen on Island of Jersey. Short, funny little men with big whiskers. It was at their shop where he had bought the diamond pendant. He must have ordered an additional work from them.

She stepped up next to him, pressing her warm body up against his side, and handed him her little tiny pencil from her notebook. "Push the button on the back. The lead lights up. It still writes just fine, but you can see what you are writing."

He stared at it. Henry realized that he could no longer tell what was supposed to be odd and what was supposed to be normal. He had never seen a mechanical pencil with luminous graphite built in. But did that mean it was inexplicable? Or just unusual?

Laureline said, "You are gaping like a carp! It is from Japan. The pencil lead glows in the dark for a few minutes on the paper, and then fades to black. Really clever, actually."

He wrote down: *Investigate history of Rose Crystal Chamber. Who built it and why? Did any of Manfred's relatives also study mesmerism?* And, as promised, the pencil strokes glowed in the dark. Then, on impulse, his hand wrote: *What if an inner Manfred lives too, tells him to slip me a clue? & where did the mermaid of Frome go to, after slaying her lover Lubberlu?*

But then she put her hands in his, and said, "Darling, I have a better idea. Simpler. Why not just stay in the chamber? Here is a couch, a lamp, a fireplace and a bottle of wine. It is an old mansion: I can bring in a chamber pot. I practically live here, now. All the moving, all the preparations for the wedding will bring me back again and again. You saw, you saw, that I can make myself just on impulse arise at night and come in. I will make a note that this should be used as a pantry or luncheon room, and to bring food. I will keep coming here on any excuse and our love will not die."

Henry nodded slowly. What if there were something like radiation, some influence, which existed in this chamber, which he could soak up? Could he acclimate himself to the chamber of memory? Grow up an immunity to amnesia like developing an immunity to poison? The wedding was soon. He had to try anything that might work.

"Very well," he said. And it was agreed.

She wrote in her book with her magic pencil, kissed him lightly, took up the dark candle, and walked away in the dark. As he heard her heels click-clacking on the floorboards, that feeling of oddness came over him again. In the dark, blindly, he wrote in his own book.

Find out why Laurel never takes off her shoes?

Chapter 8

Trapped Within the Inner World

Sunday

He woke to the wonderful sound of the bells ringing in the eight-sided bell tower in the South Wing. He saw Manfred and Laure-line, the few servants and gardeners from the house, and a surprising number of folk from the village and the south part of the island streaming into the chapel. Since there was a church in the middle of the island at a more convenient spot, he assumed Manfred had invited them there for some reason, perhaps to make an announcement.

An hour later the small throng streamed out, chatting, and entered the forest path to find their way downhill to the less strange parts of the island. Henry sat with his cheek on the windowsill, sighing, feeling like a boy playing hooky.

The time walked by with leaden steps. He wished now he had brought his books and the rough draft of his dissertation paper. There was nothing to do, and only one or two thoughts to think about. Henry was not a man well equipped for idle solitude.

There was one wine bottle left, which he nursed carefully. There was also water in the bottom of the bucket, which would last him a day or two at most.

Once or twice he heard a servant, Mr. Nodenson the Butler, or the Cook's daughter Brigit, walking through the pentagonal corridor that ran past the head of the stairs, and he called up from the foot. At other times, from the eastern windows, he saw workingmen moving crates through corridors of the gallery, and he waved or shouted.

No one was able to hear him. He screamed bloody murder, whistled, and hollered. It was as if everyone in earshot were deaf.

Once he leaned out too far, and forgot where he was or what had happened—hadn't he just been touring the house with Laurel?—But when the top half of his body was inside the Rose Crystal Chamber again, he recalled.

In the afternoon, he saw Laureline and Manfred walking in the tiny garden nestled between the gallery and the Square Tower and the Main Hall. He was showing her the stone quern. Their voices were clear, and Henry could hear each word. It was all love-talk, impish and saccharine, and it made him sick, because he knew that the false Laurel doing the talking was lying, playing a role, and the true Laureline buried inside her was drifting farther away. Whatever doubts Manfred had entertained seemed gone now.

As Henry watched, Manfred sat on the stone quern and pulled the dark-haired beauty, pretending to protest, into his lap. He nuzzled and caressed her, fondling the gorgeous girl, Henry's girl, who blushed prettily, pretended to be scandalized, and asked what the servants would say. When she jumped to her feet, Manfred gave her a playful swat on the rear, and the girl took her skirts in her hands and ran away at a fair clip, while Manfred after a moment of gawping in surprise, gave a jovial laugh and set off in pursuit. The pair circled the quern once or twice, and sped off past the barren gardens and the apple trees toward the north lawns. A crest of the hill soon hid them from sight.

Apparently Manfred had been as easily habituated to follow Laureline's wild tastes in the silly roughness of courtship as had Henry. It seemed terribly un-English; which was probably a great relief to Manfred. And why should he not be free with his lips and caresses? Why should he not put his hands where he liked? Had he not already violated his old fashioned oath of chastity? Manfred's rebellion against the fashions of the modern world lasted until a busty Cornishwoman with long legs and kinky tastes mugged him in his study, it seemed.

A black hatred came over Henry then like a mist in his eyes. He daydreamed about dropping some heavy chair or flower pot from this window onto Manfred's head and breaking his neck. It would be the perfect crime. No one could see him, could they?

Laureline, however, was true to her promise, and came to him after dark, dressed in her semitransparent nightgown and her high heels. She had forgotten to bring him a change of clothing or any food, or any way to wash up.

"I wrote it in my book," she said, "but I must have been too direct. I have to give myself a reason to bring things in here."

"You love the decorations, and think this should be your honeymoon suite. You do not want the cook or the butler around during the honeymoon, since you might be embarrassed if they heard the noise. You're a bit of a screamer, you see."

"That's droll," she said, raising an eyebrow. "In any event, embarrassment is for servants. I answer to no one, or soon shall."

"Fine. You are convinced he is embarrassed, and so you want to pack this room with food stuffs, so you can feed yourselves while the staff is on a holiday. And a chamber pot! And damn! Am I thirsty!"

"Now you are swearing like Manfred. I wonder what his problem is, with that mouth of his."

They puzzled and fretted over the exact wording of her notes to herself, trying to find a way to make them indirect enough to escape the curse. She promised to go to the cellar and get him some bottles to drink, and, once again, to force herself to return, she slipped off her nightgown, and stood there before him wearing nothing but her stockings.

The sight inflamed him; heat coursed through his veins as if his blood were flaming brandy. Her body was flawless in every line and curve. His mouth was suddenly dry, he forgot to breathe, and his heart was thunder in his chest. She pressed her body up to his for a lingering kiss, and then she was gone.

He waited, holding the nightgown to his cheek, and savoring her perfume, but she did not return.

Through the windows, he saw her, nude, rapping on the door to the master bedroom. Of course. Once she woke up to the amnesia of the outer world, what other explanation could there be for stealing naked through the mansion at night?

The black hatred returned when he saw the door open. He closed the window and drew the drapes and took up a chair, and smashed it to bits, and threw it in the fireplace.

That was the first day.

Monday

On Monday afternoon, he saw her once again in the small garden enclosed by the gallery and the Main Hall. She was dressed in a white blouse with a high, starched collar and long skirt, and a wide belt, as ever, cinched too tightly. She wore high-topped shoes, with a long skirt and straw hat, her hair tied back with a blue ribbon at the bottom of the bangs so that the whole mass was a lozenge rather than a pony tail. She looked like something out of a picture album from a century ago. Henry felt sickened and weak with hunger, thirst, and longing.

She took up a seat on a stone bench directly below his window, her legs crossed, reading a book. After a while, she took a bit of bread crust out of her skirt pocket, and tossed the crumbs to birds that gathered, while his mouth watered and his stomach growled.

He screamed and cried and reached out with his hand, but she did not hear. He dropped rose petals on her head; she did not look up.

That midnight she came again, dressed in a new nightgown, this one black and lacy. Her underwired bodice emphasized her cleavage dramatically. It could not have been comfortable enough to sleep in.

And the nightgown was not enough to dissuade him from his anger at her when he discovered she had once again forgotten to bring him anything to eat or drink.

"At least I keep remembering to come!" she said in protest. "I saw the note about the honeymoon, but that is after the wedding, and the food would go bad! I thought it was a reminder for two weeks from now. You cannot expect me to remember my true love is hiding in the house! Manfred and I believe you went away to catch up your paper once you realized how slack you've been about it."

"Actually, I could work on it now if I could think of a way to get you to go to Mr. Drake's smoke shop and retrieve my books. It is maddening here. How do hermits do it? There is nothing to think about except for every drop of water I have ever seen."

"What happened to the potted roses?"

"I've been chewing the flowers for moisture. Hold on! Write yourself a note saying you have to water the flowers!"

She said, "This time, this time for sure, I can go get some wine bottles out of the cellar for you. I'll take off my–"

"Is that your answer to everything? I am in love with a crazy exhibitionist! It's a wonder you manage to keep any scrap of clothing on you at all!"

He saw her shocked face, and wondered if he had gone too far. But the anger and frustration was still strong in him. Two days without water, and two nights of poor sleep and vivid nightmares, was making objects seem to swell and recede in his vision. He gathered up her white nightgown and tossed it at her roughly. "Here! No more running around naked for you! It does not help. And what is it with you and your shoes? What girl wears silk stockings to bed?"

She sighed in exasperation. "I am staying in a guest room, and did not bring everything I own. My slippers are at home, and I have to wear shoes to walk around this drafty mansion at night because the carpeting is not installed yet. And you cannot wear these shoes without stockings. These are the only pair in my closet that I can tell by touch match each other. I can't see anything in there because I have to leave the room to go to the closet to find a candle."

She stepped into his arms and whispered softly. "And when I wake up in the dark, and I go roaming, it is almost as if I am hoping to see my someone I love. A girl wants to look nice. I am wandering the dark halls, looking and looking for something, unable to sleep, but not knowing what I seek!"

"It will not be long now, darling!" he said, his anger subsiding.

She smiled sadly, "So you say. It might be forever."

"Then I will die in this room! I will not forget you again. In here, you love me. Outside, you do not love me!"

"Oh, but I do!" she said. "I realized it on the golf course, when you walked out on me! That is why I wanted to show off the house to you, rather than have you study. To be alone with you, to look at you, to find some excuse to stumble so that you would put out your hand! You do not know how ashamed I am, or how foolish I feel."

"I see you flirting with Manfred. You do not look ashamed."

Her eyes darted to the window, and, from the thunderstruck look on her face, it was clear that only now did she realize all he had

seen. "I've explained before," she said smoothly, "Without you, I
have no courage. Without you, my choice is between a fine income
with a rich lord for a husband, or living with my mother downwind
from the fish cannery in her freakish house on stilts, and maybe doing small theater roles for pin money, with no real chance for a career, for independence, for freedom. I've mentioned the state of the
British theater these days? I am trapped. Trapped!"

"You could work in a shop in London and rent a flat!"

"Spoken by a man who has no idea what London flats go for, or
what shopgirls have to do to keep their jobs these days. I'm penniless.
I don't even have enough to put down."

"If you married me, you'd still be penniless."

She twined her arms around his neck and stood on her tiptoes
to kiss him. "The wife of a scholar! You get meals free in the dining
hall or something. Besides, you are rich enough to buy a motorcar
two weeks ago, buy it outright, without a bank loan. Why? What's
wrong?"

"I don't remember doing that."

"You loaned me the car at the golf course. You left it for me.
The man at the front desk of the club said so."

"Yes, yes, I remember that, but– what am I doing in this room?
I should be talking to a psychiatrist. There is something wrong with
my brain chemistry. Why do we think this is a curse? Is there a witch
after us?"

"My mother is a witch," said Laureline, "but perhaps not in the
way you mean. You mean a fairy-tale witch. A cunning woman is
what witches are called in the old stories. Listen. This is no ordinary
madness. How is it influencing both of us? Did your brain chemistry
leak into mine?"

He said, "Never mind. Write yourself these two notes: first,
you have to store some wine bottles here in the Rose Chamber to

see how well they keep in this temperature, meaning you have to check every day. Second, you've realized that you keep waking up at night because you are hungry, so ask the cook to fix you a snack for midnight, wrapped up in wax paper or something, and you want to eat it up here... uh... because this is where the wine bottles are, and you need to check to see they are not going flat or stale or whatever. Got that? And remember to water the flowers. And oil for the lamp. It is dry."

The look in her eyes told him, more profoundly than words, how she admired the sacrifice he was making, and how she pitied his suffering.

"I'll try to remember to bring paper and ink next time," she said. "So you can write a letter to your smokeshop owner, what's his name."

"Mr. Drake."

She tried to leave the candle with him, but could not. Each time she stepped out into the darkened hall, she turned, saw the candle burning in the room, and went back to get it. After the fourth repetition of this, he broke the candle in half, lit one half, and gave her the other.

She left, and he watched the tiny yellow reflections of light dwindle and vanish from the staircase as she ascended, and then he watched the reflections of reflections from the unseen hall above, until all was black as pitch.

He carefully watched the distant window across the courtyard that framed the master bedroom door. But the bobbing light appeared and disappeared through other windows, and went elsewhere.

That night he dreamt of howling wolves trying to climb the south wall and force themselves in through a large double-arched window, wolves wearing jackets and caps, and one large black wolf who carried a lantern. In the dream, his walking stick somehow caught fire, and he thrust the terrible wolf-things out the window, while Manfred stood on the round signal tower, and fired the Spanish cannon at a cloud, which so angered the cloud that it shot back lightning in forked bolts, which Manfred deflected with the little green book he carried, and threw the bolts on the ground, to burn the wolves.

Tuesday

Late Tuesday afternoon, Manfred and Laurel were again in the little courtyard garden where the quern stood. Since the kitchen was in the west wing, and the view from the outbuildings were blocked from the gallery, Manfred must have assumed this was a fairly secluded spot.

Today, he and Laurel played tag, and wrestled on the grass, and Manfred had her blouse halfway unbuttoned when Henry, faint with thirst and anger, turned away from the window. Not long after, he heard them talking: Manfred had decided to take her with him on an overnight stay to the City, to meet with lawyers. Henry rushed to the window, shouting, but she did not hear. He broke a chair against the wall, to get a length of wood small enough to fit through the window, and he threw it straight and true, but a sudden gust of wind caught the wood at the last minute, and it fell silently to the ground behind the couple as they kissed and laughed. Their eyes were full of each other, they saw nothing.

He was sorry later for that last missing bit of wooden chair. He had burned the other chair in the fireplace last night, and now the wood was exhausted. He had no blanket, but had wrapped himself in the tiger rug.

That night he dreamed of Laureline's mother, Mrs. du Lac, a wrinkled and surly old stoop-shouldered crone whose dentures had been improperly made and were the color of cast iron. In the dream, she had cut off the head of a girl scout, and was cooking the body in the oven, while she ate the brains out of the severed skull, blond hair still attached, and hair ribbons still in place, with a wooden spoon.

Wednesday

Wednesday he saw no one and nothing. The gardeners and workmen had been given leave, and the cook and butler never came near enough to his part of the mansion for him to glimpse them through the windows.

He was near-delirious with thirst but had lost the ability to feel hunger. He was sorry now that he had relieved himself out the window, for he realized he could have tried the stranded sailor's trick of gargling his urine in order to kill his thirst.

He was tempted to try Laureline's trick of wandering outside without clothes, knowing he would get a drink before he returned here for his pants, but he decided to wait until he was more desperate. Because he was now not sure what his false and outer self would think the situation was with Laurel. Would Hal outside know that Manfred had slept with Laurel? And what would the reaction be? Shame? Guilt? Envy? Nothing good, that was certain. And what if that emotion drove Hal to commit some noble, irrevocable gesture? What if he flew back to the United States, vowing to remove himself entirely from possibility of temptation? It was the kind of the sacrifice that he would indeed make for his friend. And then the one spot where Henry was fully awake and fully true to himself, this chamber, would be gone.

Ideas came to him from time to time, ways to improve his situation based on techniques Hindu sufis used for banishing the effects of mesmerism, or on early tests on the subject done by scientists in the nineteenth century, or on the work of modern psychiatrists, or on other snippets of information about the nature of hypnotism that he would unexpectedly recall. He turned these ideas over in his thoughts, hoping that one of them would provide the hidden key they needed to break the curse. After a while, however, he was struck by a thought that he found tremendously disturbing.

Every single fact he recalled, every hint, every snippet, every clue, came from something that Manfred had told him while working on his dissertation.

Henry shivered. He knew these fears were false. Manfred was his best friend, and yet…

The happy thought struck him that there might be something in the chamber that broke the curse and warded off the amnesia, not the chamber as a whole. If so, he need only lean out the window, holding any candidate for this protective charm, and, if the object was normal, even the noblest and most grief-stricken version of himself would not climb down the outer wall rather than merely pull his head in the window. But he decided to remove his trousers and shoes, just in case.

The lamp from which the chamber took its name was the most obvious candidate, and it was awkward and slow, but not hard, to find the chain to lower it. In the process he discovered the location of a second and full flask of oil, and a box of Lucifer matches.

But neither lit nor unlit did the lamp protect his memory when he leaned out the window with it in his arms. With other objects, one by one, anything small enough to fit through the frame, he tried the same experiment, to no result.

But his search took him to explore each part of the wall of the chamber, which was shaped like a spiral. The far wall, where the spiral ended, was covered in wooden panels carved with images of lotuses and roses. There were no windows here, and this was the first time he had been holding a candle, so he spotted what looked like a raised boss that was worn smooth, whereas all the other bosses in the design still had their edges. It moved aside at a finger touch, revealing a keyhole behind.

He went back to his pants, donned them, got the key with the lotus design for the bow, and returned. It fitted. He turned the key.

There was a click, and a black line running from roof to floor appeared in the wood an inch to the left of the keyhole. He put his fingernails into the black crack and it widened. The whole wooden panel slid to one side.

Beyond was a stone wall pierced by a portal made of the whitest, brightest metal he had ever seen. The portal was not square like a gate nor rectangular like a door, but hexagonal. There was writing in Arabic and Hebrew and one other system of letters he did not recognize all along the edges of the hexagon in three concentric rows. Midmost in the portal was the image of two opposite triangles superimposed. There was something peculiar about the white portal that reminded him of his vivid dreams.

Henry touched the door, wondering if there were a chamber dedicated to Jewish observances hidden on the other side. He knew that there were houses with priests' holes and escape tunnels built during the bloody reigns of Henry and Elizabeth to let priests escape, and he was sure that the Jews had been driven out of England, or forced into hiding in the days of King Edward I. If there was a second keyhole in the portal, or some hidden latch or catch to open it, he decided not to try, for fear his current memories would be lost. He slid the wooden frame shut, locked the door, and pulled the silk hangings back in place. He told himself there would be a time to experiment with this door later.

He was surprised when he heard high heels clattering on the stairs, and saw Laureline appear that night, once again in a nightgown, this one long and green, almost too big for her. This time, she was carrying a three-branched candelabra, and, better still, a sandwich wrapped in wax paper, and a thermos bottle of cold tea. For once, his hunger was greater than his desire, because he wolfed down the sandwich and swallowed half the contents of the thermos before he kissed her.

"I woke up feeling a bit peckish," she said. "And this time I wore my wrap as well as my nightie, because I could not think of any excuse to give myself to smuggle pillows and blankets up here."

"You are a lifesaver! I will love you forever!"

"Oh, darling, I knew that already. I am not suffering as bad as you, but I had quite the argument with Manfred convincing him to get away from his lawyer friend in time to sleep here. I made such a fuss about hating hotels—which he knew was a total and complete lie, because I love the London hotels. So mannerly! Such high quality—and my nerves were on edge because I did not even know why I was lying to him, or why I wanted to get back here."

"My sister acted that way some times," said Henry. "With her boyfriends back in her schooldays, of which she had a lot. Very popular girl. I always thought she was acting erratic on purpose, trying to see which one she could push around versus which one would not put up with her nonsense. Like a two-year-old testing boundaries. But maybe it really is nothing like that. Does everyone have a true, inner self that whispers to him? Maybe there was something as important to her inner self in each of the cases where she seemed to be acting crazy as you must have seemed tonight to Manfred. You returned from a nice night in a London hotel to meet a man who loves you entirely, and who will break this curse for you. You and I will both see the truth, and soon. I promise."

"Before, I doubted. Now I never will again. Maybe it is getting easier to break this curse. Maybe it is like, I don't know, I have heard of cases of brain damage where you have to train a new part of your brain to do what the old messed-up one once did. Something like that? Because even without knowing why, I came back."

She gave him the green gown she wore, with its puffy sleeves and delicate lace throat, and was wearing her white nightgown beneath. He took two of her three candles, but he found he could not get her to leave without the thermos—Laurel kept returning for it before she reached the stairs.

He poured the tea into the empty wine bottle, one of the few readily-breakable things he had not smashed in the chamber.

Fed and free of thirst, he wrapped himself in the green satin for warmth, and spent an almost comfortable night on the divan, wrapped in the scent of Laureline's perfume.

Thursday

Thursday made up for all the previous suffering. This time, she appeared not long after sundown, wearing her black nightgown, and more importantly, carrying a picnic hamper, a rolled-up blanket over her shoulder. In the hamper were several meals' worth of food, two bottles of wine, two two-liter bottles of water and two six-packs of soft drinks.

"You would not believe the lies I had to tell myself to trick me into lugging this stuff into this room! I also brought a sponge, some soap, and a laver, and look! A canteen! While you might want to drink most of this, we should use some for a sponge bath. I used to do this as a nurse. Come on! Off with everything. You are smelling awful ripe."

"Meal first."

The wine took the edge off of any sorrow or anxiety. She poured a small bowl of water, beat it to suds with some soap, and set it on the battery-powered hotplate to warm up.

Henry said, "Just out of curiosity, what lie did you tell yourself?"

She said, "I wrote it in my little memo book last night. Manfred needs to move his cot and all his survival gear from that garret room to his chamber here. Wanted me to arrange it in here in a way that looks nice. I believed it only because I think the outside me is starting to listen to her hunches."

Running warm soapy water over a naked man with a sponge is sure to lead to some sort of distractions, and Henry, after the last few days, was beginning to have grave doubts about the wisdom, and the practicality, and the sanity, of his old promises. If Manfred was not keeping them, why should he?

And she insisted on disrobing, so as not to get her nightgown wet, and she suggested something that could not cause pregnancy, and so perhaps was not technically the same as having sex.

Henry's reservations were lost in his passion, and he had drunk more than a bottle of wine to make up for days of thirst, and was in the act of finally sliding her panties down the curve of her hips when they were unexpectedly interrupted by the noise of someone walking heavily down the steps outside.

Laureline leaped to her feet, picking up her nightie and clutching it to her breast. "It's Manfred!"

It was true. He was somewhere in the pentagonal corridor that circled the central nave of the priory, and his voice was echoing though the empty hall. His voice sounded angry.

She was wild-eyed. "I have to go!"

Henry said, "If you run out there undressed, the curse will convince you to go to him again!"

"You'd worry about that now?"

But she was out of his reach and ran through the door, and suddenly slowed, puzzled. He followed and tried to reach her with his hand without actually stepping over the threshold.

But she took a step in order to put the nightgown on the floor in a circle and pull it up over her body, and then tuck her breasts into the silky cups. It seemed a strange way to put on clothes, and Henry was not sure if he had ever heard of women donning a dress that way. He realized he knew rather less than he thought about what women do when no man is looking.

Again, he saw her face change like an actress going into character. She swayed gracefully upstairs, her heels clattering.

Henry heard Manfred say sharply, "What are you doing wandering the mansion at this hour of the night?"

Her reply was in a soft and sultry voice, too low to hear.

"I did not send any note about moving that cot. Why would I ask you and not the Levriers? With all the noise you made, I thought someone had broken in. You know we had trouble last night."

Henry felt a tremor run through his body. He left the door and followed the curve of the wall, peering behind the drapery every three strides. He finally found a window not like the others. It was larger than the square transparent ones facing north, and, unlike the stained-glass windows facing west, these opened on hinges.

Outside, he saw the south wing, the chapel, the bell tower, and the signal tower. In the moonlight it was impossible to see clearly, but the grass seemed to be torn in places, like the divots left by golfers, and in one spot the grass was blackened and burnt.

Sighing, wondering about sanity and insanity, dreams and reality, and what sort of flamethrower would leave a perfectly circular burn mark on the grass, he returned to the hamper, eager to open his next wine bottle. His hand touched something cold and metallic at the bottom of the hamper. He drew it out, jingling.

It was a pair of furry handcuffs, metal hoops lined with black mink, key still in the lock.

He raised an eyebrow. Perhaps he knew less about women than he thought. A lot less.

Friday

He was awakened by the sound of her footfalls coming down the stairs. There she stood like a vision in the light from the candle she held.

Henry stood, his head spinning. He was not sure of the hour, or even the day. It had been an unexpectedly warm night, so he wore only his shirt, the same he had been wearing for a week. Before he slept, he had imbibed far too much wine in a rush of despair, and the spirits were still in his blood, blurring his speech and fogging his eyes.

But he could see she was pale with horror. "What is it? What's wrong?"

She placed the candle on the mantelpiece carefully before throwing herself recklessly into his arms. Her shoulders shook. "The wedding plans have been moved up! We only have until the end of the month."

"What?"

"And I've made travel plans to go visit my sisters in Quedlinburg to sew my wedding dress and give Manfred the uninterrupted time he needs to study without distraction. But that is not the real reason. He is worried that I have been prowling the mansion at night, or sleepwalking, especially when there has been trouble in the village. He thinks the house is haunting me, affecting my thinking! He wants me out of the house!"

Henry knew he could not survive for three weeks in this one room, not without an ally bringing him food and drink.

He said, "What if you buy me a plane ticket to—where the heck is Quedlinburg?—to come with you? We'll have to make up some reason why you'll return to this chamber with the ticket, where you will remember yourself and give it to me. And then I will write myself a note telling myself to use the ticket, so that when I leave the chamber... I will, uh..."

Laurel raised her head and narrowed her eyes. "Quedlinburg is in Germany, in the Hartz Mountains where the witches live. Are you the kind of man who would spend a week traveling with your best friend's fiancée in romantic surroundings, and seduce her, and carry her off, and marry her? Or even tell her you love her? No matter what?"

He did not answer and did not need to answer.

She said, "We are out of time and out of options. I am leaving tomorrow for the continent. My outside self thinks you are hiding in your little room in the smokeshop, frantically writing your paper, and I won't see you until the wedding day. You've been a week in here. What has changed?"

"You've remembered to come each night...."

"Because I cannot sleep! And I leave things here, like lunch hampers and nightgowns, so I have to get up and retrieve them, thinking I am losing my mind! Which I am!"

Henry said, "If I step outside, I am probably simply going to leave, thinking it best for you and Manfred. Why can't you just tell him you don't love him, and you are only after him for his money? Why can't you come clean?"

"Why can't you? You've never confessed your feelings to me! You barely say *boo* to me out there! Everything I do out there to draw you closer drives you farther away. You have to be the one to speak, to act! You! I have made a fool of myself throwing myself at you. Here! It is time for you to act."

And she threw off her nightgown, and once again stood before him, her breasts heaving, her skin flawless, her beauty perfect, maddening, dizzying as wine. She was not wearing any undergarments, and her bottom was bare. There was no barrier of fabric, no matter how slight, between him and any part of her.

He said, "If you walk around the house naked, the curse just tells you that you are trying hard to seduce Manfred, and it sends you to his room."

"It is my role to put the courage into you," she said in an implacable voice. "Like a good little cavegirl."

"You already tried leaving your clothes here. It was a disaster. And when Manfred sees you nude, he does not do as I would—well, damn him to hell."

"Give me your shirt!" she said.

"It stinks," he said. "I have not changed it in a week."

"Well, who knew you were so delicate?" She smiled archly. "And they say smell brings back memories better than any other stimulus."

"The plan is to wear my shirt outside? Will that force your outside self to remember I am here? I guess it is worth a try."

"Just hand it to me."

He did, and so stood there just in his skivvies. She smiled and tossed the shirt over her shoulder out the open door. He shouted in astonishment. "I hope you have a way for me to get that back! It is cold in here at night."

"Not this night. It will be the warmest of your life."

She stepped over to the hamper, drew out the handcuffs, and slid close around him, wrapping her arms tightly around his tall, strong, wide body, her naked curves mashed up against him. He heard the noise of the handcuffs clicking shut behind his back. Then he heard the key tinkle as it fell back into the open hamper.

He said, "It is not going to work. Even if we walk out like this, the curse will make up some farfetched explanation."

She said, "Not if we roll out right in the middle of what we'll be doing."

"Wait, what?"

She said, "After the wedding, you are not going to live here, but I am, and I do not want to step into this room one day and remember that I let the love of my life, my true love, get away from me because of his stupid scruples. I don't care if it is your upbringing, your religion, your childhood trauma, or whatever it is. You have to pick. We are out of time. Choose me or choose your convictions. It is one or the other."

She started kissing him, but he could not back away, and if he stooped down as if to pull her chained arms over his head, this merely thrust his face into her breasts, and she yelped as if this hurt her wrists, and then there were tears in her eyes, and he could not hurt her, not even to extricate himself from this.

And he was not sure he wanted to be extricated. What was he thinking? This woman was willing to break all the rules of Heaven and Earth for him, literally to chain herself to him and throw away the key. And she was beautiful beyond all comparison.

Weakened by hunger and wine and lack of sleep, besieged and baffled by manly passion and woman's tears, he surrendered to his desires.

Chapter 9

The Master of Wrongerwood

Archimage and Architect

Henry woke in the dark, at the sound of approaching boots. He was filled with a warm euphoria, a sense of victory and greatness, before he felt the heat from the girl sleeping next to him, and remembered why.

He had gone to sleep a boy; now he was a man. Loveplay had been more awkward than he would have thought, elbows and knees in the way, and hisses and grunts and moans and cries that in another setting would have seem absurd, in those moments of supreme passion, were perfect. For the second time, she had knelt. For the third, they had been in each other's arms, in a position he was sure missionaries taught to pagans so that they could look their wives in the face, as one man should only look to one wife, unseverable, indissoluble, bound together forever…

But why this feeling of guilt, of embarrassment, of shame?

Because she was not his wife. He had looked in the face of a woman pink with passion, her eyes like burning emeralds, mysterious, ecstatic, wondrous, and yet it was a wonder meant for a marriage bed.

"I suppose if this all works out in the end, I can stop worrying about…" he started to murmur to her, as he turned, intending to take her in his arms, and kiss her. He could still smell her scent, feel her warmth, her nearness.

And he fell onto the floor in the tangle of sheets. She was gone.

Now the footfalls sounded again, a man's heavy tread, not Laureline's doe-like tip-taps. There was a figure at the door, dimly seen in the starlight from the windows.

The silhouette reached to one side of the door. There was a click as he threw a switch. Suddenly electric lights from a dozen bulbs hidden behind silk panels in the ceiling blazed forth, dazzling.

It was Manfred, fully dressed, and wearing a long tan coat. His hands were in his pockets and he held a hunting rifle tucked in one elbow. He stepped over the threshold, and winced as if a sudden pain had jabbed through his brain. He frowned. He scowled. And this time, it was not merely his heavy brows.

Henry had fallen asleep naked with his head and chest on the floorboards and his legs still half on the divan, twisted in the blankets.

If his friend really had betrayed him—if Manfred's mesmerism really were the force behind their memory losses—the deadly truth would now be laid bare.

Mandrake, without a word, tossed a rumpled ball of cloth at him. It was Henry's shirt, which had been laying on the staircase. Mandrake kicked an ottoman closer to the divan, and sat with a sigh, neither taking his eyes from Henry, nor putting his rifle down.

Henry rose to a sitting position on the floor, pulled on the shirt and buttoned it up hastily, looked left and right for his pants, and, not seeing them, seated himself gingerly on the divan, and pulled the blanket into his lap.

"Henry," said Mandrake in a casual voice, "this question may seem rather odd, given where you presently find yourself, but do you realize you have been living in my house for at least a week, in hiding, here in this room?"

Henry looked at his friend intently, "When you stepped in here, did you remember another life?"

Mandrake paused and then said slowly, "Yes. I knew Dame Hathaway quite well, in fact. I spent my summers here as a child, and I came into this chamber often. It was built by John Dee, Queen Elizabeth's Archimage, in the last years of the Sixteen Century, using the instructions smuggled to him by Giordano Bruno. It is a memory mansion. This room in particular preserves memories that charming or cunning otherwise smothers. When I was young, there was not so much forgetfulness at large in the world, and the difference between inside and out was smaller."

Henry gritted his teeth. "In here, in this chamber, I remember that Laureline and I are truly, passionately, faithfully and eternally in love with each other. She does not love you."

Mandrake nodded. "I know."

Simple Solution

"W– what?"

Mandrake said, "When you are outside, how did she and I meet? Compare it to your memory when you are in here. What does that tell you?"

Henry said, "I hadn't really thought about it."

Mandrake shook his head. "A week alone to meditate in the Rose Crystal Chamber of John Dee, and you did not use the opportunity to put your thoughts and memories in order? It is a good thing you have me around to help you over the stiles, then. I am being forced to marry her."

Henry nodded. "I knew I remember Dame Hathaway was pushing the arrangement."

"Pushing? Blackmailing. But I had to be made to forget that, because otherwise I would have resisted too much."

Henry's heart leapt as his doubts evaporated. It was not Manfred who was responsible for their situation! His friend was as much a victim as he and Laureline were.

For the first time, it occurred to him that perhaps Manfred was studying mesmerism for the same reason Hal studied Giordano Bruno: His friend's real self was urging him to work to break the spell.

Mandrake continued, "I had to be placed under a love charm, and dote on a woman I can barely stand to be around, a snide and sarcastic demimonde."

"Don't speak that way of her! I love her!"

"You can have her!" said Mandrake impatiently. Then, with a sour smile. "Unless, of course, if I read this right, you already have *had* her."

Henry felt the black anger that possessed him before stirring in the depths, reaching out for him, but at the same time, a bright bubble of laughter burst from his lips.

Mandrake scowled all the more. "Explain the joke to me?"

Henry said, "It is all gone! It is all fixed. I have been living under such a weight!"

"What the devil are you going on about?"

Henry said, "Well, you and she are not in love and she and I are. I can take her from you with a clean conscience."

"More than that. With my blessing! You have no idea how much trouble she's caused for me just so far. The old caretaker, Mr. de Jardinier, was so offended with her, for the way she mocked Dame

Hathaway, that he resigned on the spot rather than be the one to unlock the doors for her. You have his keyring."

Henry said, "I suppose that if my outside self seems to steal her from you, that is it not really a betrayal, if you, deep down, really are pulling for me."

"The curse cannot last past a proper marriage ceremony. As soon as you put a ring on her finger, and you are man and wife, the charm on me will snap like a twig, and I will come to my senses! Betray me? Breaking up my marriage to that woman will save me, and her as well."

"Then my problem is solved! Thank God!" said Henry with another bright and cheerful laugh. "What a load off my mind! But— hold on a moment—if you think she is such a bad woman, why aren't you trying to save me?"

"She is marrying me for my money, Henry! But if she marries you, she trades all of the great and ancient House of Wronger- wood for living in your rathole above a smokeshop in Blackbird Leys. Good Lord, man! If she does that for you, she's more faithful than Penelope! You'll never deserve her."

Henry remembered the first time he danced the waltz, how the ballroom spun. It was like that now with his thoughts. But if he held his eyes on one fixed spot in the room, turning his head to keep it in view as he twirled, he could dance without being dizzy. He fixed his eyes on one thought.

"Then you don't want her."

"Not a bit."

Henry pulled up a bottle of wine from the hamper. "Then let us toast!"

Coven of the Countess

Mandrake said, "You will forgive me if I don't feel like celebrating. It should be clear that my cousins were murdered, and my great Aunt."

Henry said, "I thought it odd that you mourned them so. Your true self knew them well."

"It was my habit, each time I came here, to meditate and pray in this chamber. So stepping in here again immediately brings them to my thoughts. Not only did the charming make me forget about this house—you recall that I told you that I never clapped eyes on it?—you were caught up in the charming as well, because you are my friend. Your previous visit here last summer, and the one before that, had to be blotted out, as well as your memory of how and where I met Laureline. Also erased, I assume, were the memories of any number of lawyers and record keepers, in an attempt to throw my claim to Wrongerwood into disarray, and carry off the furnishings, turn off the power—all this was done to make me not want to stay here. I am glad I had enough strength of character to resist that charming impulse."

"How is the power back on?"

"The spell is breaking. Mr. Twokes, that stubborn old bluenose, turned out to be hard to charm. The lawyers are able to read and remember the will, clear up liens, get matters back in order. The power company turned everything back on at midnight on the dot. It is Saturday morning just now, before sunrise."

"And the lightbulbs?"

"I suppose the Rose Crystal Chamber hid itself from the eyes of the workmen who came to strip the mansion during the months after Aunt Sibyl's death, and before anyone remembered that I was the heir next in line. I assume Countess Margaret wanted the time to search the place."

"Who? No, wait, I remember her: She is the one who introduced you to Laureline."

"She is rather more than that. Countess Margaret is one of the coven of the Witches of England who preserve the island. She made you and Laureline forget your growing love for one another because it interfered with her plans."

"But I thought she was Dame Hathaway's friend?"

"I wager she snared Aunt Sybil during those long stays in London, convinced her no longer to return here at regular intervals and break any witchcraft clouding her thoughts. I need proof that Countess Margaret killed my family, but once I have it–" He lowered his eyes to the floor, teeth clenched, and left the threat unspoken. Henry, at that moment, lost any doubt that Mandrake was capable of murder.

No Such Thing

"But there is no such thing as witches," said Henry.

"No?" Mandrake looked up sharply. "If Morgan le Fay was not a witch, how did she contrive to shatter the Table Round?"

"That is just a story."

"A story of history, yes. And Merlin?"

"He—just a legend, some Christian retelling of pagan tales of heroes and gods."

"And are there truly no pagan gods? No power that answered when those sad and ancient people prayed and danced and sacrificed? Building Stonehenge and monoliths from here to Russia, cutting the throats of horses, raising mounds and digging tombs—that is a damn lot of effort to no purpose, isn't it? You'd think they would have noticed before they did so much work that it never worked."

Henry laughed. "Good lord, old man! I do believe you are serious!"

"Answer the question, please."

"You mean, do I think pagan gods are real? Gods like Odin and Oberon and *Osiris*?"

"I was thinking more of Moloch and Asmodeus, but you may answer as you'd like."

"Of course they are not real!"

"Then who or what did I foreswear and defy when I was baptized? When I swore off the devil and all his pomps, and vowed enmity to all the devil's angels, who was I talking about? When the Christians overthrew the Roman Empire, they kept all the institutions of man intact. They fought only one foe, and overthrew only one enemy. Who did they fight, if not the pagan gods? The powers of the air, the prince of this world? When a third of the hosts of heaven followed Lucifer in his fall, who fell?"

Henry sighed. "I know you think demons are real..." he began in a condescending tone.

"If demons are not real, what did Our Lord drive into the herd of swine at Gadarene?" And, when Henry had no answer, Mandrake said, "You see the problem with your modern American education, where everything in the past is forgotten? The problem is that you forget the simple principles of logic as utilized by Aquinas or Aristotle. You cannot have it both ways. Either the supernatural order exists or it does not. Either there is another world alongside this one, invisible, haunted, filled with powers and terrors we cannot imagine, and wonders beyond all joy, light beyond light, or—"

"Or what?"

"Or the whole lot of it, from Christ to Krishna to Cuchulainn, is all a bunch of rot, and nearly everyone you have ever met is a damned fool for believing a word of it. And there is no life after this one, and no dreams come true, and we are born of nothing and come to nothing. That is the choice."

Henry said, "Either stark, hopeless atheism, or I must believe in witches and spooks?"

"Yes."

"No. Men can tell lies and make up stories about God and spirits as easily as any other topic. God could be real and magic fake. You know that! That trick you did at No Talent Night, when you pulled a dove out of your sleeve! There are reasonable positions between those two extremes, old man. Reasonable halfway opinions."

"Out there, I grant you, in the outer world, there are reasonable halfway opinions," said Mandrake with a solemn nod. "That is one reason why this chamber was built. Because those thoughts we think out there are fogged with the fumes of Lethe, the river of death, which Adam set free at his first act of rebellion. Mermaids sing death in their songs, and witches brew death in their cauldrons. Out there, a man can believe Christ is divine, but cast out no demons and performed no miracles. And so belief slowly ebbs, wisdom is lost, and men become shallow and vulnerable. Out there, it is reasonable not to believe in curses, and to believe our memories cannot be influenced by charmings. What about in here? What do you believe in here? Tell me, if you were a witch, and could fog the minds of men, surely the first thing you would fog out is the memory of the fog?"

"What do you mean?"

"If you could mesmerize others, the first false belief you would implant in your victims is that there is no such thing as mesmerism. No one can fight a foe he thinks does not exist. He cannot even arm himself. Come now! Your conclusion might be different if we held this conversation out there. But in here—why was this chamber built, if not as a protection from witchery?"

Unwritten History

Henry said, "Do you know when and why this chamber was built?"

"Yes, but this is a history not anywhere written down, for what the men of Sark say, they do not write down."

"Go on."

"Queen Elizabeth I was one of the first to study diligently the art the Catholic Church had forbidden to mortals, and she formed the first of the Coven of White Witches protecting the Island of England. By her dark arts she raised a storm and scattered the Armada. Sir Francis Drake, the most famous of the English privateers, was given a looking glass in which he could summon winds and tempests.

"And so it was that for many years we flourished and grew, until the empire on which the sun never set was protected by these uncouth, unseen means. The power of the White Coven was broken after World War Two; that is why Hitler put so much effort into studying the occult, why he collected rare items of mystical influence like the Spear of Destiny, and why the Soviets forced men like Lysenko and Rejdak to study parapsychology so diligently.

"So after the war, something spiritual was broken in the spine of Britain, and now the witches use their arts only to their selfish advantage, and so more and more of the mists of amnesia rise from elf-lakes and buried kingdoms below the hills, and sweep across the British Isles. The Irish barely remember they are Irish any more."

"About the murder of your cousins—I heard folk in the village, three men or four, talking about it. They blame you."

"I'd prefer you tell me this outside, so that I can remember it clearly."

"But I dare not step outside."

"Of course you can."

"But you will forget you don't love Laureline—and I will forget I do!"

Mandrake shook his head. "Everyone knows you love Laureline. I am the only one who does not see it, and even I suspect it."

"But you and she—I saw you!"

"What? You think I am being very intimate and cozy with her? It is an act. My outward self does might not recall all that was blotted out of memory, but he is canny enough to play along and see which card is turned next. If I call off the marriage now, that gives the enemy too much time to plan. The next group to attack this house might not be one that can be easily driven off, like those rowdy boys we drove off the other night, or that nuclear scientist from a decade ago."

"Even so, I dare not go out."

Mandrake stood up. "You merely need to trust your true self. If your love for her is not strong enough to be heard in your heart even through the deception fogs of witchcraft and enchantment, it is not true love. And if it is true love, then you cannot be afraid. Come back out with me."

"And what will happen?"

"There is a small, still, quiet voice in you that always speaks truth. Forgetfulness can numb that voice, but never smother it entirely. If you listen to that quiet voice deep inside you, you will win her."

And so Henry walked out of the door with Mandrake, arm in arm, friends before they crossed the threshold and friends as they trotted up the stairs, both suddenly convinced and seeming to remember that Hal had been at the house all that week, studying diligently.

Chapter 10

The Feast of Saint Guthlac

Graduate Student

Hal sat on a hardbacked wooden chair in the office of the College's Tutor for Graduates. Dr. Vodonoy sat behind a desk piled with books, folios, and manuals. The computer monitor was an old-fashioned square box that looked like someone's grandfather's black-and-white television, and it also had a stack of books piled on it. Between the stack to the left and the stack to the right, the florid and square face of Dr. Vodonoy could be seen, like a full moon rising between mountain peaks. He was a Fellow by Special Election in the Senior Tutor Department.

"Your adviser says you have missed two meetings in a row, to discuss your paper," he said in a censorious tone. "By this late date, not only should you have turned in an abstract to your adviser, Mr. Pettyworth, but given him a list of your Literature review as well. The subject approved by the Committee was on the Substitutionary Atonement in The Matter of Britain. At the time, several members of the committee cast doubt on the appropriateness of the subject. A bit too, ah, theological, shall we say? More than one of them said to me privately that bringing religion into the Arthur myths was controversial, and may be seen as rather inappropriate, considering the backgrounds of Mr. al-Asiri and Dr. al-Wuhayshi. Even insensitive.

A word to the wise should have been sufficient. But you insisted, so I went out on a limb for you and the topic was approved."

Hal nodded, looked over the top of the man's head to the window, and the sky outside. It was a fine blue day, with but few clouds as white as ewes, drifting lazily above the domes and spires of the campus buildings.

Dr. Vodonoy raised his voice. "And yet when asked what has been accomplished so far, you were able to tell your paper adviser only that you had read one or two books on amnesia cases, one on state-related memory, and the biography of the astrologer and mathematician John Dee!"

Hal was unconcerned. He said breezily, "The subject of memory retention techniques and memory loss is related to the thesis topic in several ways. In the story of Tristram and Iseult, for example—"

"Perhaps you had better use those *memory retention techniques* of which you speak so highly, Mr. Landfall, to remember what the date is! Most of the other candidates are polishing up their table of appendices by now! Have you even begun? Do you have even one word written on a piece of paper?"

Hal said, "Too much drafting and redrafting tends to take some of the spontaneity and zest out of academic writing, in my opinion…"

Dr. Vodonoy sat back. "You are going to perform several months' worth of work in mere weeks? The examiners will tear you to bits like mad dogs. It will not be a pretty sight."

Hal shrugged.

"If it were in my power, Mr. Landfall, I would expel you here and now. Unfortunately, there is no requirement that you meet with your adviser, nor keep him abreast of your progress. The only requirement is the paper, properly presented, on an approved topic, embodying original and significant research, and it must be your own work. Since it is perfectly clear to me that you have done no work at all, but either bought or intend to buy a dissertation written by another, I assure you that five minutes after you turn in your plagiarized fraud, I will have you before Dean Schubert, who is chairman of the Graduate Student Ethics Committee."

Hal knew he should take the warning seriously, and do his best to placate the Senior Tutor, but there was no help for it. He simply laughed, unable to tamp down his buoyant feelings. "Don't be such a worry-wart! You'll give yourself pemphigus! I could write this paper in my sleep. Original work! The world has no idea of what I know about King Arthur. Did you not know how he fights his battles, over and over and over again, in dreams. Do you know how many stalwart warriors and chiefs he slew, when the banners of the Saxons streamed against him, and he alone recalled the Roman tactics, Roman honor? He was fighting for Christ against you pagans, you witches and enchanters! You have taken over the halls of Academia, and called up the blinding mists from the elf waters roaring darkly beneath the hollow hills!"

Dr. Vodonoy's face grew dark. "You clearly are drunk, Mr. Landfall!"

"No, I–" Hal blinked. What had he just said?

"Again, drunkenness is not grounds for expulsion, but plagiarism will be. I am looking forward to blasting your hopes and dreams, but I must wait until the deadline falls like a guillotine blade. And, no, there will be no extension on account of illness, or drunkenness, or even insanity. Good day!"

Daily Crossing

Hal, a thin cigar in his mouth, one hand in his pocket, twirling his cane, and with the bright sun high overhead, strolled happily and unhurriedly back to his flat above the smokeshop in Blackbird Leys. Sure, it was the bad part of town, the haunt of 'chavs' and lowlifes. But Hal had never been harassed by them: even the toughest boy seemed for some reason to steer clear.

Why so light on his feet this day? He had found a way to visit Laurel every other day or so. It was only a bit over two hours from Oxford to Weymouth by motorcar, and he had come across the brilliant idea of drawing out all his savings, and the money he had set aside for his remaining school expenses, in order to buy a yacht. It was a small boat, but fast, and able to cross the fifty-four nautical miles to Alderney in three and a half hours, and it was only ninety minutes more to Sark after that. This meant that every day he left at six o'clock in the morning, he could reach Laurel and enter the Rose Crystal Chamber before two o'clock, and if he departed before sunset from Sark, he could be back in bed in Oxford by midnight. Of course, this schedule would be thrown off by classwork or study, but he could skip those. And horrible distractions like the Graduate Tutor insisting on seeing him! The nerve of that man.

Hal decided he needed more time with Laurel. Schoolwork had to wait. After all, he was doing so well on his studies, and was so far ahead on his paper, he could afford to take this week off. That would leave him with all of next week to start and complete the dissertation!

Now, why it was that this one room in Manfred's spooky old house held such an attraction for him, he did not know. And, with no money now left for rent or food, he practically had to make the daily pilgrimage to Laurel, to see her, to...

No, wait, what was he thinking? Laurel was marrying Manfred in less than a month! He was traveling all this way to see Manfred, of course, and to help him along with his studies. Manfred seemed unaccountably worried about how the dissertation paper would be received. Hal wondered why.

It was late in the day when Laurel met him on the lawn in front of the house. Perched atop masses of coiffed hair was her broad straw hat. Apparently it had been returned to her after that night it fell from her head in Wrongerwood Forest. She wore a short, sheath dress which displayed her figure to its best advantage. Hal wondered for the first time why she never seemed to get cold? He had not once seen her dressed as warmly as a person should be.

She seized both his hands in hers, and in a bubbly voice of enthusiasm described how she's hit on the idea of inviting her sisters to come here, to England, to Sark, to help with the dress and the wedding preparations.

Hal said, "You cannot just buy a dress in a shop?"

Laurel drawled, "And be a laughingstock? There are traditions to be upheld, you know, and appearances. In any case, I found this letter in my handbag, inviting them, and laying out all the plans. It was in my handwriting, but I don't remember writing it. I cannot seem to sleep at night, I am so excited. Manfred thinks I am sleepwalking—or perhaps sleepletterwriting—but, just between you and me, it is nice to have an excuse to knock on his door at night... well..."

His heart bumped oddly. He said, "You look a little sad. Having second thoughts?"

She raised her shoulders and her eyebrows in an exaggerated shrug that, to him, looked adorably girlish. "All brides get cold feet."

"Well, the clever ones run off with the best man," he said with a grin.

Laurel said, "Good heavens, Hal, are you making a pass at me?"

"I must be doing it wrong, if you have to ask."

"Aren't you the bold one! I should slap your face!"

He put his arms around her, and hugged her tight, pinning her arms to the sides. "Be careful! If you slap me, who knows what I might do?"

He gazed down at her as she stared up at him, startled. Her expression was haughty, but in her eyes, he saw something else, a frantic innocence that pierced him to the very center of his heart. It reminded him of an animal, trapped at the back of a canyon in its efforts to escape a wildfire—watching as its crackling doom approached, yet unable to do anything to alter its fate. But Laurel was as tough as steel and as resilient as bamboo. What could possibly so frighten such a fearless girl?

The wedding. The wedding was her wildfire. She did not wish to marry Manfred, and yet she could not contrive to escape.

Staring down into the helpless agony of her eyes, Hal felt his universe tremble as it came to him, with a terrifying certainty, that it was he, and not Manfred, that Laurel loved.

No. It must be his imagination. Perhaps, her agony came from the tightness of his grip. Perhaps, he entirely mistook…

Manfred came pacing around the corner of the eastern wing at that very moment, staring at the ground. Hal released the girl and stepped away. Laurel, her cheeks pink, drew back her arm to slap him. Hal grinned and proffered his cheek. Laurel hesitated, and looked over her shoulder at Manfred. It was not clear if he had seen anything or not.

Manfred looked up. "What is all this, then? Having a tiff? I want my bride and best man to get along, you know."

Laurel smiled her dazzling smile and laid her upraised hand on Hal's shoulder. "Oh, I was just asking Henry to step into the Rose Chamber with me, to look at swatches."

Oddly enough, Hal had also been tickled by a strange urge to visit that Chamber again, but for what reason, he could not say.

Lovers' Quarrel

Memory returned. They were in the silk-lined chamber beneath the silver dome. Laureline had somehow cajoled her outer self into replacing the smashed furniture, stocking the chimney side with wood, and moving a small icebox in here, some futon mattresses, and other little comforts needed for a lover's nest.

Henry said, "That was a very good sign! That last scene—Manfred saw, and he was not angry. The Out-of-Doors you is coming around!"

But Laureline was angry, almost panicking, her eyes like green fire. "Your brutal antics are ruining everything!"

"Brutal antics?" he asked, entirely confused. "Weren't you complaining that I was not caveman enough for you?"

Laureline ignored him and charged on. "Manfred has seen you traveling between here and Oxford for days now, doing without sleep, ignoring your school! He's getting suspicious and angry. Even my other self is starting to hate you! You are so creepy!"

He shook his head as if to clear away the mental cobwebs. He said, "I don't think you know your outside self very well. She is about to come around. She is falling in love."

Laureline's eyes flashed. "She's not."

Now it was Henry's turn to be angry. "Well, she would be, if you were inside her doing your job, and pulling for me!"

"Don't throw the blame on me. Things are worse than ever!"

Henry said, "How can you say that? The spell is breaking! It is working!"

Laureline said, "No, all that is happening is that your out-of-doors self is losing his mind, getting more desperate, taking longer and longer chances to see me. It smells of desperation."

"We only have two weeks left. There is no harm in me being away from school."

"You fool!" she blazed. "Women hate desperation! We can smell it like a dog smelling a hidden wound that has started to fester! No, no! We have to try something more reliable, something that will get you to come into this chamber every day."

"So you *do* think the spell is breaking?"

She kissed him, and he forgot whatever it was he was going to say. He pushed her down onto the rug, and when her hair fell out of her hat, it spread like a black pool for a yard in each direction.

Not long after, she leaned over him, kissing him on the chest and neck and lips, and saying, "Henry, I have a plan, a foolproof plan, that will ensure you must return to the chamber each and every day."

He said, "You are far too worried. The spell is breaking–"

"I tell you it is not. We must take bold steps."

After a little more kissing and snuggling, and a daring game involving chilled baby oil and hot fudge and a blindfold, he was not in the mood to argue. "Whatever you say, darling."

"Here," she said with an odd smile, "Drink this!" and she handed him a glass of wine she poured from a small black flask she took from the cooler.

"To us!" he said. Her manner was so odd, and the look in her eye so bright, that initially he took only the merest sip. But it was delicious, so he drank it eagerly, downing the whole in one searing swallow.

Then he had to lay down, because a feverish dizziness was coming over him, and a sensation of ascending into the unimagined heights of deep space, beyond the nearer constellations, to where the stars were strange and sang in the silver voices of women.

Nausea

Hal woke in a strange room, feeling sick. The mattress was rough and lumpy, and the bed was sort of a boxlike affair built into one side of a slanting wall. It had been made for shorter sleepers: his head and feet brushed the opposite walls. There was a dormer window admitting light that dazzled his eyes and made them water. He was in an attic, but one where all the exposed wood was lacquered and polished, and the drywall smooth and white. There was another bed opposite, two narrow doors, and a staircase leading down.

It was not until he stood that the nausea assailed him. Aches and pains clenched his limbs.

On his feet, shaking and sweating, he looked out the window. He recognized the tiny street on which no motor vehicle had ever run. Across from him was the Stocks Inn, and he saw the constable, who was also the Island's postmaster, on his bicycle coming out the back door.

From the position of his coign of vantage, he knew which house this must be: Mammy Levrier, whose boys were working as gardeners at Le Seigneurie.

His gorge started to rise. He staggered over to the two narrow doors. One was a closet of shelves stocked with children's toys from seventy-five years ago, a blue schoolbus made of metal, a set of solid wooden blocks, a toy space helmet from the days before the moonshot, a Raggedy Anne doll. It was odd how sturdy and well-preserved they were. Hal had never seen toys that were not built to fall apart in a year. He found his clothing, neatly folded, in a wooden drawer beneath.

The other door contained a porcelain sink-bowl beneath a mirror, and a porcelain toilet bowl. The light was a naked bulb worked by a pull-chain. He managed to get the lid open before he upchucked the contents of his stomach. At first he could not see how to flush it, but then he saw the water tank on a high shelf, connected by pipes to the bowl, and another pull-chain.

Hal dressed himself and went down the narrow stairs. Again, the woodwork was finely done. To his left was a kitchen, with a sink and washbasin beneath a hand-pump, a larder and an icebox with a big metal handle. To his right was a den, with a collection of geodes and semiprecious stones stored neatly along the walls under glass. Here was a large easy chair facing a small television, and a few paces beyond that, on a nice rug, a large dining table under an unexpectedly fine chandelier. Everything was spotless, well-kept, clean. He stared in puzzlement at the several wolf heads stuffed and mounted on the wall. One particular head was huge and shaggy beyond normal proportion, looking like something from before the last ice age, a dire wolf. The paws of the wolf were stuffed and mounted as well, and formed the gun rack on which several well-made American hunting rifles were resting.

On the wall opposite was an ornate booth with a statuette of the Virgin Mary, and rosary beads hanging on little brass hooks. He stared and saw among the rosaries a chain without beads. It bore a large silver image of the crucified savior as the pendant. Hal touched his own bare neck. That was the very crucifix he had picked up the other day from the Brising Brothers, not very long after he bought the diamond pendant from them. Someone in the house must have hung it here, in this little shrine, for safekeeping while he slept.

Hal stepped over and took it down, running his fingers across it. It was a handmade item, with no twin in the world. Two scrimshawed ivory pieces to the left and right of the crucifix displayed a Roman soldier with a spear, and a slaveboy holding a sponge on the end of a staff. Beneath the pendant was a medallion smaller than a dime, showing a graybeard rabbi carrying a cup overhead, almost touching the nailed feet of the dying man. As with the dolphins on Laurel's necklace, the work was almost impossibly fine and small.

Hal looked around, worried that if someone saw him take his pendant back, he might be thought a thief. He shouted, and was rewarded with a stab of pain through his head and his joints. There was no one here. He knew Mrs. Levrier was in a hospital on Guernsey, and the boys were no doubt on the northern end of Sark, working on the gardens behind Wrongerwood House.

Why was he here?

The front door looked handmade as well, and by someone who took pride in his carpentry. It was arched, made of polished boards over an inch thick, and held in place with massive wrought-iron hinges and hasps. The door could have shrugged off a battering ram.

Hal found his boots by the door, newly polished and smelling of oil. In a can next to a tightly curled umbrella was his hawk-headed walking stick. Here on a hook was his coat. In the coat pocket was his memorandum book. It was too dark in the kitchen to read.

He stepped outside, and sat down on the little steel box where the milkman put the daily bottles. There were flowers in a little well-tended strip of garden to his right and left, and the only traffic on the road was the mailman on his bicycle, and a plow-horse pulling a haycart coming the other way.

In the book was a ferry ticket to St. Helier Harbor. With his pounding headache and fuzzy memory, he could not recall where that was. On the back of the ticket was the image of two crossed golden axes on a blue field. He had no idea what that meant.

Rented room from Wolfhounds. Beware the pale, gaunt man.

"I should go see a psychiatrist," he muttered. He did not recall writing that note, nor what it was about.

Reminder: left medicine with Manfred.

That made more sense. Hal had suffered some sort of powerful allergic reaction to something, perhaps a bee sting (he still felt the pain of the sharp sting in his forearm), and Manfred had offered to run his antihistamine through some filters to strengthen it. And, naturally, it would have been dangerous to stay in the house until whatever it was that provoked his allergic reaction was isolated.

Of course! The memory was coming back now. He had to return to Wrongerwood House immediately for his medicine, and to do whatever else Laurel wanted him to do. That only made sense.

But then there was another note: *MUST go to Brising Brothers and ask for package: I promised Manfred!*

Hal clenched his teeth. He wanted (oh, *how* he wanted!) to go to pick up his medicine and see Laurel again. And Sark House was only a short walk up the island's one road to the north end. But then there was that word *promised*. Also, Laurel would not be home regardless. She had insisted on borrowing his yacht, since she had wedding plans to make, florists and bakers and such to meet in London, and she had asked so nicely, saying how convenient it would be not to be chained to the schedule of the one, lone ferry that sailed by the morning tide and the evening tide, twice daily, no more.

Well, now he was chained to the ferry schedule. Looking at his watch, he realized he had just enough time to haul his aching body to the boat and collapse into a seat, if he were to make it at all. Going up to Sark House meant catching the evening ferry which meant, in effect, deliberately breaking his promise.

There was nothing he hated more than breaking a promise, even over the smallest things.

He waved his stick at the haycart. It was a modern-looking thing of green metal with rubber tires, shock absorbers and springs, but pulled by a long-maned old nag. A farmer named Beaumont sat on the bench.

Hal wiped his nose, gritted his aching teeth, and said, "When you see Liam, tell him I have taken the ferry to St. Ouens, on Jersey."

Beaumont smiled, and said in French, "You seem unwell, my sir. Must you travel? I will give you a ride to the dock."

Hal climbed up behind him, his joints aching. "I don't have a way to lock the door."

"There are no locks on the doors here, except in the Seigneur's House. And that is to stop the ghosts from coming out, not the robbers from getting in."

The Parish of Saint Ouen

The journey was a disaster. He had diarrhea on the ship, and lost control of his bowels, and ruined his pants. Passersby on the street of the port town of St. Helier watched in disbelief and disgust as he limped through the street, stinking, trying to find a hotel. He checked in, had the bellhop take the pants to be cleaned, and then sat on the bed, sick and shaking, while the hours passed. Eventually the bellhop returned, and, when Hal had no money for the tip, the manager arrived, asking him to pay immediately for the room. When it turned out that Hal had nothing, could find none of his traveler's checks, and that his credit card was exhausted, the manager, in a fine Gallic fettle threatened him with jail, and the bellhop (who seemed to think Hal was a dope addict) threatened him with a beating. Hal managed to make some phone calls from the manager's office, and send some messages, and get his sister Elaine to wire him some emergency funds.

By the time he was released from the manager's office, the sun had set. He had missed the ferry back to Sark.

He was also destitute of money for a bus or cab, so he had to walk the five miles from St. Helier's at the south of the island to St.

Ouen's village in the north. He faded in and out of agony during the walk, which took twice as long as it should have. He was glad for his cane, and, for once, actually made use of it with each step.

At the start of his tramp, in the moonlight, he saw the ruins of the Twelfth Century hermitage where Helier was martyred by Vikings. During the Reformation, that hermitage was closed and rebuilt into a fortress by Queen Elizabeth. And at the end of his long walk, hours later, he saw the silhouette of the La Rocco Tower in the Saint Ouen Bay, illumined by the gleam of the lighthouse, looming like a rook from the chessboard of a giant. La Rocco Tower had been erected during the Napoleonic wars, one of thirty round towers raised to defend the coastline.

The weight of history soaked into the ground was like nothing he had seen in America, no, not even in places like Williamsburg, where he had gone to school before Oxford. He wondered if all these ruins, and fortresses built on hermitages, and warlike towers each were visited by the ghosts of men who defended them in life, and whether their battles were fought over again forever until doomsday.

It was late in the evening, but the streets of the town were crowded, and colored lamps were hanging on wires over the square. Folk in shaggy costumes, wearing masks of fierce animals, were dancing and cavorting in the square. Hal waved at a couple, a boy with a sparkler and a girl with a wineglass, and asked if either knew the way to the Brising Brothers.

"But yes, my sir!" said the girl, red-cheeked and glancing-eyed with the wine. "The shop you seek? He is there, beneath the old windmill. The main street is closed for the procession of relics. You must find the back way."

"Are they still open at this hour?" shouted Hal over the sound of the raucous music.

The boy said, "You've had too much. Are you unwell? Do not drink any more."

But the girl said, "It is the feast of Saint Guthlac of Crowland! He lived in the stinking fens and swamps where the monsters and devils dwelt. He was friends with the wild animals and had the gift of prophecy. He held the marriage."

Hal's head was pounding. "What marriage?"

"Saint Guthlac convinced a Sir Lanval, the poverty-stricken knight exiled from Camelot, to wed rather than to slay the mermaid he caught. Each year we celebrate the marriage of the water-woman to the knight, because she gained a soul. When the church bells rang the wedding, and she stepped over the threshold, her tail fell off, and she became a mortal named Tryamour. All the old families in this parish are descended from her. See!"

The girl pointed to a procession of figures in papier-mâché heads, led by a bishop in a miter of absurd size and proportion. Behind him was a man in white armor adorned with ermines, and a sword of tinfoil, and a woman hidden in her wedding veils. Even as Hal looked, rockets went off, and bells rang out, and the bride threw off her veil, revealing a pretty young brunette beneath, with the wide and expressive features of a Gallic woman. Amid many whoops and rowdy cheers, the bride shook her hips, flourishing the long silly-looking fish tail trailing from her bustle. The bishop touched the tail with his crook, the woman untied the fake tail, and, while the crowd roared, she whirled the tail over her head and sent it flying into the thickest part of the crowd, where women young and old leaped to catch it. The crowd threw rice, blew tin whistles and sent spouts of champagne into the air.

The boy said, "Look there! That is one of the brothers, it is he. Him you seek, is it not so?"

He pointed to a man so short, that Hal wondered if he were

a dwarf hired for the celebration. The bald little man was dressed like a burgher from a hundred years ago, complete with watch fob and waistcoat, and sporting an enormous set of side whiskers. He was walking into a dark and narrow space between two buildings, evidently to avoid the commotion of the beast-bride and her knightly bridegroom.

Hal, leaning on his walking stick a little unsteadily, stepped into the alleyway. Just then, Hal saw a pale, thin hoodlum dressed in filthy rags crawl out from beneath a trash dumpster. The crawling hooligan grabbed the little man by the ankle.

"Hey!" shouted Hal. "What is going on?" He could not believe it was a robbery. The noise and lights from the festival were only a pace or two behind him. Any number of people near the head of the alley would have seen everything clearly.

The pale man looked up, his eyes filled with insane malice. The man's face was so white, Hal wondered if he were an albino. The pale man had discolorations around his mouth, like bee stings or cold sores.

The pale man stood, and stooped over the little man, licking his face.

Hal took step forward, and raised his walking stick threateningly. "Now, you let go of him!" But the gaunt man looked at him with such a dark look in his eyes that Hal hesitated. Just then, another one of the cramps and muscle spasms that had been plaguing him that day struck his arm. His elbow joint was aching. He dropped the walking stick with a clatter.

Hal drew out the crucifix he wore on a chain around his neck, and held it up. The gaunt man looked like he was trying to stifle a sneezing fit. The gaunt man shuddered and twitched, doubled over, and then suddenly collapsed.

Hal turned, picked up his walking stick, and looked behind him.

They were within plain sight of a dozen people in the main road. Why had no one noticed? Why had no one come to help, or even raised a voice? Perhaps the alcohol was stronger or the music louder than it seemed.

The little man was shivering and trying to straighten his old-fashioned clothes. He had fallen, and there was a cut on his neck. He was holding his handkerchief there to staunch the blood. Hal helped him to his feet. The little man said to Hal, "I remember you. Come."

Hal said, "Shouldn't we call the police?" He pointed at where the gaunt man had fallen down, but the gaunt man was no longer there.

The little man was already a half-dozen paces down the alleyway. Hal followed, feeling as if he were in a bad dream or was the butt of a bad practical joke.

Twelve steps more, and the little man opened a metal door in the rear of his shop. Inside were glass cases, row upon row, as fine and beautiful as anything Hal had ever seen in the finest shops in London or New York. There were also antiques for sale. Hal gazed in admiration at a suit of black and gold armor refurbished from some museum, inscribed with images from elfin myths of swords and swans and wounded kings, bleeding lances and cups seated among the stars, and an arm clad in shimmering samite flourishing a blade from the midst of the lake waters.

"Yours is scale," said the little man, "Set with images of the ermine."

Also here was a second dwarf seated on a stool, a twin to the first, except that his scalp was snowy with hair, and his mustaches drooped like those of Fu Manchu, dangling past his jaw. He had a jeweler's loupe in his eye, and he was tapping delicately at some bright thing shining in the confluence of several goose-necked lamps.

The first one said, "This is one of our special order customers from Sercq. He saved me from the Great Gaunt Man not a moment ago, at terrible peril to his life and soul."

Hal said, "Wait a moment. You mean that ragged, starving bum outside your back door?"

The second one peered at him, and his right eye seemed swollen and enormous when seen through the lens of the loupe he had forgotten to remove from his eye. "The Mists of Everness have fogged his wits. He is surely sunken deeply in her charms."

The first one said, "How are we to know, brother, that things will work out well? We send him to his death. The Gaunt Man is strong, stronger than before! No arms of our make can prevail against him!"

The second said, "The air of Earth beclouds our eyes as well. We must trust in all the things we have forgotten, for the Fisher King would not have sent us into this world unprepared."

Hal said, "Listen, if you boys have been drinking too much at your little *Mardis-Gras* here...."

"You have lost the count of time," said the first little man, exasperated. "That was thirty nine days ago. This is the Feast of Saint Guthlac."

Hal said, "I am here to pick up an order for Lord Manfred of Sark. I'm—I am afraid I don't remember what it is, exactly. I wrote it down in my book..."

The second little man hopped down from his stool, the tools jangling in his apron loops. "We remember. Come with me, please, sir. Our special order customers must go deeper into the shop."

He walked between the tall cases of many cut and polished stones set in rings and earrings, broaches and pins. Here were amethysts, and jacinths, chrysoprase as green as grass, peridot and beryl. Yellow chrysolite, red sardius and sardonyx, emerald and carnelian, blue sapphire and purple jasper.

The little man in front of him, with the Fu Manchu moustache, stopped at a blank wall and gestured toward the jewel cases. "You see our approaches are warded. You may tell the Lord of Sark we cherish our duties."

Hal said, "What is going on? What is this place?"

The little man behind him, the one with the enormous side whiskers, pulled shut a metallic grating behind them, and locked it. He said angrily, "He does not know us. His spirit is corrupted with morphine alkaloid of opium, a witchbrew."

The second one said to Hal, "We always pay our debts. For the lifeblood of my brother, whom you saved, we should like to gift and grant you with an amethyst stone, whose virtue is to bring sobriety, not only for inebriation but also for over-zealousness in passion. Here is an amethyst taken from the ring of an Archbishop, who threw it in the sea when the Parliament decreed King Henry to be greater than Christ, for His Eminence wished in that hour for the wine to blind his memory."

"Uh, really, it was nothing." But the little man thrust a ring onto Hal's finger, and the purple stone winked like fire. The ache immediately began to throb less and less, and the room spun more slowly.

Without a further word, the first little man slid open a panel in the wall. Behind was a door that Hal was certain he had seen before, perhaps in a dream. His dreams at Wrongerwood House had been so vivid.

The door was made of white metal, brighter than snow, and hexagonal in shape. In the middle was the Seal of Solomon, two opposite triangles crossed. Passages from the Gospel and the Talmud were inscribed in concentric rows along the edges of the door, and the Enochian script in which Noah had written his book of prophecy, the only written language of the world before the Flood.

The two little men now donned thick goggles of smoked glass. The first one took out a key, the twin to the one in Hal's pocket, which had a silver-white lotus inscribed in the bow. There was a loud click as the bolt shot back. The portal began to open. A nimbus of light escaped through the widening crack, and the rush of music beating in a hypnotic fantasia: lute and zither, rebec and bamboo flute, buzzing reeds and sounding brass.

Henry squinted against the blinding brilliance. He stepped forward, and the air seemed as thick and fluid as the bottom of a deep pool.

Chapter 11

Hue and Cry

Captain Hezekiah

To his infinite surprise, the two Brising brothers insisted on finding him passage back to Sark that very evening. The first brother gave him a note written in strange letters to a certain fisherman whose houseboat he described with great peculiarity: a small black tug with a squat iron chimney adorned about the prow and stern with the bones of whales and teeth of sharks. The captain's name was Hezekiah. This captain must have had very good eyes indeed, for he stood on the gangplank to his small steamboat, and read the note in the night, with no lamps nearby, and not even the moon.

He was not French, but spoke in a thick accent of Southern England. "They pay their debts, the sons of Albrecht, sure enough, but are skinflinted enough in collecting them! You have any charms to ward ye? They are worthless. Throw them in the sea. Call upon your name saints!"

"My name is Henry," Hal answered, climbing aboard. "And I am not, ah, what you might call a churchgoing man, so I don't know what my name saints are."

"Do you charge into battle with a sausage for a sword? Barmpot! Saint Henry of Conquet is yours, as is Saint Henry of Uppsala, and

Saint Henry II the Holy Roman Emperor. Saint Henry Walpole the Martyr, or Saint Henry of Sweden! Call on them."

There was an awning aft beneath which was an open coal bin. Hezekiah took a billows and blew on banked coals of his engine, and spat and cursed, until the fire was reborn. With efficient motions of his rippling arms, the old sailor man began to shovel coal into the grate, which opened and shut like the mouth of a demon, letting hot sparks and red leaping light escape into the night each time the iron teeth snapped open and shut.

"There are women in the channel and witches in the air, and they say the Gaunt Man flew back to the hollow caves the Nazis carved in Brecqhou. Hell take him! Old Captain Hezekiah knows the better nooks, even with the tide against us, even in the dark, and I can find where John Allaire diddled with his doxy on the south coast past the pools of Venus and Adonis, while on the north coast in his tall, old house, his lady lay alone and pining. Come!"

But the pains in his limbs, and the sweating, overcame Hal soon, and he slept before the lights of Saint Ouen village were out of sight aft.

Hal woke in an undersea cave, in the middle of a dark pool. The cave mouth he could hear but not see behind him, and he saw the starlight on the waters.

The captain handed him a tin lantern, and pointed to an ancient dock. Between two stalactites covered with barnacles and bright shells was a stairwell, almost a ladder, leading straight up a natural chimney in the rock. Captain Hezekiah told him which wall to follow so as not to get lost in the empty caves. "You'll be aland in the old smuggler's tunnel at the south island's end. Recall the law! It is the *clamour de haro* and it is old Norman law, used in all these islands, but only in Sark does the memory keep! You must say the Lord's prayer where a Christian man can hear your words, to show

you are no warlock, nor heathen, nor deceiver, and then cry out
Haro, Haro, Haro! À mon aide mon Prince, on me fait tort!"

Hal blinked in confusion. "And the prince comes?"

"All unlawful acts must cease until the matter is heard by the
court. You must should register your complaint with the Greffe Office within twenty-four hours, or the cry can be annulled for sitting
on your rights. You know the Lord's Prayer?"

"Um. *Now I lay me down to sleep?*"

"Barmpot!"

Commotion under the Stars of Sark

Hal emerged from the mouth of one of the old silver mines in Little
Sark, the southern half of the island. A chain ran at knee height
between two posts carrying a tin sign, no doubt the name of the
mining company long defunct, or perhaps a warning to keep out.
He stepped over it and walked past the pumphouse and an empty
shed to the dirt road leading north. The sound of the waves on the
seashore was all around him, dimly in the distance. He covered the
tin lantern and let his eyes adjust to the starlight, for the stars were
bright indeed tonight, and seemed closer to the Earth. The Milky
Way was a silvery river in the heavens, bright and clear, which was a
sight he had never seen from the brightly lit streets of Williamsburg
or New York or Oxford or any other place he had lived. It was an
amazing sight: he now understood why Sark was called a Dark Sky
island.

With his lantern dark, and the aches in his limbs diminished
to an occasional twinge, Hal tramped beneath the stars uphill and
down, and granite boulders protruded from the lush grass to either
side of the path as he went.

He came to the narrow isthmus called *La Coupée*. The path leaped boldly along this sheer ridge of rock two hundred sixty feet above the sea, with an abyss of air to either side. There were stone posts linked by cables to the left and right, but the wind-gusts from the sea made the footing uncertain despite this railing, especially in the star-filled dark.

He was halfway across, and had another fifty yards to negotiate, when he saw two groups of men in leathery, dark coats and dark caps, perhaps a dozen in all, struggling roughly with each other. In the starlight he saw them rolling on the ground in awkward wrestling, or throwing wild punches. The strangest thing was that they were making no noise aside from hisses and grunts.

There was a solitary figure standing tall and pale-faced in the starlight at the far side of the airy isthmus, a thin man with naked legs, wrapped in a blanket or cloak. He stood looking on, and the starlight was reflected in his eyes.

Hal knew, because Manfred had boasted, that there was no crime on Sark. The two jail cells of the local volunteer constabulary were reserved for tourists. So he knew this scrum could not be as desperate as it seemed. It was probably mere boyish roughhousing. But to fight here, in this narrow space with an appalling drop to either side, was madness.

Hal stepped forward, waving his walking stick in the air. There was a bright flash: Hal had accidentally banged the cover of the lantern open and shut, producing a momentary blinding dazzle. "*Notre Père, qui es aux cieux, que ton nom soit sanctifié, que ton règne vienne, que ta volonté soit faite sur la terre comme au ciel!*" he shouted.

He now saw that the fight was uneven, that it was ten young men against two. Hal broke into a jog, feeling anger in his limbs, a blush of heat in his face. His bellowing must have disturbed some large osprey or albatross nesting nearby, because a winged shape launched itself from the stone bridge and soared away over the sea. The pale man standing at the far end, beyond the commotion, was gone, even though there was not really any place he could have hidden.

He was now close enough to see that the two boys being harassed were Liam and Burt, the Wolfhound brothers who had been doing gardening work at the manor house.

"...*Et ne nous soumets pas à la tentation, mais délivre-nous du mal!*"

Hal strode toward the young men boldly, flourishing his walking stick in the most menacing fashion he could contrive, feeling ridiculous.

"Hear me! Hear me! Hear me! Come to my aid, my Prince, for someone does me wrong!" Hal cried in French.

To his astonishment, that worked. The fighting stopped, and the young men stared at him in wonder and fear. One of them, a scruffy farm lad with a beer bottle in his hand, fainted away on the spot, and fell to the road. The nine others broke and ran, whining like dogs, sidling past Hal and pelting away down the narrow isthmus toward the abandoned silver mine.

Hal helped Liam to his feet. "Good lad!" he said soothingly, petting the young man's hair and scratching under his chin. "What happened here?"

"There is trouble at the House, sir," said Liam. "You'd better hurry on up. Burt and me will see that Luc finds his way back home." He nodded toward the drunk boy lying motionless on the road.

Without waiting for more words, Hal jogged, ran and walked the two miles past Convanche Chasm, past the hills called Le Grand Beauregard and Le Petite Beauregard, up Mill Lane to Chasse-Marais, past the Chief Pleas House, the Inn and its one lamp, and up the one village street. Then he was among fields and pastures, and then he plunged into the dark woods.

He came suddenly upon four men in fur caps with thick beards leaping up and down in front of the main doors of the house, gnashing and snapping their teeth. They were armed with bricks and bats. The image of the lion hanging above the heavy doors seemed to frighten them, for they kept darting closer to the doors, trying to hurt it. Evidently a swung bat or thrown brick had already wounded the figure, because some of the gold was scraped away from the image about the paws and mouth, revealing a red gold underneath, in long red streaks.

As before, Hal called out the hue and cry, *haro, haro, haro*, and waved his walking stick in the air. Hal swatted one or two of the rough-looking hairy men on the back or legs with the walking stick. Manfred or one of the servants must have been watching from inside and wanted to help him, because, just then, the porch light came on, dazzling bright, and burned out, going dark again after one eye-dazing flash.

And, as before, the men broke and ran, two men helping a third who limped, although Hal was sure he had not struck the fellow that hard.

Hal banged the door and called, but no one answered. He used the key whose bow was decorated with the gold lion head to let himself into the main door.

It really was quite extraordinary, Hal thought to himself, that these rustic folk had so much respect for the law that they would go home and go back to their beds just when someone raised the hue and cry. Extraordinary! Hal shook his head sadly, thinking of the crime-ridden streets of New York.

Inside, the manor house was dark and silent. Provoked by a strange impulse for which he could not account, Hal climbed the stairs and headed for the upper gallery circling the nave of the old priory, seeking the Rose Crystal Chamber.

Love's Bitter Fruit

Memory fell into his mind.

The purple divan beneath the silver dome now had a silk curtain draped in a circle all about it. An electric heater was here, coils red like hot coals, and cast a shadowless pink light across the floor. Within was Laureline, asleep, outrageously voluptuous, her lips as red as blood and skin as rosy-white as snow seen by dawn, her black hair spilled across pillow and floor as a scented flood. On a little end table next to the divan was a stoppered bottle and a hypodermic.

His gaze traveled slowly from the line of her neck to her naked shoulder, down the slopes of her torso to the valley of her waist, and then upslope again to the rounded hill of her hip, with rolling slopes of long thighs and calves trailing away in the distance. By the time his gaze had traveled this landscape of luxurious flesh back from toes to head again, he saw something that made his heart lurch.

There were odd bruise marks, set like fingerprints, upon her neck, and her black lacy negligee was ripped along the back. As he frowned at this, he saw her eyes were half-open. How long she had been watching him, motionless as a cat, from beneath half-closed lids he could not say.

Henry's eyes traveled back to the bottle and needle. He said sharply, "You *addicted* me? What is in that bottle? Morphine? Heroin?"

Laureline sat up. The brassiere of the ripped, lacy, black negligee strained to contain her breasts.

"It was necessary," she said, her voice groggy from sleep.

"Necessary?" His voice snapped with cold fury.

"There was no other way to make certain, absolutely certain, that you would return here!" she said, turning her back to him, then picked up a comb of gold and ran it through her rippling yards of hair. "How was I to know that the Outer You would not suffer a spasm of conscience and go flying off to America until after the wedding? You are too addicted to foolish notions of wrong and right, niceties of honor: I had to act to protect us, since you will not."

He said, "We discussed this. The spell is breaking! Now that you and I have been, ah, intimate…"

She turned again, and smiled a sharp smile with no humor in it. "You mean now that we have rutted like maddened weasels in heat? No, there was no other way." She pointed with her golden comb at his walking stick. "Leave that here. It has got to be at hand."

"At hand for what?"

Laureline raised her golden comb again and then frowned slightly, touching the bruises on her neck as if to soothe their ache. Like someone suddenly recalling themselves after rising from the oblivion of sleep, her eyes grew wide and her whole aspect changed.

The slow, sweet smile of the woman combing her hair vanished. Instead, her eyes blazed like those of a she-wolf, half in terror and half in wrath. Her half-naked body trembled with fear and rage, flushing bright red from cheek to neck. The diamond pendant in her cleavage winked and caught the rose-red light, like the trinket of a mesmerist glinting as her bosom rose and fell in the passion of her words.

"He saw us, you fool! You and your groping hands! You don't know how to hide your expression. You had your octopus arms all over my body, and he saw it. He knows, I tell you! He knows what we did in this chamber! Mandrake was waiting for me here last time I entered, sitting there, just there, in that chair! Who knows for how long—all day, perhaps. Waiting. Waiting for her to come in."

"I see," Henry crossed his arms, refusing to be distracted by her frenzy. "And he must have told you–."

But she was still speaking, her voice a tremor of wrath and terror. "Mandrake raised his foot and kicked the door shut. He smiled this little, hard, frozen smile like I have never seen. He said all sorts of mad things, about how Lords of England need an act of Parliament to get a divorce, and how this Countess was a witch who had enchanted him, and somehow I was to blame as well. He could not escape her, but now he had found a way out. The only way out!

"It was terrible." Her body trembled as she spoke. "He was out of his mind! Possessed! He said there was only one way to make sure he would never marry me in the outside world. With no more words than that, he rose, he grabbed me by the neck; he started to strangle me!"

Laureline clawed at her own throat, panting, eyes wild, as if she still felt the strong fingers at her throat. "I kicked and screamed, but what can I do? No one outside this room could hear me. I clawed at the door handle. We fell out over the threshold, and all at once his strangles turned into embraces and kisses, because outside, in that world, we love each other. The next time, by whatever impulse, I happen to walk into this Chamber, and he just happens to be here, it will be my last hour on Earth!"

She jumped toward Henry's tall body and clung to him with desperation. She looked up. He frowned, perturbed and uncertain, his mind numb with shock, unable to process first the barbaric behavior of his beloved in drugging him and now the accusations against his best friend.

There was terror in her eyes and tears on her cheeks. "I cannot even run away! I cannot remind myself outside that my death is waiting, waiting for me here! As soon as I step outside, I am the happy bride about to marry the Lord of the Manor. Don't you see, you've killed us both. My excuse for coming to see you here has been that I was making up the Rose Crystal Chamber to be the honeymoon suite for Manfred and me—he will come in here on the wedding night—and–!"

Sobs smothered her words. She made other sounds, inarticulate, broken. Henry could no longer make out what she was saying. From her expression, it was clear she was seeing her own young body lying motionless, dead in her marriage bed.

Her tears were too much for him. He caught her up in his arms. His heart overflowed with sympathy for her. He could see it all. She was desperate, trapped by this curse, which now had become deadly. Whatever she had done to draw him back to her was justified.

As for Manfred—Henry would have gladly killed anyone coming between him and Laureline. And Mandrake, for all that he had sounded so reasonable when he and Henry had spoken in here, was still the only person Henry knew with a knowledge of mesmerism.

And yet...

She whispered, "Outside, you and I are cowardly, ashamed to admit our love, but in here we are true, we are better, we are strong, we are not afraid! Not ashamed of our truth, not afraid to cast aside all the petty little rules and laws of properness and propriety! How I hate to see you, like a giant tied down by the little strands of Lilliputians! You can break all the world's rules with one arm, and with the other, create for us, for you and me, a world where we can be ourselves, true to ourselves, a secret place of love and passion to endure forever. Can you make such a world for me? Are you strong enough?"

"I will do anything for you," he said with simple grandeur.

"Then leave your cane, as I said!" She hiccupped as she spoke, gulping air. "Take out your memorandum book and remind yourself to ask Manfred to step into this room to talk about, oh, something interesting. And then you are going to hit him with that walking stick in the head and kill him."

Henry merely narrowed his eyes.

"You must kill him," she cried, her voice shrill. "You must!"

Henry said, "I cannot kill my best friend."

"You would rather he kill me?"

"He was perfectly calm last time I spoke to him in here. He must have just been angry. Surely, he will not be so wrathful the next time."

She started at his words, her eyes growing wider. "B-but, Henry! My love! You did not see him! His eyes!" She shivered touching her neck again. "He was clearly mad! I mean... insane, not angry. Madmen can often fool people with their calmness for a little while."

"Nonsense! I have known Manfred for years. He is not mad!" said Henry, though he could not help remembering some of the strange things Mandrake had said about demons and witches.

"But what if– What if he is insane in this world, and he needs the outside world to be sane?"

Henry was startled by the idea. He had never considered such a thing.

She said, "It is not impossible, is it? We are in love in here, but not out there. What if he is insane in here, but not out there?"

Henry swallowed, "I do not know what to say. Or even what to think."

She stood on tiptoe and kissed him. She whispered bravely, "You will find the strength."

Henry opened his mouth to speak, but he had no words, no excuses. The reality was simple and stark. If Mandrake were mad, no doctor of the outside world could help, no treatment. Yet Manfred in the outside world was sane and good. Henry had never seen him show any sign of temper out there. But in here...

Henry remembered the murderous rage upon the face of Mandrake, as he spoke of the death of his aunt and cousins. Manfred might be a man of peace, but Mandrake was clearly capable of such a violent crime.

And the wedding was soon, and getting sooner, and the best man would no longer have an excuse to be staying overnight. Then Manfred would carry his happy, giggling bride in over the threshold to this room, this chamber. Their eyes would grow wide as they remembered, and while the well-wishers outside cheered and threw rice, Mandrake would choke the life out of the girl, and her green eyes go dark.

Laureline's wide green eyes watched his face carefully. She spoke in a slow, soft voice he had to strain to hear. "You must, Henry. This is our only chance at happiness. Think of it. Once outside, you need never remember this chamber again, or what happened in it. I will be a widowed bride, yearning for comfort; you've already begun to waken to your love to me. He simply will be out of the picture. We will remember all this as some sort of accident, as if he had been surprised by some ragged beggar, or torn by a wild animal."

"No," he said, "No, I could never hurt Manfred." But the hope that surged through him at the thought of having her to himself, so easily, so simply, left his voice weak.

What had really happened in the chamber between Mandrake and Laureline? Had she perhaps done something to anger him? If Laureline had tried some trick on Mandrake, similar to the one she tried upon Henry with the hypodermic and the drugs, he would not be able to entirely blame the man for his wrath. Or perhaps the unknown forces arrayed against them had found a way to influence Mandrake within this chamber, to convince his friend that Laureline or Henry had some part in the death of his family?

Or had Mandrake deceived Henry during their last conversation, perhaps in a desire to lure Henry back outside where he could not remember the truth? Had his friend, or his friend's insane alter ego, been the one who had cast this spell after all?

Had Henry been deceived by Manfred's friendship all this time, like a dupe?

The idea of Mandrake, or anyone, laying their hands upon the woman he loved in violence transformed Henry's blood into boiling lava.

Laureline pried the walking stick out of his hand and pushed him gently back on the divan, murmuring, "Shush, shush, my love. We can speak of this later. Later…" and she smothered his words with tearful kisses.

It was perhaps an hour later when she resumed speaking of her fears. Hour after hour she spoke, sometimes weeping in his arms, sometimes cold and threatening. She flattered and cajoled and demanding and argued and screamed and threatened to kill herself, and then joked and pouted as if what she asked were no great thing after all. She told him it would bind the two of them together, seal their love in blood, forever.

His strength drained away and was lost.

He agreed.

The light in the stained-glass windows was turning from gray to pink with the dawn. Up she rose in the half-light, and donned her stockings and shoes so slowly it was as if she had never seen her own legs before, and was delighted at their proportions and beauty. She drew a black silk robe about her shoulders, the same hue as her hair, which was unbound and floating about her.

"I will go to bring him here. Smite him with your fathers' walking stick and slay him. Take it in your hand and stand behind the door to take him from behind. There must be no errors. Oh! And before I forget: write yourself a note to lend me the key he gave you to the Silver-White Lotus Chamber next door. Mandragora won't let me go in there, and it has been bothering me."

She walked out the door. Her heels clicked with her light, rapid footfall as she went up the stairway.

Chapter 12

The Silver-White Lotus Key

The Pink Rope

Henry stared at the hangings and decorations of the chamber. Once or twice he went over to the large window facing south, and stuck his head and torso out, so that, for a moment, he forgot the terrible deed he had agreed to do. The front lawn was a torn mess of wolf prints and scorch marks, and the paws of what could only be lion tracks showed clearly in the bloodstained mud. What this mystery meant, he was too weary to wonder. He was sick of madness, tired of inexplicable events, and now he just wanted it to end. He had given his word to the woman for whom he would gladly have given the world. And now...

And now his world was gray and airless. He felt as if a coffin lid the size of the night sky now covered the Earth from horizon to horizon, as heavy and musty as the carved sarcophagus lid of some cursed Pharaoh whose name was effaced from all records and monuments. It was a world of death, without hope, without light, without life. He had already betrayed his friend, and now he was to kill him: or else he was to betray the girl whose life depended on Henry now, solely on him, and stand idly by while she died. And then he would leave the Rose Crystal Chamber, forgetting she was murdered by her husband, forgetting that he loved her, forgetting all… was that the price of being innocent? Merely not ever looking at one's sins?

Every wrong he had ever committed in his life came flooding back to him, great and small. The candy he had stolen from his mother's cabinet as a child. The fat kid he had beaten up in grammar school. The pornographic magazine he had kept at the bottom of his sock drawer when he was in high school. The time, on a dare, he had run across the stage naked during some school play. Stealing cigarettes from his father's desk.

And then older, darker things. His mind was like a mob, a shouting crowd, all condemning him, all convicting him of crimes, of evil thoughts, and evil deeds. And yet what could he do? Honor demanded he be true and loyal to Manfred; and honor demanded he protect and love Laureline; and Mandrake meant to do her harm. Every sense of decency in him demanded Henry that he do the murder as he had promised. And yet the thing was impossible.

Henry looked up, and saw a way out. It was a coward's way, but it was an out. It took only a few moments to find a stout cord hidden behind the draperies covering all the walls, to tie a noose. The rope was a bright pink.

He lowered the rose-shaped crystal lamp that gave the chamber its name. He tied the knot tightly to the final link in the chain, and hauled the chain back into position, looping the chain securely several times over the cast-iron stanchion.

A way out.

"Is there any other way?" he asked himself, looking at the noose. It seemed horrible that the rope should be pink, such a sweet, feminine color.

"But you are not strong enough to resist Laureline," he told himself. And what if Mandrake walked in and tried to strangle her again? Even the imagination of her soft, fragile, beautiful throat being marred made him tremble with rage. To see it with his eye would drive him over the edge of madness. He would surely kill his best friend to save her. Henry had no doubt in his mind about his willingness and ability. Even the knowledge that his best friend was touching her, caressing her, coupling with her was enough to make the prospect of killing him enticing. And now, to have an excuse, a reason his conscience could not condemn—the temptation was too great.

He climbed up on a chair, adjusted the noose around his neck, and wondered if he were supposed to say a prayer before doing this. Somehow that did not seem right.

Henry's thoughts spun and swirled like water down a drain. His mind and soul were empty save for one thought, more a picture than anything he could put in words: Mandrake will no doubt kill her once she steps over the threshold, but by then, Henry would be safely dead, in a happy oblivion, a swinging blob of meat, safe.

A small, quiet voice in his mind told him that this was wrong, utterly wrong. He put his neck in the loop nonetheless anyway, kicked the chair away.

Then his legs were kicking in the air, jerking comically and he was swaying, an erratic pendant. Suddenly, he knew what he was doing was wrong.

Desperate, he struck at the rope with his walking stick, that he found himself still holding in his hand. The rope parted and dropped him. The stick struck some of the lightbulbs: there was a flash of light as two of the bulbs shattered.

He coughed and writhed on the floor, drawing in great ragged gasps of breath. Then he knelt, the noose still around his neck like a halter meant to lead a bull. Henry stared at the cut end of the rope in puzzlement. It had been neatly severed. He looked at the cane in his hand. The eyes of the German hawk in the handle gazed back at him cryptically. Henry clearly recalled setting the walking stick by the door. He could not have been holding it when he tied the knots, for that required both hands. And no one carries a walking stick when he climbs a chair to hang himself.

There was no way it could have found itself in his hand. Henry looked up at the lamp. There it swayed, a bit of pink rope dangling down like the necktie of a drunk, rocking back and forth like the lantern of a ship at sea in a storm. This was an oil lamp, with no bulbs to break. And its red glass was unbroken.

A Simple Sacrifice

He had climbed to his feet, and was righting the chair on which he so nearly ended his life when he heard from the stairs the lighthearted chatter of Laurel and the somber replies of Manfred.

"You'll love what I have done with the chamber..." she was saying as she stepped into the room. Her eyes suddenly widened as her memories struck. Her eyes darted from Henry's face to Manfred, who was smiling genially, his foot passing over the threshold.

Lithe as a lioness, Laureline leaped to the small end table where lay the syringe and her golden comb. Out from a little drawer she drew a kitchen knife as long as her forearm. With a harpy scream, she launched herself at Mandrake slashing with the knife and making a shallow cut on his brow and cheek. His eyes grew dark and stormy as his memory returned, and he fended her off, slapping the knife spinning out of her grasp, grabbing at her wrists, wincing as she bit him.

The limbs of the thickset man and the short woman were intertwined. Her spine was bent back almost to breaking. Perhaps he was manhandling her, or perhaps he was murdering her. There was blood on his face, and more blood on his forearm, but whether the knife cuts had been shallow or deep, Henry could not see. Laureline was screaming for Henry to come save her, save her.

Henry stepped forward and parted them. Mandrake was not a weak man, but he was smaller than Henry and no match for him.

"Now!" shouted Laureline. "Henry, now, strike now! Hit him!"

Henry took Laureline by the upper arm and Mandrake by the shoulder and forced them apart. He did not let go his grip, but looked them eye-to-eye, turning his head.

Henry saw no madness in the eye of Mandrake.

"What is this all about?" asked Mandrake grimly. "Why is there a pink noose around your neck?"

Henry said, "She says you mean to murder her, and that you already tried once."

"Nonsense," Mandrake said.

"She says that you are lovers, and that when you–"

"More nonsense. I never touched her."

"I saw her knock on your door at night!"

"Then you must have seen me turn her away. It would corrupt the honeymoon for a bachelor to covet and embezzle to himself the pleasures a wedded husband by such dire oaths of lifelong faith and selfless love alone can win. After all I have said—is that what you think of my character? That I am a murderer and a fornicator?"

Laureline hissed, "You cannot believe him! You dare not! Why would I invent such a story? Women don't lie about things like this! He will kill me as soon as he is alone with me in this room." But her eyes were filled with a swirl of dangerous emotions.

Henry said calmly, "Manny, I cannot take the chance you might be lying."

Mandrake said, "It looks like you damned well have to, old man! Unless you have something else in mind?"

Henry said, "Very simple. We all three step out of this chamber. I close and lock the door. Then I melt the key."

Mandrake said, "What will that do?"

"If none of the three of us ever return to this chamber, my poor outward self never remembers that I am in love with a would-be murderess. The two of you end up with an unhappy marriage, but alive. You see? Then it does not matter who trusts who or which of you I believe. The door is shut. We have all made a sacrifice of our personal happiness to save the others, even though we will forget why we are unhappy. We will do the right thing, but not know we had done it." He took the keyring out of his pocket, and held up the key with the red rose image for its bow.

Laureline said, "My idea is much more fun and delicious!" And she reached back with her free hand and snatched up the little bottle of heroin. "You promised me his death. I charge and compel you to abide by your promise!"

Henry then felt all the pains of that morning tremble through his bones. Sweat was pouring from his skin and stinging his eyes. A pounding dizziness swirled into Henry's brain. His thoughts scattered like a cloud of insects. He felt his bowels loose, and the strength of his sinews unknit. Laureline pulled her arm from his shivering and nerveless grip. The keys dropped to the floor with a bright chime of noise.

Henry found he could not prevent himself from throwing his body at Mandrake, any more than he could have prevented his finger from flinching away from a hot stove. Henry's vision narrowed to a black tunnel.

He saw his own arm, moving by itself, striking toward Mandrake's heart with his walking stick. As his eye fell on the amethyst ring, however, he regained control of his hand and turned the stick aside, so that it struck instead against Mandrake's upraised arm. A flash of light went off.

Mandrake with his other hand pulled a small green book from his coat pocket and held it up, saying words that came from his mouth with a sound like a trumpet.

The darkness burning in the corners of Henry's vision receded, and the pains in his limbs were gone. He found himself on his knees, his walking stick in his hand. Mandrake was lying on his back, his right arm deeply cut, bleeding heavily, the little green book still clutched in his left hand.

Neither man was in a position to stop her when Laureline stooped, snatched up the keyring, and ran in a clatter of heels and a lilt of girlish laughter around the curve of the chamber toward the white hexagonal door at the far end.

Chamber within Chamber

Henry rose to his feet, threw the pink rope off from around his neck, and strode angrily after her. He could hear her heels echoing from around the spiral turn. An inner panic told him to run. He increased his pace.

He came into view just in time to see her stepping into the beams of blinding light issuing from the open portal. The sound of strange music was all about him, lutes and buzzing reeds, the throb of horns and beat of tambours, the skirl of bamboo flutes.

He blinked and tried to focus his eyes. He could see the chamber beyond the hexagonal portal: Each wall was covered with floor-to-ceiling looking glass of beaten and polished silver, and the panels between the mirrors were covered with mosaics of diamond grit, spelling out words in a language he did not recognize, the cursive script that looked like scimitars, kukri knives, and pothooks. The walls met at obtuse or acute angles, as there were nooks and bays opening out from a nine-sided rotunda. There was a tall dome or perhaps a chimney midmost into which four tall silver pillars, inscribed with spiral lines of writing in Hebrew and Latin, disappeared, their capitals hidden by the lip of the dome. Directly beneath was a silver-basined pool on which floated lotus blooms. The webwork of reflections from the pool danced across the roof, and were reflected in all the mirrored walls.

Laureline splashed into the middle of the pool which was up to her mid-thigh. She turned toward the portal, her expression one of awe and astonishment. She threw back her head and laughed a deep and throaty laugh. Her long hair lifted and spread to either side of her, pushed by some motion of the air Henry, from his position outside the silver-walled chamber, could not feel.

She rose up off the ground as if pulled by unseen wires, and passed behind the lip of the upper dome.

That sight was not so strange or shocking that it made Henry forget his friend, lying motionless back around the curve of the wall. Henry ran quickly back to where Mandrake had fallen, and was relieved to see him sitting up. Mandrake was trying awkwardly to staunch the flow of blood from his right arm with his left hand.

Henry ripped off the hem of his cloak to bind up Mandrake's arm. "Sorry, fellow, but what did she do to me?"

Mandrake said, "I've never seen anything like it. A shadowy line of smoke came out of the little bottle and reached and touched you. It had fingers. It was an arm. A freakish thin arm made of shadow came out and grabbed you by the heart!"

"And how did you stop me? With that book? You made the pain go away."

Mandrake shook his head as if to clear a fog from his thoughts. As he sat, clutching his bandaged arm, his face began to look more calm, less bewildered. "No, no. In the excitement of the moment, we are forgetting the exact order of events. All that happened was this: When Laureline showed you the bottle, you were overcome by temporary insanity, willing to do anything to get your next fix of heroin. So, when you rushed at me with your sword, naturally I reached into my pocket for the first thing I could find, which was my book. I threw the book and it knocked the bottle of heroin out of her hand. The moment you saw the heroin was gone beyond all recovery, you snapped out of it. That's all."

Henry looked back and forth, and then down at Mandrake. "That could not possibly be what just happened here."

Mandrake said, "Certainly it is. Look there." And he pointed at the broken shards of the bottle on the floorboards. It had struck the stones of the fireplace and shattered.

Henry pointed silently to the little green book with brass clasps still in Mandrake's hand.

Mandrake stared at the book in surprise.

Henry said, "If you threw the book, why is it still in your hand? And if I struck you with a walking stick, why is your arm lacerated rather than contused? The flash of light I saw also went off the last time I swung this stick. The first time, my mind convinced me I had opened a tin lantern; the second time, that some bulbs in the lighting fixture had broken. And, thinking back, I remember the same light when I stuck open the cellar door downstairs. But that lamp there is an oil lamp, and it is not broken. This time, the deceiver, the curse, whatever it is that makes us explain away what we are not allowed to see, it could not come up with anything convincing. It was caught flatfooted, presented with a strangeness too extraordinary to cover over."

Mandrake fished a tiny key out of his pocket, unlocked, and

opened the little book in his hand. "The first half is in Aramaic. The second half is in Koine Greek. Those are not languages I read."

Henry said, "And when did I learn how to field-dress wounds? Come along. The answers will be in the next chamber."

Mandrake said, "What is in the next chamber?"

"The same as this, only one step further in." He blinked in confusion. "What happened to Laureline? Wasn't she just here? We were talking about… something…" He snapped his fingers. "The inner chamber! She was trying desperately to get into the chamber."

Mandrake leaped to his feet. "Dear God! You're right! Lorelei was just here. The moment she stepped over the threshold, we forgot her." He began loping around the curve of the chamber, running toward the far wall. "She could be doing anything with the papers in there!"

"Papers?" Henry ran after.

"Contracts and covenants. Legal documents. Estate papers, wills, that sort of thing. The Deed to the Wrongerwood House. Mr. Twokes, the other lawyers, and I have been going over the wards and bounds pretty carefully these last few days, setting things in order."

The hexagonal portal was open, and silvery light was shining in beams from the mirrored walls of the inner chamber. The music of flutes and zithers poured out. Laureline was not in sight.

Henry said grimly, "Let us go in. We are not who we think we are."

Their ears popped as they crossed the threshold. Each man staggered and blinked as an inner and deeper life poured into his soul.

The first man said, "My name is not Henry Landfall."

The other said, "I am Mandragora."

Chapter 13

The Third Life

Landfall and Lanval

Sir Henwas Lanval of Avalon was blinded for a moment. He passed his hand before his eyes.

Now he hefted the sword of ancient days in his hand. The blade was Galatine, and had been carried before him by Sir Gewain, also called Sir Gwalchmai the Mayhawk of Camelot. Sir Gewain had challenged him that the eyes of Lady Tryamour, Lanval's beloved from the Elfinlands, were not more fair than the gray eyes of Queen Guinevere. The matter was put to the trial of tourney, but Sir Gewain lost the famed blade to Sir Lanval. The peculiarity of the blade was that it shined like thirty torches when it struck the ill-begotten or accursed. Small wonder that, even in the world of men, Sir Lanval never let the hawk-shaped grip from his hand.

This very day, this far-famed blade had slain two of the talking animals, wolf-warlocks who took the shapes of men, as they contested the narrow way, or sought to force the doors; and the light of the sword had driven away the Dark Prince, greatest of the Soul Eaters, who fled from the brink of Le Coupee on wings of membrane. The Great Lion of Sark had risen from its eternal sleep before the doors of the House when the wolfish men approached, and Lanval with his sword had come to the aid of the noble beast.

And on previous nights, he had departed this chamber, some charm of the Silver-White Lotus Chamber allowing him to keep his memory for an hour even in the dull airs of the outer world. He and his blade had flown to the aid of Mandragora. They had fought side-by-side, defending the house from the Dark Prince's servants and the talking animals that besieged it in battles that he later remembered only in his dreams.

Lanval looked down at himself. He was clad in white, with hauberk and winged helm forged by the dwarven craftsmen of Brising, slaves of Albrecht who had escaped his dark world. The white surcoat was adorned with the image of an ermine spot beneath three roundels.

They also had repaired for him the great sword Galatine, that had so unjustly and treacherously been used in his hand to break the wards and shatter the back-gate of Wrongerwood House, and allow the Unpitying Fair Damsel, Lorelei of the Lake, entry into this sacred house. She by her spells had been attempting for two years to enter that house, but had never been able before then to bring her memories. Always before, she had been powerless inside here, forgetting all her arts. The sword had not been broken, but in sorrow its fair light had been quenched when Lanval, or, rather, Hal, had used the sword's virtue to force the door to the cellar here.

The dwarves had used the hoof of the White Ox of Oxford to burnish the blade to gleaming brightness once again. With a tremor of fear, Lanval now recalled his battle of riddles with the water-monster Vodonoy to recover the ox hoof. Lanval blessed the mist which had hidden that true scene from his eyes. The mist had disguised as well the smoky cave no foe dared approach, where Lanval slept, for he slumbered in the coils of a baptized and repentant dragon of monstrous size. To his eyes then, it had seemed nothing more than a tobacco shop.

The knight turned and looked at Mandragora the Thaumaturge, who was dressed in his robes as a blackfriar, with his scholar's hood upon his head, and the book of miracles in his hand. Lanval said, "How could I have been so confounded by such small things? Why were my eyes so blind? We were at war, deadly war, the whole while."

He looked left and right. The many mirrors and many nooks of the chamber were confusing to the eye, but he saw no sign of the green-eyed girl.

Mandragora said, "My aunt and cousins were slain by the mermaid's song, and made to drown themselves. Lorelei forced the old caretaker away from the house, but good hap allowed me to find Gwent mab Nodd, called Nodenson, who was the knight of the black-scarred face still keeping watch over the Badbury Rings. The caretaker's keys I gave to you."

"Ah, that is why she cried out his name when she ran afoul of his protections in the cellar. And the Wolfhound brothers? Are they talking animals as well?"

"Yes, but baptized, and they rend the other wolfenkin as wolfhounds rend wolves. They are the Hounds of God, the *Canes Domini*."

"Many talking animals escaped! And I did not slay the Dark Prince, who is the chieftain of the blooddrinkers. We must see to the walls!"

"You forget the day. On Holy Saturday, when the world mourns Our Savior in the tomb, the evil wights are bold to assault the strongholds of ancient memory. But now is Easter Sunday, and the bells of Saint Peter will drive them forth. We must deal only with the Unpitying Fair Damsel found here. And quickly! For I see her mischief!"

One of the mirrors had been opened like a door. Behind was a cabinet made of dark wood, and piled high with parchment bound with ribbons, scrolls, librums, folios and quartos, grimoires, manuals, and books with iron padlocks.

Lanval said, "Is anything missing?"

"Of a certainty," said Mandragora. "But what?"

"Wait! Now I recall. I saw her spread wings and fly upward."

"Wings? Then she is something worse than a mermaid."

Sons of Smokeless Fire

Mandragora and Lanval stepped to the brink of the lotus pool, and stared upward against the light overhead, which poured in through a crystal dome. The four pillars upholding the dome had hollow capitals in the shape of iron cages. The bars of the cages were wrought in the twisting shapes of runes and sigils, and the four letters of the Tetragrammaton were written on the four sides of each cage.

Within the cages were djinn, creatures of pure fire. It was from them the light came, along with black clouds and fumes that filled the dome above.

Mandragora raised the green book in his unwounded hand and spoke words that rang and echoed like golden bells tolling. *Qui facis angelos tuos spiritus et ministros tuos ignem urentem!* Immediately a wind stirred in the silver-white chamber, and the black clouds cloaking the dome grew transparent to their sight. Now they saw Lorelei in her true shape, short-haired but winged like a black swan, laying elegantly atop a cornice that ran around the lip of the dome. She was a foot or two from the bars of one of the pillars. The folded wings which now draped her naked body past her hips, in the outer world, had looked to their spell-caught eyes like hair.

Lanval hefted his sword and saw how high above them she was, forty feet or more. "I have no bow and arrow. How can she fly? I thought she was a mermaid, a river daughter, or a nix. I thought she hid her fish-tail in shoes enchanted to give her legs a human seeming."

Mandragora said, "No, she merely likes shoes, since she had none to wear in the unpitying fair world from which she comes. She dances the elf dance on lakes in the moonlight, craving praise and sorrow of men, their love and their grief. The legs are hers. But what is she doing?"

And then he cried out in anger and woe, for Lorelei, smiling archly, took one of the papers from the sheaf she held and thrust it in through the bars of the cage. The paper touched the chained foot of the iron-winged djinn, and the cage bars vanished like vapor, and the dome sagged where the pillar's support was absent. A crack appeared in the crystal. The djinn arose in a clatter of iron wings, fires before him and behind, shouting triumphant blasphemies and defiance against heaven. The being of fire whirled near the top of the dome, a tornado of dark smoke, with branches of further darkness reaching upward from its blazing skull like the tines of a crown.

Lorelei looked down with mirth and malice in her emerald eyes. "Ah! Is my little poppet come to play? My lover who I, with such labor, enchanted to adore me—what can you do now, now that you have played your part, and opened up this door to me? Here are the writings, oaths and contracts signed in blood, by which the older things trampled by Arthur were made sanctified. And look! I have set one free! It is your doing, lover! If only you had kept your word, kept your purity intact, kept trousers on and let the luscious and forbidden apple linger sweetly without a taste—but that was too much to ask, was it?"

She pointed at Mandragora. "Go, son of fire, regent of Iblis! Nasir al Khuddam! Slay the wonder-worker!"

But the voice from the fire said, "First free my brother Shasir, and my sisters, the *jiniri* Hassa and Massa!"

"Burn! Burn and consume, for Mandragora is the scholar by whose grammarye you are bound! His tales that penance will return your long-lost unsmoking forms to you, clean and bright, were but lies to deceive you."

The tornado of fiery darkness flew down, and the roar was a storm.

Mandragora held up his book, and around the book when it opened, there came a rainbow which burned like an emerald. And the fires of the rainbow, Lanval saw, were words written in the three languages of Man, the Latin of Europe, and the Aramaic of Asia, and the Hieroglyphs taught to the Pharaohs from long-drowned Atlantis. Thunder and lightning fell from the black cloud all around Mandragora.

Lanval stepped between the two. His shining sword parried the first bolt of darkness, and then a second, but the force of the Djinn was too great for him. Electric shock threw him from his feet, and a screaming wind flung him against a far wall, and the silver was dented.

Mandragora flung aside his cloak, and, behold, beneath his robe was full of stars. He stepped over to Lanval's fallen body, his book of emerald brightness still held high, and stood with one foot to either side of Lanval, crying out, "*Statuet turbinem in tranquillitatem et silebunt fluctus eius!*"

The black wind tore at the chamber to the left and right, throwing tiny fragments of silver and diamond here and there, and great wet sopping lotus leaves, but the roaring force did not touch Mandragora nor Lanval.

"Henwas, can you move?"

Unpitying Fair Damsel

Lanval groaned, saying, "I don't know if I can—I cannot feel my hands and feet. I am pretty badly burnt."

"Can you reach into the pocket in my sleeve and pull out a little silver mirror?"

Lanval coughed, and stared at the blood which spilled out over his chin and breast. His white mail coat was blacked and stained, and from his blacked skin of his arms, raw redness oozed. But he managed to force his numb and trembling fingers into the pocket of Mandragora's strange robe, in which stars and comets burned and turned.

He withdrew a small eight-sided looking glass smaller than his palm. "I have the glass. Now what?"

With his wounded arm, Mandragora reached into his billowing sleeve and pulled something out, something alive. Lanval marveled when he saw it. It was a dove.

"Hold up the glass in front of my familiar's eyes."

The effort pained Lanval greatly, and his charred fingers left red stains on the little mirror, but he held the glass, trembling, before the bright eyes of the little white bird.

Lanval expected to see some change in the bird, but the little creature merely stared blankly at the mirror, cooing.

Mandragora said to the bird, "Comforter, great spirit that flies between my tower in Elfland and my place of exile here, fly to my chambers in the Otherworld and return with my wand. You will forget who you are when you go, and will think yourself nothing more than a lost bird, but by my art I will place in your mind the suggestion that you want to carry a bit of bright straw that you find back here, back to the hand that feeds you grain. Now go!"

Around them, the djinn roared and lashed at them with black wind, but it could not reach through the green emerald rainbow. Mandragora tilted the book in his hand, and the top of the rainbow opened outward, forming a road or chimney up which the little bird quickly passed. The bird flew past the djinn, past the tops of the pillars, and found a small crack in the dome, and passed out beyond.

Lorelei from above the two men dropped a mocking laugh, her wings flapping lazily, as she fed a second document into the bars of a second pillar. Loudly over the wind of the first djinn still battering the emerald barrier below her, she cried to the trapped spirit, "Once I release thee, great Shasir, older than Adam, pass quickly over the walls into the Sleepwalking World. You will forget who you are, and think yourself but a thunderstorm, or some other natural disturbance of the air. Slay the Talking Animals protecting this house. Find the Dragon-Prince of the Soul-Eaters, the Impaler, and bear him here on wings of storm. Go!"

With a deafening noise, the crystal dome was broken from the two remaining pillar tops and flung away into the high blue sky, toppling into a thousand bright shards that fell no man knows where.

Lanval saw the dove, a white speck against the red light of dawn, flying away from the house.

Lorelei called down sweetly, her voice loud and shrill over the wind: "My master, the Prince of the Soul-Eaters, is nigh, living in a gutter, drinking whiskey that will never soothe the craving for blood that torments him. His host is gathered here, each one called by a silent voice inside him, called by their true selves, burning!"

The black whirlwind now broke the circle of green light protecting Mandragora, caught him up in the air and flung him headlong to the far side of the silver chamber.

Mandragora, on hands and knees, bruised in his face, nose running blood, shouted back, "You shall not prevail, Lorelei."

"Watch and see!" she called.

The black-crowned whirlwind left Lanval and hurled itself upon Mandragora. Again, he opened his book, and three columns of light, green as spring grass, softly arose from the floorstones around him. The windstorm drove him to his knees, but the tongues of forked lighting flew wild, striking the silver walls, leaving him unharmed.

Lorelei flew toward the next tall column, reaching out with a document toward the iron bars that held one of the two remaining djinn bound in place. But she mistook the wildness of the winds the djinn had let free, and a sudden turn of the wind flung her downward.

Lanval, despite his pains and wounds, made a prodigious leap then, while she struggled with her wings against the gale, and grabbed her slender ankle. He was twice her weight and more: down the two fell into the lotus pool. She sputtered, and he sighed at the ease of his burns, which vanished away in those magical waters like a dream.

Lanval, his strength restored, and Lorelei found their feet. He twisted her arm behind her, and placed the tip of his bright sword between her perfect breasts.

"Call off the djinn afflicting Mandragora! Send it out swiftly to protect the Wolfhound brothers!"

Lorelei held a handful of dripping papers and parchments. With a furious gesture she cast them into the air, where the whirlwind caught them and spun them to each quarter of the chamber. "I release my power of command over ifrit, djann and djinn! Nasir is now his own master! Whom do you think he will slay?"

The djinn roared with laughter.

Mandragora called out to Lanval, "I can hold off the creature until my wand is brought. With that, I can force the spirit back into a brass bottle."

Lorelei called out gaily, "And if my Master arrives here first, you both will be consumed by inches, screaming!"

Lanval shifted his grip on her, pinning both her elbows behind her folded wings. The dark-haired beauty arched her back and smiled alluringly, teasingly, at Lanval, ground her shapely hips against him.

He held her to him, threatening her with his sword. He shouted to Mandrake to bathe his wounds in the pool.

Mandrake said, "The same contract binding the djinn permits that the pool they are forced to guard may cure what wounds they inflict here. Its waters will soothe no other ills."

Lorelei cooed in a mocking, dry tone to Lanval, "Sweet lover, what do you recall of the World of Exile? Were you born there, among the death and suffering and pointless misery afflicted by an uncaring and distant heaven? Or was it all taken from you? All your poor, pathetic memories? Have you never wondered how we came to be here, living like this, disguised as Sons and Daughters of Eve?"

"I am the son of The Grail Knight. My father showed me the cup when I was a boy, still with heaven's innocence in me, so that the shining rays were visible to me: and in the Blood of the Grail he anointed me."

"And after...?"

"We moved to New York, and he opened a used bookstore."

"Fitting mission for one of the boldest knights of the Table Round!"

"Silence, lilim, daughter of Lilith!"

"Should I be silent? Or should you know why we dwell here in utter unmemory and amnesia? Here is the tale of the Exiles! The triumph of the Father of Dragons was nigh. He is that same worm that tempted Eve with knowledge; eating also of the Tree of Life, the subtlest of creatures could never die, and grew with every passing year, till the land could not hold him, and even the sea was in torment to hold his bulk. He took his tail into his mouth, and his stinger tail piercing his own tongue, wrapped the whole world in his scaly belly. His hunger is such that he must eat, and he gnaws faster than he grows. The world was about to be split like an egg, when the Exile was proclaimed. All of us, friend and foe alike, knight and wise man, elf or scaly drake, was flung into this place of forgetting! It is not the spell of witches that robbed you of your glories, Son of the Grail Knight—it was heaven's last desperate act! The final burning of all bridges back through the perilous woods and wilds of myth and lore to the gardenlands of paradise! The way is closed, and all of us lost ourselves, as a stopgap to stave off utmost defeat—a defeat for you which is now at hand!"

The sword grew dimmer in his hand, and Lanval saw with horror that its virtue came from his own heart. As soon as his spirit failed, the sword would again go dark, and then he would be defenseless against both djinn and lamia alike.

Mandragora called out over the noise of the winds, "Each passing year, their forces dwindle in number. The Sons of Light, even forgetting all their triumphs, do not forget their virtues; but the Children of Darkness, forgetting their black crimes, sometimes turn away from their vices, charmed by the simple humans we here live among."

But the emerald columns of light around him had bent and broken, and the dark wind was driving him back, step by step, toward the hexagonal portal, trying to hurl him back into the world where he was a scholar, not a magician.

She laughed. "It is not our numbers that dwindle each day, but yours! The Silver-White Lotus Chamber was built to spread the narcotic power of the Lotus Pool across all the worlds on the wings of captive genii, so that the dream is not interrupted. Now that we possess the pool, it will only be a short time until we discover how to break it, and wake the world, and show them the serpent that circles the globe! Men can only have the heart to stand against us when their eyes are held, and our true power and true beauty and dark majesty is hidden from them—how do you think they will prevail against the naked forces of the night world in all our terror and glory?"

And the bright sword Galatine grew dimmer yet, and the girl touched the tip with her tongue, and it did not draw blood. "Your sword is getting dull. Having trouble keeping the blade erect? Are you suffering from cutlery dysfunction, Sir Knight?"

The White Wand

There was a flutter of white light in midair, which, at first, Lanval thought was a trick of the many looking glasses. Then he saw the dove, with a slender sliver of straw in her beak, fluttering down from the broken dome to land on Mandragora's shoulder.

Mandragora knelt and took up the sliver of straw the dove had dropped. He whispered a word, and immediately the sliver grew into a wand of white wood, a fathom tall and as big around as a man's thumb.

Suddenly the whirlwind seemed to have no power over him. The air howled and battered him and threw lotuses and water from the pool, nails and diamonds and shards of silver from the walls in reckless spirals, but not even the hairs of his head were disturbed. He stepped over to a silver wall, opened a panel as if it were a medicine chest, and took a flask made of metal from it. He raised the staff and spoke. "*Et daemones credunt et contremescunt.*"

In a moment the wind had stilled.

The Dark Prince

But at the same time, a black and whirling cloud surged down from the sky and filled the space where the dome once sat. There was a roar like thunder, and a flash, and from the cloud a man was dropped down into the lotus pool.

It was a long fall, and Lanval looked on with alarm, while the green-eyed girl in his arms shrieked in exaltation. The falling man was thin to the point of starving, dressed in rags, his pale skin showing through the many rents in his garment. He struck the water, but somehow, did not sink. Lanval stared in startled recognition at the pale and gaunt face, the bleary eyes, the mouth ringed with cold sores.

The water drenched him, and it was as if the false memories of the outer world were washed away. He stood, and he rose until he was taller than a man, a Dark Prince, dread and grim and pale of skin, iron-crowned and armored. He reeked of blood, and slowly, ominously, a pair of great, black, leathery wings extended from his shoulders.

Lanval wished he could flourish his crucifix, but it was under his hauberk, and there was no squire at hand to unlace the mail shirt and allow him to reach it.

The Dark Prince held up a mace like a scepter, and from the ball of the mace, almost too thin to be seen, came dozens, hundreds, or thousands of fine wires, red with human blood, issuing like strands of hair. The strands reached up through the broken dome to the cloud and spread in all directions out of Lanval's sight.

The Dark Prince spoke, and his voice echoed from the hollow places in his chest like the voice of a man buried prematurely echoing from his coffin. "All my slaves into whose hearts my little thorns I put, I hold up this my truncheon, and make the threads of little thoughts grow tight. Come to me, in this place. Come all the worlds of the night." He lowered his gaze onto Mandragora. "Wonder-Worker! How long do you think to hold that power of heaven at bay? You wrestle with a thunderstorm! You cannot prevail, any more than you can bring the dead to life."

Mandragora threw the wand clattering to the silver floor. Immediately it burst into bloom, flower and leaf. It was a dogwood wand, for the flowers were small and white with dark eyes. "There is a heaven above the middle airs of the world, where no air stirs, and the shadow of this grim spot called Earth never brings the night."

The Dark Prince did not bother to reply, but the scorn on his pale face was plain. He turned his face toward Lorelei. She was still struggling in the single-handed grip of Lanval, kicking at his shins, and snapping at his face. And still the Dark Prince made no attempt to aid her.

Instead he said only: "Daughter of Lilith, child of tears, you have done well this day, and brought victory within my grasp. But your task is not yet complete. See that you set about it! As for me, I go now to find the sources of this well and poison them with the poisons from my mouth."

And, even as he spoke, his armor turned to crocodile scales, and his jaw elongated, his skull narrowed and flattened, and his crown became the horns of a dragon. Arms and legs shriveled to nothing, and from his spine a new body nine yards in length sprouted, finned like the body of an eel, but with a tail like a scorpion. His body was like that of a great snake, his beard like that of a goat, his teeth were those of a lion. Only his eyes were the same, terrible and cold as the eyes of no innocent beast of prey nor carrion eater ever could be.

He dove into the water of the pool, and somehow, in pure defiance of the laws of earthly geometry, even though the pool was no deeper than two feet or three at the most, the dragon sank down and down, seeming to grow larger as he did, and was lost to sight in the murky distance.

Lorelei laughed and laughed. She ignored the sword at her heart as she cried out in maddened glee, "This is the best day of my life!"

The Seal of Solomon

Mandragora whistled to his dove, who flew up to another panel, one which Lanval had seen opened before, filled with parchments, books and scrolls. The dove poked around the papers, cooing and billing, and turned her pale head toward Mandragora with a motion of the wings that seemed just like a shrug.

Lanval was still holding the dripping, wet girl. He saw the problem. Mandragora had taken up his staff again, and with it charmed the second djinn who had brought the Dark Prince hither on his wings. Mandragora had managed to stuff both of the freed and immense djinn into the absurdly small brass flask. Now he stood with the staff touching the mouth of the brass flask, but there was no stopper, no way to seal it.

"Looking for this?" Lorelei still had her elbows pinned behind her back, but she twisted lithely to one side, and was able to bring her left hand snaking over the curve of her hip. On her ring finger was a golden ring inscribed with four Hebrew letters, and set with a dark stone bearing the Star of David. "I took it from your papers when I found the covenants your djinn were forced to sign!"

"Is that what you need to stopper the brass bottle? A moment and I will have it from her," said Lanval. He sheathed his sword, released her elbows and grabbed her left wrist. But now her wings unfurled, and she was half in the air, and he was being battered by her pinions, and she was offering him kicks and curses and ineffectual blows with her small and delicate fist.

But Mandragora said, "The ring of the Seal of Solomon cannot be removed by force. Like all rings of power, it can only be freely granted."

"And if I kill her?" asked Lanval.

Mandragora said, "An unarmed girl? It is not in your nature. And no, even then the ring will not serve."

Lorelei landed, and, ceasing to struggle, she pressed herself against Lanval and ran her hand over his armor, seeking he knew not what. Annoyed, he caught her other wrist, and they stood there eye-to-eye, like dancers before the waltz.

She tilted her head to one side, and pouted and said, "Wonder-Worker, what would sealing away but two djinn do? Once the Dark Prince of the Soul-Eaters finds the root of the fountain of the lotus, he will envenom the waters, and the dreams of the lotus-eaters that you have used to blot out all the ancient glories of the darkness from the minds of men shall end, and mankind awaken to the terrible, unanswerable truth!"

Lanval said, "The chivalry and wisdom of all the earth are not so easily overthrown!"

She showed her white and perfect teeth. "As easily as Camelot was cast down, Sir Fool. Your Arthur knew of the fornications of Guinevere, but for the sake of the realm, and to prevent the accusation and trial of the friend of his heart, great Lancelot, he hid the truth, and so the Table Round was shattered, and so bastard son and faithless father slew each other, Mordred and Arthur, and the wound from the spear of Arthur was so great, that Mordred's shadow was broken on the ground, for the sunlight passed all the way through his body!"

Lanval said, "Arthur is in Avalon, recovering from the wound that Mordred dealt, and the years and seasons in that land have no power to pass away, save when the three fair queens grant them leave to go. Here in the mortal world, time flies. There, time tarries. Evil prevails but for an hour."

"An endless hour, as eternal as the fires of Hell!" she exclaimed. "How have you not discovered it yet? It is not clear? You are in exile here, robbed of thought and memory, because you are one of us. You are evil, a servant of the darkness. The only difference is that you do not know. Heaven does not need your help, and neither will your deeds unmake your crimes. You will be as damned as we, unforgiven, for any goodness that forgives evil condones it, and to condone is to aid, and to aid evil is to be evil, is it not? The only way heaven retains its precious purity is by condemning its knights and defenders to the flame once heaven is done with them."

"I am loyal," said Lanval.

"To your lusts!" she said. "Each time we met, I stole a little of your force of will from you, so that the days had no meaning, and your duties went undone. Remember your dissertation paper? Remember how you never worried about finishing it? That was my enchantment, draining away your ambition!"

"What? A paper?" he scoffed. No force on earth killed love as quickly as the realization that one had been played a fool. He clung to this, struggling to tear his heart back from her uncaring clutches. "Do you think I am vexed with such petty things as this?"

"You promised your teachers, did you not? So you broke your word. This made my enchantment stronger, for next, I was able to lure you to the island of Sark, you and your lovely bright sword, to meet with Manfred and tour his house, while Manfred was about to be eaten alive by the sea-hag, my mother. Had you been diligent, the lure of seeing me on outings would have passed you by, and the deeper lures I sank into you later."

And, when Lanval had no answer to this, she turned her head. "How did you escape her, by the way? My mother, I mean." This last she called across the chamber, to where Mandragora was standing, holding the wand with both hands, with the open brass flask on the floor beneath the heel of the wand. His expression was weary. She said, "My mother Ran was worshipped as a goddess in times of old, and the blood of children spilled into the sea to feed her, and your King Arthur took that all away from her. How did you survive her?"

Mandragora said, "I was unafraid, because her grisly hut on chicken legs, filled with the bones of her victims, looked to my eyes like an ill-kept middle-class house. I thought I was a student visiting the home of my prospective inlaws, and so I was polite, even though greatly tempted not to be. And I said my grace before the meal, and so I was not thrown into the soup pot and cooked. What fairy in the history of the world has ever slain a mortal man who was courteous?"

She sneered, "The djinn have not such niceties to mind. As soon as your wounded arm is wearied, and you drop the wand again, the djinn will tear you limb from limb!" Then to Lanval, she said, "Do you see how he suffers, how he bleeds? All this is your doing. Every night we came together in unholy concupiscence, I drained a little more from you of your manliness and might, a little more of your virtue and purity, until you were my puppet and his betrayer; a wretch who has dealt a grievous wound to his friend.

"Will you claim that the mists clouded your vision, forgetfulness fogged your mind, and so you did not know how dire the penalties would be? But you did not forget right and wrong, for these are the same in all worlds. You will never see the Grail your father saw now!"

He released her wrist and drew his sword, which blazed like thirty torches with his wrath. She saw the death in his eyes and screamed in unfeigned panic. A small, quiet voice in his heart told him not to strike. He seized her by the hair, which was short, but still long enough to take in hand, and cut off a great hank of hair on her left side, from bangs to ear, leaving stubble.

"Let that be a sign of your shame," he said, "Even when you depart this place, and the comfort of forgetfulness is around you, you will still be half-shorn. Half-bald, and today is the wedding day. You will need to hurry to find a wig or an opaque wedding veil!"

"I have no need to leave this chamber, ever!" she said, flying up out of his reach. Then she saw her reflection in the silver walls, and she clutched her marred hair with both hands, and began caterwauling and weeping piteously, in woe for her offended vanity.

"Marriage is a sacrament," Lanval answered. "It will give you the right to enter these grounds, not as thief, but as mistress. That is what you creatures are seeking, isn't it? The dark powers need the sons of light to grant them lawfulness, honor, and praise. To come here again as the bride and mistress, you will not miss your wedding."

Her eyes were full of hate. "Then I will host a full house of guests. More and more of us are coming, and more, summoned by the Darkest Master. Once you step away, you both will forget that the two of you are nothing more than a bridegroom and his best man!"

Lanval gazed levelly at her lovely, malice-filled eyes, forcing himself to acknowledge what his lady love had become, what she had ever been. It was not this creature that he loved, but a pure fabrication, a fiction. He was like a man who had fallen in love with a character played by an actress in a movie or a television show.

Their love was nothing. It was pure fantasy. Invention, if not delusion.

And yet, his memory recalled to him in vivid clarity, the moment when he grabbed her in front of Wrongerwood House, and she had gazed up at him, the unguarded anguish of her heart visible for an instant in her eyes.

It had been a trick, of course, another fancy of his mist-clouded mind.

And yet, a small voice whispered very softly to him that in this unguarded moment, he had seen the truth, that only love, true love, could reach so from one soul to another.

He dismissed the lying voice as the faint remnants of his Rose Crystal self.

Mandragora called Lanval over, and then, unexpectedly, tossed the unstoppered flask at Lorelei. She caught it more by reflex than design.

Something small and jangling dropped from between her breasts when that happened. Lanval saw it was the keyring of the seven keys. It was yet another impossible thing, for she had been naked except for her diamond pendant this whole time, and could not have been hiding the keyring in her hand during all these struggles and commotions.

And yet, the keyring had fallen from her neck. He saw the diamond of her necklace held within it tiny images of the shoes and clothing she had discarded, and a scrap of her dress, including the pocket where perhaps the keys had been held, was sliding back into the surface of the diamond, shrinking and vanishing.

The little dove flew up and snatched the keyring out of midair, and, laboring mightily, managed to bring it through the air to fall at Lanval's feet.

To Lanval, Mandragora said, "Sir Knight, take the wand from my hand, and hold it touching the floor like so. By my Art, I have made it so the winds cannot harm us until they snatch that wand from your hand. Do not let it from your grasp!"

Lanval snatched up the keys, and then took the wand in hand, and leaned on it. Lorelei above him, seeing this, upended the flask upon him and two dark tornadoes flew out.

The winds tore at Lanval, and pried at his hands, and bruised his arms, but the wand seemed somehow to be as sturdy as an iron

pillar gripping the core of the world, so not only was the wand not
snatched from his hands, it did not move an inch. Lightning and
black fire fell around him, but, as Mandragora had promised, it did
not harm him while he held the wand.

Mandragora took out a little velvet box from his pocket, and
held it up. It was the wedding ring for tomorrow's ceremony. With
no ado, he threw it into the little lotus pool. As had happened with
the dragon, the mirrored silver bottom of the pool seemed not to be
a bottom, to be much farther away than could be accounted for, and
so the ring, too sank out of sight.

Lorelei drew a pin from her hair, and transformed it into a knife.
She swooped toward Mandragora, but now the little white dove flew
up and flapped its small and gentle wings in her face. She screamed
in horror and panic, and flapped her vast black wings and flew up
and away. The dove chased her to the top of one of the broken pillars,
where the two female djinn still groaned and cursed.

Mandragora said to Lanval, "Henry, look in that little mirror you
took from my pocket. Gaze into your own eyes until you recognize
yourself. By my Art, I place in your mind the suggestion that we
have both been through an uproarious bachelor's party, during which
I lost both of the wedding rings, his and hers, and that I dare not
go to my own wedding without having them replaced. My best man
and I will go to the Brising Brothers in the middle of the night, where
we will pound on the doors until they let us in."

Henwas Lanval said, "What does this mean?"

"It means there are enchantments beneath enchantments and
worlds within worlds here, and many things long prepared against
this day. Dvalin and Grer will make a fine and fair ring for her hand
tempered in the tears of widows, and me for my wedding band will
bestow the Ring of Youth to replace what I have lost. And this will

cure any poisons spewed by the dragon and keep the living waters of this fountain hale and pure."

Lanval gritted his teeth, because the wind still roared and tore at his hands and fingers. Then, of a sudden, the two dark clouds were drawn up out of the chamber into the dome. Lorelei drew the two djinn into the brass flask she held, covered the mouth with a cork of lead, and impressed the seal into the lead with the ring she wore.

Lanval straightened up, limbs shaking and ears ringing. "And what does that mean?"

Mandragora said softly, "It means Mistress Lorelei has just realized that if the djinn slay the bridegroom, there will be no wedding this afternoon, and she will not be mistress of this house; and even more to the point, if she does not prevent them from blowing down the house or drowning all of Sark in tidal waves, there will be no house for her to be mistress of."

Lanval looked up at where Lorelei cowered atop the pillar, held at bay by the tiny flapping wings of the dove, and its angry little cooing-calls.

He said, "Now what?"

Mandragora said, "Now we leave."

"We leave!"

"We have to take the morning ferry to St. Ouen to beg a ring from the Brisings, in order to catch the evening ferry in time to return for the wedding."

Lanval said, "You cannot be going through with the wedding?"

Mandragora said, "Even if I vowed to break the engagement, my vow would be forgotten once I breathed the airs of the outer world, and I would be forsworn. We would not be allowed to leave this chamber alive if the Dark Prince and his thralls were not convinced you and I were needed for the wedding. Do you think the Light is all-powerful in the world of men, or the world of elves?"

"The Light is omnipotent in all places!"

"Including the places in your heart?"

Lanval was silent, and his cheeks were hot with shame.

Mandragora said, "We who serve the light are weak, and half our service is treason. That is why darkness triumphs, despite how stupid and self-destructive it is. Come! For an hour or two let us walk one last time in the fields the mortals know, in the world where the sun shines by day. We will forget our hard service, our treasons great and small, and the mocking laughter of our foes. It is the compassion of heaven that allows us this respite."

Henry and Mandrake emerged into the Rose Crystal Chamber a moment later, and Hal and Manfred a moment after that emerged from it, laughing over the misunderstanding, already forgotten, that had ended when Manfred fell and cut his arm painfully on the fire irons. Then both men stopped and looked back at the door, wondering what might be keeping Laurel so long.

At that moment Manfred put his hand in his pocket and a look of shock came over his face. For, as he informed an astonished Hal, he had somehow lost the wedding ring!

Chapter 14

The Consummation of the Wedding

A Second Silver Room

The Silver Lotus Chamber in the back of the jewelry shop of the Brising Brothers was smaller, an eight-sided chamber with a pool in the middle, from which only a single pillar rose, holding a captive ifrit at the apex of a smaller dome in a lantern of iron. There were chairs here and a workbench, and a little ways down a silver corridor, a forge and anvil as well. The chairs were a trifle too small for both men.

Mandragora had visited the emergency room of the Island Medical Center at St. Aubin, and his arm was now stitched, wrapped in antiseptic tape, and benumbed with painkillers. He listened carefully to Lanval tell of the various episodes and incidents which had happened, or apparently so, to Hal and Henry.

"How could anyone not be insane in such a world?" Lanval asked bitterly. "We are carrying out missions for an unknown master, for reasons we know not, and whatever is gained or lost in each turn of the card is hidden from us. And my mind and soul were being influenced by that Unpitying Fair Damsel! How is any man to know right from wrong?"

Mandragora said, "Such talk ill becomes a knight of the Table Round. When you besiege a castle, or defy an unknown knight with black and blank shield to combat, what might be gained or lost is not known. No one knows the full consequences of his acts in any world. That is why the laws are unchanged in all realms, the same in all circumstances. Without that, they could not be followed."

"I did not follow them in any case," said Lanval, heavily.

"In the mortal world there is no way to turn time backward on itself, restore and undo the many trespasses, breaches, and offenses we commit, and so there is no true escape from condemnation. We are fortunate that this is not the only world there is. In a higher world there is a magic water which washes all wrongdoing clean, and no waters of earth have that power."

Lanval said, "Why is this water hidden?"

"It is not. Le Seigneurie in Sark is a great and splendid house, a fortress unvanquishable against the endless hosts of the besieging darkness, and greater far within than it seems without, even as a mortal man is. But there are other houses with memories older than those of English lore, who are bulwarks even greater against the foe, and the demons tremble when their bells ring out, or their standards fly. To us, they are quaint old haunts visited by grandmothers, but to them they are as terrible as an army with trumpets and lances."

Lanval said, "Nonetheless, you seem to think the evil will be victorious this day."

Mandragora said, "The world of men is dark and ruled by darkness. Who says otherwise is deceived. But we are not without hope of final victory, albeit the cost will be terrible. Who knows? Perhaps even the tears of that loss can be wiped away."

"Is there no way to escape your marriage to that witch?"

Mandragora sighed. "As soon as I step outside, I forget that there is any reason not to marry her, and, ironically, she is no longer a witch."

"She seems kinky enough. I bet she has a whip and leather lingerie somewhere in her toys."

"Then pity her. People do not turn to such things out of idleness, no matter what some might claim, nor just for sport or seeking to startle jaded nerves. These are the heraldries of despair, born of a desire to demean and unmake the sacred joys of the marriage bed. In order for the tantric magic to gain power over you, it had to be perverse to nature, that is, outside the normal realm of human emotion."

Lanval was annoyed. "What does that mean?"

"In realms where the image of Man is not sacred, and the gift of sexual ecstasy no longer is a source of divine joy, in other words, in any realm where what is hale, and whole, and right and fitting are all trampled and twisted and made abhorrent, in such a realm and there only is where the creatures of the darkness have power."

"Be that as it may," said Lanval, "There is one more realm we have not yet seen." And now he held up the last key on the ring of seven, the key whose bow was inscribed with the image of a black six-petaled flower. "As with the Rose Chamber, what occurred in the Silver-White Lotus room could not have been real."

"Why say you so?" said Mandragora, surprised.

"I held a little stick no fatter than my thumb against the force of a hurricane. A tiny dove that came out of your sleeve like a magician's trick held back one of the Unpitying Fair Ones."

Mandragora said, "The wise know that the things of the world seen with eyes are less than shadows on a cave wall of puppets and dolls held up against a bonfire's light. That fire is a fair image of the sun, and those figurines are fair figures, but until we discover an exit to the cave, we will not see the truth. The wise man learns to trust his soul before he trusts his eyes, and such wisdom is not found turning the leaves of the books of scholars. That wand was a branch from the Tree of Life, whose roots run deeper than the world. While you grasped it, you could not be moved."

"And the dove?"

Mandragora merely shook his head and smiled. "You have been told many times about the Comforter, and you have forgotten."

"How can I fight, if I see nothing aright?"

"As all men save Adam before the Fall have fought. Blindly."

"Your words do not comfort me."

"Then seek for comfort where it is found, not in words of men! And yet you see our mission before us aright!"

"Howso?"

"We must enter the Silver-White Lotus Chamber before the wedding, so that Lorelei will have no power to command the lion to rest and call the wards and barriers to part. The Ring of Youth has the virtue to unpoison the wellspring of the lotus dreams, and drive the *dracoule*, the little dragon, to the surface. But even your blade will not then prevail to drive the Dark Prince from the chamber. We must find the final door, and open it. There is no victory for us in the silver world nor the red, and it either must be in that final, most inner chamber, or none at all."

"And if there is no victory at all?"

"Must you ask? Then the Dark Prince poisons the dreaming fountains of the world, and all men see the naked face of evil wrapped around the earth, too vast for earth or sea to hold, and either they go mad, or they bow down and serve and worship it."

"Then let us hope we both have deeper and more inward selves who see a way out of this maze of forgetfulness and darkness."

Both men knelt and prayed before departing the jewelry shop, and they ate the bread and drank the wine a prince of light had brought down from heaven and left for them there.

The plan miscarried badly.

The Well-Wishers

All the common folk of Sark were there, in the Edwardian chapel beneath the octagonal belltower, and many from Guernsey and Jersey as well. The noble families of England, Wales and Scotland sent their parties, and where they went, so came gentlemen of the press; and Laurel's family from the Hartz Mountain of Germany was more extensive than expected.

Hal and Manfred kept looking for excuses to break away from the well-wishers before the ceremony, as each was prompted by some unspoken urge, some urgent thought that something vital to the wedding had been left in the Rose Crystal Chamber, which was to be the bridal suite. It was also the room in which the bride and her maids were now making their preparations. So Mrs. du Lac, the Mother of the Bride, and Margaret, the Countess of Devon, acting in the place of Manfred's late mother, stood guard against Hal and Manfred, and would not let any male enter into the newly decorated chamber, nor see the bride in her equipage, lest they see too soon, and bad luck ensue.

Laurel had braided her long hair and wound it into a kind of lopsided turban before fixing it in place with pins and a coronet of roses, all hidden beneath a veil. It was a strange coiffeur reminding Hal of an old man combing sideburns grown long to cover his bald spot, and he wondered why she did it. But then again, who could explain the eccentricities of women?

Then the ceremony commenced, and it was too late. Hal, sweating and nervous in his tuxedo, was so distracted by the fact that the Price of Wales himself was present, that he almost missed the nod from the Archbishop of Canterbury when it was time to pass the ring to the bridegroom.

The urgent desire to enter the Rose Crystal Chamber vexed him, although he could not recall why it was so important. What had he left in there? He had been drinking heavily during the riotous stag party, and his memory was blurred. Something embarrassing no doubt had been left sitting in some obvious spot, some terrible thing he had to remove or hide before the happy couple entered it for their joyful nuptial consummation. He was just glad that when they dressed the bride, no one had noticed it, whatever it was.

He had been to his sister's wedding a few years ago, and he knew that, as soon as the wedding mass was over, the photographers would press forward, issuing commands with the barking authority of prison guards, for photographers were no respecters of persons. So he waited until the mass ended for his opportunity.

But it would have been discourteous indeed to step away from the reception line and miss shaking hands with the royal family, and so there was no opportunity then. After, Hal had to give the toasts both sincere and risqué that followed, and at that point, the male guests all decided as a group, including the young Marquis of Carabas and the gray-haired, but grinning Duke of Devonshire, to hoist Manfred on their shoulders and haul him bodily to the honeymoon suite in the Rose Crystal Chamber, peers and lords mingling with servants and tenants unabashed, shouting ribald advice, while the ladies and their maids hurried a blushing Laurel into and through the throng, keeping pace with Manfred.

And then it was too late. The happy mob was streaming into the upper corridor. What else could Hal have done? Could he have stepped into the cheering, riotous throng and belabored them with his walking stick? Hal thought Manfred looked a little panicked, but he remembered no reason why Manfred should be worried, not on this, his wedding day, aside from the worries every bridegroom is right to worry.

The door to the Rose Crystal Chamber was locked, but Laurel's mother stepped over to Hal and pushed him toward the door, and all the men cheered. Laurel said, "Allow me!" and plucked the keyring from Hal's fingers. Again, what else was he supposed to do? Argue with the bride on her wedding day?

The throng put Manfred down, and a dozen hands picked up Laurel and shoved her into his arms. Manfred put an arm around her shoulder and another under her knees, smiling to all his well-wishers, "The Roman and his Sabine Bride need a little privacy now, you barbarians!"

Meanwhile she leaned from his arm, reached out with the key, and undid the lock. The well-wishers were all standing behind the happy couple on the stairs rank on rank. Hal, more by instinct than reason, tried to close the door against the laughing, raucous, joyful throng, but they came down the stairway, and it would have been easier to halt an avalanche.

The Ill-Wishers

Then they were within the Rose Chamber, brilliantly decorated, and the cheering became a little more hoarse and sinister. Henry looked up woebegone at Laureline. Their eyes met, remembering both their constant and deep love for each other, and her look of shock and guilt. Henry knew she had recalled her attempt to have Henry murder Mandrake. Mandrake, for his part, finding himself holding a woman whom he was being forced to marry, whom he did not love, and, in fact, who had tried to kill him opened his arms and dropped her, reaching for the keyring.

But the roaring mob, looking rather more shaggy than they should have, with green eyes that glowed like the eyes of wolves, called out in gruff and hoarse voices. The Duke of Devonshire, gray and lean like a famished wolf, and the Count of Carabas, grinning like a panther, heard the Countess Margaret shout out a command, and the two grabbed Mandrake roughly by his arms. Laureline's blue-dressed maids of honor, her sisters, had grown strangely more beautiful and alluring than they had appeared even a moment before, and now moved with a sinuous, boneless grace, like undersea creatures, and one of them picked up the keyring and returned it to Laureline before Henry could move.

Henry was taken roughly by the shoulder by Laureline's mother, Ran du Lac. The old woman seemed to have miraculously put on about one hundred pounds of blubber and fat, and turned her skin an unhealthy shade of pale green, her teeth to iron, and her scent to the rotting odor of old fish. Henry stared in bewilderment, aghast. Another young thug in a tuxedo seized his elbow, and one particularly shaggy-looking farmlad from the village bit his wrist and pried his walking stick from his hand.

In a moment, cursing and struggling, the throng moved around the spiral curve, and Laureline had worked the lock to the silver hexagonal portal. Into the wall it slid, allowing light and music to escape.

A Rout of Monsters

With roars, shouts, howls, and yips of excitement, the throng of people shoved themselves into the chamber, dragging Manfred with them, and then the talking animals, walking mermaids, lamia, maneaters, ghouls and witches, their apparel glistering, and making a riotous and unruly noise. They threw down the bridegroom Mandragora, and bound him fast with chains.

The bride's mother was now a four-hundred-pound toad-like thing with a gaping mouth full of jagged teeth like a shark. Her three sisters from Germany were singing and swaying on the surface of the waters, creatures of appalling loveliness, but with eyes devoid of humanity or pity.

The bride now threw aside the veil, and unfurled her dark and swanlike wings. "Oh, my beloved! Shall I not couch with you this day?" And her sisters stripped the bridal dress from her, and the bride in mockery lay down and wound her white arms and legs like snakes around the bound and helpless Mandragora, and she bit his neck and licked his blood.

Henry Landfall was pulled over the threshold easily, but Henwas Lanval, champion of Camelot, was not so easily taken. He threw the monsters from his arms, which now were garbed in mail, and smote a beast who tried to bite his neck, but was now prevented by the aventail of his winged helm. He fell upon the talking beast who had taken his sword, grabbed its snapping jaws with both gauntlets, put his knee against its back, and reared and broke the vile creature's spine.

The sword was in his hand, and the first wolf-faced monster who staggered back, blinking and blinded, died from a blow through heart and lungs, that also cut the gargoyle standing directly behind. Blood splashed across the white surcoat, and stained the proud ermine there, warm and glorious.

Over the screams and shrieks and roars of the beast-men and the blasphemies of the magicians, Lanval cried out the name of Arthur, and took a step, sweeping the blazing blade in a mighty sweep to the left. Paws and claws and tentacles and heads, human and inhuman, were swept away in a prodigious spray of blood, as the magic sword parted flesh and bone. He swung the other way, and men with the heads of hippogriffs and wolves, and rodents, and bears and all the vermin that prey on man or his livestock, were severed from their bodies. He drove the blade up to its hilt into the throat of the Duke of Devonshire, a corpse-mage who had used his own dark magic to raise himself back from the dead into hideous mockery of life. Lanval laughed the laugh of madness. No one else in the chamber was armed, no one else was armored. With his back to the door, he could slay as he willed, like Arthur himself that glorious, red day at Badon Hill!

With a mighty swing he decapitated the catlike and inhuman head of the Count of Carabas, but the head rolled rapidly away, eyes blazing brightly, yowling for help.

And those yowls were answered. Up from the pool in the center of the chamber stood the pale and grim prince in his black armor and blacker crown. He spread his vast wings of membrane, and spoke a word of blasphemy, so that all in the chamber were thrown to their knees or hindlegs, save only Lanval.

The Dark Prince pointed one long white finger at Mandragora. Lorelei had an athame, a witch's knife, driven a quarter-inch into Mandragora's neck. The Dark Prince said in a bloodless voice, "Throw down your sword and surrender, and I promise you will pass freely from this chamber."

A small voice inside him told him not to listen, but the mother of the bride reached into Mandragora's mouth with a pair of scissors, and cut his tongue out. The sight was so horrific that Lanval was drained of strength. He presented his sword to a gargoyle with the head of a bat.

Nine monsters grabbed Lanval, forcing him to the ground. Quickly chains were twined around his arms and wrists, legs and an-kles. A baboon-creature bit through the leathern straps and yanked his helmet off, and seized his hair in its stinking paws. The baboon pounded Lanval's face into the floor over and over again, breaking his nose and dislocating his jaw.

The bat thing proffered the great sword to the Dark Prince, who took it in hand. There was a hiss as the grip of the sword burned the unholy hand of that prince, but the gaunt man neither winced nor cried out. The light of the blade died, and the metal turned black.

Next, without a word, without a sign of remorse, the Dark Prince stepped over to where Mandragora was chained and tongueless and helpless, and drove the sword into the intestines of the wonder worker, and upward into his vitals.

Lorelei released the chained man, her fingers trembling before her mouth, her eyes wide, shocked. "No!" she cried.

Blood and offal and the fluids from other organs gushed out. The tongueless, inarticulate and lingering scream of Mandragora was horrible beyond description.

And the cry went on and on and on. Lanval forced his head backward against the grip of the baboon-thing. The flesh around his eyes had begun to swell, but he could blink through his own blood to see what was happening to his friend.

A minute passed, and then two, and still Mandragora did not die. A voluminous wash of red blood like an apron poured out of his opened stomach, over his legs, and into the lotus pool, and more blood poured out, and more, and still it did not cease to pour. Mandragora cried out again, but then closed his jaws, and hissed, and ceased from crying. Instead, jaws clenched shut, he stared at the Dark Prince unblinkingly, his face expressionless.

The Dark Prince said, "Did you say *no* to me, my pet?"

Lorelei's eyes were round with panic. "Indeed not, Master! I was cheering for you!"

"Women are weak weapons. You always fall in love with those you lure."

"Not so, dread and dreaded Master! My heart is cold and dead!"

"Bah! A woman's heart. Turn him prone."

Lorelei, with shrill little grunts of effort, receiving no help from any in that chamber, managed to roll the chained body of her husband onto his face. She pointed to the wedding band, gleaming like the sun. "My master, he wears the Ring of Youth, which restores all wounds. While he wears it, he cannot die, and I cannot be mistress here, and all of what is his be mine. Unchain the hand!"

Mandragora was roughly pulled by two large wolfish animals into a sitting position, his intestines in his lap, and his left hand, the one that bore the ring, behind him. Each monster in the chamber took its turn trying to pull the ring off his finger. It would not move.

The Dark Prince said, "Larger than they seem are all such rings, for the weight of worlds is held in little things. It must come willingly from his finger, or not at all."

Lorelei said, "What shall we do? His blood is sacred while he wears that ring, and may counteract the poisons you have spread into the pool, my Master."

He pointed at Lanval. "Sever the hand of the knight and bring it here!"

A creature with the head of a boar said, "He is armored by the Brisings' lore. No weapon of ours will bite."

But Lorelei said, "Galatine will cut him. For me, for my sake, he, willing himself woe, sought to end his life. That a miracle preserved him is not to his credit: the sin makes his armor unwhole."

The Dark Prince took the sword, and stepped over to Lanval, while the baboon pinned Lanval's chained hands to the floor. Lanval jerked his arms when the Dark Prince swung, and shoved the baboon's skull into the path of the descending blade. The head of the baboon burst into flame, and fire gushed from its mouth and eyeholes, and the body danced and twitched and died. Lanval smiled.

The blade did not want to cut him. Sometimes the blade turned sideways in the grip of the Dark Prince, and sometimes it missed and struck the chain, and twice more Lanval, in his wild struggle and his fury, managed to wrestle some hapless creature of the many holding him down into the way, so that they were struck instead. But the Dark Prince neither smiled nor grew tired, and his spirit was greater than the spirit in the darkened blade, and at last the thing was done, the blade cut through wrist bones and blood and flesh and rang against the floorstones beneath. Blood spurted, bright and red, from the veins in Lanval's stump.

The Dark Prince lightly tossed the severed hand onto the bloody mess that was the lap of Mandragora. "Place the ring on the finger of Sir Lanval, and his life will be saved, your own forfeit. Or keep your hand closed, and watch him die, and endure now and always an eternal pain like your master, the Fisher King. Slaves! Pull Lanval to the lip of the pool, and let the blood from his wound pour in and pollute it. We shall watch as Mandragora watches him die."

The creatures pulled Lanval to the pool's edge. He was directly across the chamber from Mandragora, and rough hands and crooked claws pulled the lolling head of Mandragora upright, so he had an unobstructed view of Lanval. Oddly, Lorelei was kneeling next to Mandragora, both her hands on his shoulder, looking at him anxiously.

Lanval said, "Don't do it! In the name of God and Christ, do not let them prevail!"

As a cruel sport, and to silence his cry, the monsters held Lanval's face beneath the water for short, and then longer periods, until he breathed water into his lungs. This made his heart race, and the rush of blood from his stump grew faster and stronger as his skin turned pale and more pale.

There came a roar of triumph from the chamber. The monsters and abominations all began cavorting, and the lamia and lilim began to sing. Through the haze of blood in his eyes and bloodloss in his veins, through the reddish waters and his swollen eye-bruises, Lanval squinted and saw Mandragora, quite dead, and the Ring of Youth thrust onto his own severed hand, which lay upon the floor.

A beast had taken up Galatine, its blade as black as mourning weeds, and thrust it through the breast and heart of Mandragora, until an inch protruded out his back and scraped against the floor.

Then the eyes of Lanval went dark, and his soul was not in his body.

Birds and wolves were tearing strips of flesh from the face and body of Mandragora. Lorelei, next to the still-warm and bloody corpse of her husband, had her hands in her face, her shoulders shaking, and next to her, taller than a man, the Dark Prince loomed, staring down at her. For the first time, his face showed expression, a hatred and jealousy that stretched his mouth and narrowed his eyes, and made all the muscles in his jaws twitch horribly. He was biting his own tongue for spite, and the tongue tip was writhing between his teeth like a dying worm. The small voice in his heart told Lanval that the Dark Prince hated with a bitter hatred the fact that when he died, all his slaves and serving women would cheer. Ran, the mother of the bride, was crouched like a shapeless vast toad at the feet of the Dark Prince, and, like him, was ignoring the celebrations and howls of victory, and watching Lorelei.

As she knelt, weeping, her tears hot on her peerless cheeks, cheeks he had kissed so many times, Lorelei let out a sudden high, sharp cry. Without any other fanfare, her black wings fell from her back, disintegrated into a cloud of feathers, each of which floated gently to the ground.

"Let her be killed, O Master," the bitter old green-faced hag croaked and pointed at the now-wingless form of her daughter. "Some enchantment in this house has replaced her heart of stone with a heart of pink and girlish flesh."

Lanval heard over the noise and commotion, for he opened his eyes, and found himself, not chained and maimed with his head in the pool, not with a dozen creatures on his back (he could see his old body across the chamber, motionless) but instead inside a new body, his flesh pink and uncalloused, untouched by sun or time, which had grown on the instant out from the hand no longer severed. On his finger gleamed the Ring of Youth.

He stood, even while the commotion of beasts and warlocks were calling out, "Hurray! Hurray! Our bride is made the mistress of this house this day!" Here was the sword Galatine. He plucked it out of the breast of Mandragora, and shouted as the light of thirty torches exploded from the blade. While the Dark Prince glared and blinked, and the obscene obesity of Ran clutched her blinded eyes and screamed, Lanval plunged the sword first into him, and then into her, killing them both stone-dead in the blink of an eye.

The monsters in the chamber, taken unawares in the middle of their cavorting celebration, screamed and yowled. Yet more than half were shouting still in triumph, unable to hear the warning cries of their fellows. They had not seen their tall Master die.

A white dove landed on the naked shoulder of Lanval. "Do not forget your Lord nor your promise! You are not here to slay, but to unlock the inmost truth."

"The key! Where is it?"

He knew where it was. He reached down and took the necklace from between the breasts of Lorelei. She did not resist, nor did the chain, for the cunning of the dwarfish craftsmen made the catch come open at his touch, and the keyring dwindled and hidden inside the reflections of the gem popped out into the solid world, and jumped into his hand.

The dove flew up, and to the left. Lanval followed, striking down any pale-face witch or wolf-toothed talking animal who rose to stop him. He threw aside a large and silver looking glass where the dove landed and pecked. Behind was a door as black as night, eight-sided, and midmost was an image of a flower of six petals, painted red. Beneath the flower was a lock and ring. He inserted the key and twisted, and sheathed the sword, pulling on the ring with both hands.

He could see nothing before him. All was black without any sight or sound. But behind him was the smell of blood, the sound of a weeping girl, and the roar of monsters.

"Behold the Black Iron Moly Chamber," said the dove.

In he leaped.

Chapter 15

The Place Beyond Falsehood

The Life Beyond Life

Harry could see nothing, nothing at all, except the whiteness of a small shape he realized must be the dove, and yet, he could feel the peace that extended from it, shining upon his soul, as one might feel the rays of the noonday sun. The bird was growing larger, glowing. It had become a being of light, larger than a man, larger than an elephant, perhaps larger than the universe, and it flew ahead of him, urging him to follow.

They passed down a colonnade of tall, pointed arches.

He heard the sound of rushing waters before him and behind, and the sound was like that of one of the great sea caves hidden below the island, but somehow he knew this was much larger. Once only he turned and looked back, and saw a small round chamber that seemed to be orbs within an orb, the outer layer covered with stars like the robes of Mandragora, and the inner layers each lit with its own small lamp, one glass sphere within another, and a tiny dot of blue at the very center, smaller than a doll's house.

Ahead in a round place surrounded by a ring of slender pillars, was a table and two chairs, a bottle of wine and a loaf of bread, and tableware of silver and gold. There was a quietude here, a silence, that reminded him of the most solemn halls at Oxford, of the most ancient libraries nestled away in some mountainous retreat, vast and somber. When the being of light stepped next to the table, she blazed more brightly and drew aside a part of the darkness with her hand, so that he could see.

Harry saw his father Henry standing there, hale and whole and alive.

Behind his father stood smiling in silent joy his four grandparents, one of whom he knew only as a child. And behind them, in older clothing, his eight great-grandparents, and in the light he saw a great crowd of people standing, rejoicing silently, in concentric ranks around him, each in costumes older than the previous rank. Only the front two ranks he recollected from photographs in family albums. Those further away came from times before photographs.

And the memory crashed in on him that at his father's funeral, his father had been standing next to mother in her wheelchair, speaking to her, and she speaking back. Father had taken her hand, and they had danced on the grave, laughing, defying the empty victory of death.

Later, Father took the widow into the Black Iron Moly Chamber in the center of the church where the ceremony was, and spoke to her of many things, sad that she, for a short time, while she lived under the delirium of mortal life, would not remember seeing him. But he came by every day for lunch, and spoke with her, and read to her from the newspapers, and when he touched her hand, she remembered herself and her wits no longer wandered. Because of her love, she left her wits in the rose and silver chambers, to see him and be with him, well aware that her son thought her senile.

And not just his father.

The young man looked deeper into the chamber and deeper into his memory, recalling his own marriage. Adam, the father of the noble race of Man, a man of heroic build, tall and handsome, dressed in nothing but his own glory, had met with Arthur and Lanval after the battle of Badon Hill. Adam brought the marriage gift to the bride, to Tryamour the fair sea-fairy, by welcoming her back into his family and lineage, and Saint Guthlac had blessed the union.

It was Guthlac who, much later, after the supposed death of Lanval's wife, when duty called Harry to England on the mission—for he was in the armed services, merely not those of America—had introduced Harry to the Drake who ran the smoke shop. This drake had woken from the dragon-dream of greed and avarice after baptism, but he was still cunning and mighty, and schooled Lanval carefully on his struggles with Vodonoy, who delighted in drowning the hopes of students.

And now Harry remembered walking the campus, and seeing all the masters and professors of Oxford back to the cowled monks who had been ordered by Alfred the Great to found the school wrestling against the sea monsters who now possessed it.

All the people thought dead were still alive, still walking on earth, building, talking, making, doing, and only from time to time, in special chambers where the mists of forgetfulness were forgotten, did the mortals see the ancestors who lived among them.

His father held the chair and sat him down, and poured the wine for him. Then his father broke the bread and blessed it, and put a morsel before Harry, and before the empty chair.

All at once, the light was gone, and the vast chamber was empty, though the peace and solemnity remained. The only light came from a seven-branched candlestick in the middle of the table. The roar of unseen waters was still about him, but distant.

But now Manfred sat across from him, all his wounds healed, a look of peace and ease such as he had never imagined grim Manfred could wear shining from his smile.

"You seem happy," Harry said.

Manfred said, "I remembered all my family whom I thought dead. They walk among us, and talk to us, and, when we see them, we remember. And we remember we have felt no loss. All the chambers of my mansion are occupied, and if I am not with an aunt or uncle or forefather from the Middle Ages when I step into the study, I will meet Semiramis or Iapetus in the kitchen. As soon as my eyes were turned away, however, I was lost and hopeless again. Such was the curse of forgetfulness."

"What crime brought that curse on mankind?"

"Ask Adam. It is for forgetfulness Methuselah prayed at the locked gates of paradise when Adam died. I will not say it is not a curse, but I will say far greater good comes out of it than even the most wild optimist has dreamed. I am not going away to my palace beyond the stars in the heaven above heaven now that I am—"

"Dead?"

"Awake. You are still a sleepwalker. The Earth is wounded and is suffering amnesia until her soul heals. Then the bandages will come off, and the perfection we were meant to dwell inside will be visible to all, remembered and unhidden. No one is dead. No one has ever been dead."

"And Tryamour? If the mermaid I married in the Middle Ages is still alive, I should have resigned myself to being chaste in my affections, rather than dreaming of marrying Laurel du Lac, so as to avoid unremembered bigamy."

"Marriage, of course, ends when the dream called mortal life ends. That is the wording of the vow. We who are awake neither marry nor are given in marriage, but the joy we have so far exceeds carnal pleasures that what you have is merely a pleasant dream. We have the reality. She will be far closer than any wife when you return here on Doomsday, and holier than matrimony. Erotic love is singular, because it is precious and sacred, but divine love can be shared, because it is more precious and more sacred."

"Tryamour is why I volunteered, isn't it?" For more memories were coming back to him. "It was Tryamour who urged me to go. My sister heard my dead wife's voice, and that is why I was sent away from my mother, despite how the family needed me!" He shook his head sadly, glad that each time he reviled himself for his heartlessness, he had been innocent as spring rain.

Manfred nodded. "My marrying Lorelei actually acted to grant her a soul. The dwarves gave her the ring of tears, and with it, even a witch in the silver chamber can cry. She will come to love this house, since, once fully out-of-doors, she will recall only that she loved Manfred, and that he died on the wedding day."

"I suppose she will be angry that I stabbed her mother. Or was that a dream as well?"

Manfred said, "A sleepwalker does take real steps, and sometimes he stumbles. Lorelei will remember that the horse drawing the bridal carriage down the car-less road of Sark was startled by a gaunt, thin bum, who was trampled, and the carriage overturned, killing an old duke, a young count, and Mrs. du Lac. And me."

"What happens to Laureline, now that she is a widow?"

"Her anger and resentment will be recalled only if she goes into the Red Crystal Chamber. She will there recall that you and she conspired to kill him, and know she had a hand in his death. Perhaps by an overdose of morphine, or perhaps you beat me over the head with your iron-hearted walking stick: the chamber will decide. Her true evil nature will be recalled only if she goes into the White Lotus Chamber. But she will recall one other thing as well."

"What is that?"

"I will tell you at my funeral. I have already used my spirit to suggest to her that she go find the Old Gardener, who is the only one who knows how this mansion is set up. Living with the Old Gardener, and wearing a soul freshly bestowed, she will come to love this house and this life, and the human world, and will no longer busy herself with destroying it."

"But in the silver version of reality—whatever reality might be— have not the dark powers won control of the chamber?"

"Do you think she will allow any of them back into her house, now that it is hers? Their victory would never have been possible, in any case. All the terrors and powers of the Night World, we recall here, in the Iron Moly Chamber, that they are no more than thoughts and inclinations, temptations, appetites, suggestions. To harm Man the law does not allow. But they may, by their dark suggestions, by their soft and secret words, they may persuade a man to destroy himself. That, the Law does not forbid."

The young man sat for a moment. They said grace, ate the bread and drank the wine. Because he was warned the bread was very precious, he held his napkin under his jaw to make sure not a single crumb fell and was lost.

After the meal, he sat with his head in his hand, looking down. The floor here was dark stone, but every flagstone was cut with the image of the moly flower. Manfred neither moved nor fidgeted. He supposed that the imaginary limitations of life within mortal and impatient flesh could not annoy nor tempt his friend, now that Manfred was awake, and the long nightmare of ignorance, pain and loss was over.

Eventually he spoke again. "It still hurts. It was still terrible. We took desperate risks. I was so tempted, so confused, so confounded. I could not tell right from wrong. I tried to kill myself. I hated you. I broke my vows. I never did do that stupid paper."

"You did it the first month in the Rose Crystal Chamber and promptly forgot it. In the Silver-White Chamber, you remember the gifts your late fairy wife Lady Tryamour gave you, and so you had a purse forever full of gold. Here in this chamber you have a treasure more precious than gold which never runs out."

"Which is why I could buy motorcars and yachts and still be a penniless student."

"You were never truly a student. Oxford has fallen to the enemy, and you were there to protect me."

"And what about my mother? What was the truth there?" But it was coming back to him now: Elaine, who was also a champion of the light, was beset by winter storms and evil hounds, and by her own husband, who had sold his soul to darker powers. His inner self served the wild wine-god of ancient Greece; his outer self had a drinking problem. His father had put his mother, one of the greatest champions of them all, into a dark house where her bright light had been dimmed.

"I will be traveling to talk to your mother, who can see me, and to your sister, who cannot," said Manfred, "Pray for us that we might prevail, for hers is a battle as grim as yours. What is your question?"

He had only one question. "*Why?*"

"Why what?"

"Why was I allowed to be placed under this love charm by this green-eyed witch? Why all this risk? All the pain? What was it all for?"

Manfred said: "To save her soul."

All for a Lone Soul

He waited for Manfred to say more, but Manfred merely sat there with the unearthly patience of a man who recalls that he is immortal.

He said, "All this we went through? It was for that horrible woman? To save the soul of a night-world creature?"

He intended the words in anger, but even as he spoke, he could hear the note of awe and wonder in them.

Manfred said, "Is that not enough, to save a soul? She is a young woman, no more, no less, though one who thinks herself a witch."

"Then is there a great red dragon wrapped around the world, or not?"

"The dragon is far more terrible than that! He is larger than worlds; he is wrapped around every human heart. The world-serpent we recall when we step into the silver chamber is far gentler than the terrible iron truth. You would go mad and perish if you saw him as he truly is, a spirit invisible and impalpable, as bright as the morning star, and far more fearsome than his children, Sin and Death."

"But even if the metaphorical stuff is false—"

"Not false! It was a sacrament, a symbol for a reality too deep for your eyes to see or your mind to grasp. You saw her naked soul. Poor girl! She believes herself to be a monster, a seducer, a siren who lures the unwary innocent to destruction on the rocks of her indifference! This was her sin, and she was proud of it. It was real. It merely was not literal."

"All right, so it was real, but not literal, but even so, what was it all for? Even if I am not literally a knight of Arthur, then why do I feel so much pain?"

"You are the knight of a nobler prince by far. Who do you think provided us this bread and wine?"

"But why all this pain?"

"It was so that my bride would shed a single tear over my corpse."

"It was so much pain, too much! For one girl? For one tear? Is that all?"

"Is that all? That tear is heavier than the weight of all the Earth."

He started to answer, but his voice was choked. Now the wonder he heard in his voice was broken by a sob. He sank to his knees and wiped the tears from his cheeks, saying, "Thank Heavens! Thank the Heavens!"

And he saw a light smaller than the morning star rising in the east, yet it was brighter than the sun.

He beheld the place where he stood. He was in a pond of many little islands, some paved with stone and some bright with green grass, connected by little arching bridges. All around the pond was a garden of flowers and grape trellises, arbors of cherry trees.

A second star rose, and it was also as bright as the sun, and he squinted, half-blinded. Beyond the groves and gardens were hills of beauty, a green land where the glory of spring and summer and autumn were all combined, for the many-colored leaves of fall grew on the same branch gay and brave with the buds of Eastertide. The whole land was garden. Great forests of ancient trees were arbors, and nowhere was there thorn or canker, rotting bark or dry branch. It was as if every unfruitful branch had long ago been cleared away and burned.

A third star rose in the east, and he was dazed by the brightness of it. Yet, dimly, blinking, he saw the mountains looming in the west, scarp on scarp to peaks so white the snow seemed like flame in a furnace. And in the east, an ocean. He longed to trek the miles and leagues toward that ocean and plunge himself in it, for somehow, without knowing how he knew, he knew the waters of that sea were living and alive, deep with passion and power unguessed.

More stars arose, and the whole arch of the Milky Way, and each of the ten billion stars, was brighter than the sunlight of a cloudless noon. The heat from them pierced him through, as if each cell in his body were alive for the first time. He covered his eyes, hoping he was not blind for once and all, and he fell forward on his face.

For the stars were singing; singing for joy. He heard the voice of his father in the chorus, and of other friends and loved ones he had hitherto thought were gone forever. Their joy echoed from the mountains, and the mighty voices of the Seven Seas replied.

> *A single soul alone is saved! Rejoice!*
>
> *Which hellish power a briefest hour purloined.*
>
> *Each light of Heaven, lift pure thy voice.*
>
> *An endless soul to endless joy is joined!*

The Iron Chamber of Memory

Perhaps he fainted, perhaps he slept, but somehow, he found himself on his feet again, and Manfred holding his elbow.

"Hold still," said Manfred. He felt something cool and sweet touch his eyes and ears. "This is the juice of euphrasy and rue, a flower that grows in paradise, as on earth. It will restore the strength of your senses, which are overtaxed."

He opened his eyes. It was dark again, but he could still hear the lapping of the waters on the island where he stood. He could see Manfred, and a small circle around him, but no more.

Eventually he found words, "And what happens now?"

"Life goes on!" said Manfred with a smile. "You may exit the chamber through this door, the door of forgetting."

He pointed and there became visible a distant crystal sphere, set with stars, which held the pathway back up to the Silver-White Lotus Chamber. "And will I go though there, the Gates of Glorious Memory."

Then there came visible in the distance, hanging between two pillars, a gateway set with the sign of an amaranth flower. The bars were gold and intricately wrought. "From the Chamber of Golden Amaranth, I can return to the world of men with no memory loss. I will be able to see and talk to you, and we can meet at lunch times, or during times you will later believe to be dreams. We shall still be friends, you and I, even though, to you, I will be wrapped in a mist."

"That does not seem a very good deal for me."

"Will you not rejoice for my joy! I have won the race! I have passed the test. I gave my life for my friend, and now many crowns and triumphs and ovations await me."

"It will be lonely."

"Only for a while. Only as long as the dark dream of mortal life and the fear of death remains. Come now, even the pagan sages speak of the lives beyond this one. Even now, you forget what you are!"

"What am I?"

"A deathless champion of deathless light. You, of course, will be saddened by the loss of me, even as you come to realize that you love Laurel. She, likewise, will hear the small, still voice inside her, reminding her she loves you. In time, you will have everything you dreamed of. Almost everything. The Grail is in this room, and you cannot see it, and may never again. Sorry. Some of the things out there in that world of many deceptions are real."

"Is that why this chamber is dark again?"

"This chamber is not dark. We are in the light of a thousand suns. Your eyes are being held, so that you do not look on what you are not allowed to see. I wanted you to speak with your father, but you are only allowed to talk to me."

"Because of my suicide attempt?"

"That, and other things."

"But I will just go back to that horrible dream-world of delusion and forgetfulness and commit more wrongdoings!"

"Not if you stop breaking your word, and live like a man. No one forced your surrender to your darker impulses but you! But, hidden in the mists, there is forgiveness to be found too, and the path back to the light. It is a hard path, but you will receive the help you need at every step. The vision of the Grail is at the end of that path, and also Him whose cup it is."

"No, I mean I am about to betray you yet again! You are still alive. Am I to go back, deliberately, knowing that I am to fall in love with the long-haired Laureline! Is she not yours?"

Manfred scoffed. "Don't talk nonsense. In no sense was she mine. I never touched her, I never truly loved her. She lied about that, as she did about most things. In the Red Chamber, she was someone I was suspicious about; in the Lotus Chamber, she was my mortal enemy. Be at peace, my friend. You will love her and she will love you."

"But no more did she truly love me," he protested. "That was simple lust, and seduction so that a lamia could get close to me."

"Ah, but the Grail is in this House! Lust is a dangerous thing to play around with, especially for a young woman. How easy for that base desire to transform into golden love!"

"What happens now to you?"

"Holidays and sport! As for me, my whole family is waiting, all the way back to my most remote ancestors, and we are going hunting in the place humans only see as a dark forest beyond the house. Our game? We hunt lost souls, we huntsmen of the light and our wolfhounds run before us! We are looking for our next Lorelei to turn into a Laurel."

"But when I go out there again, I will think you are dead. Won't I be sad?"

"Not if you listen to the small, still, quiet voice deep inside you."

Epilogue: The Dark Boneyard

By one of those queer and ancient laws with which some corners of the British Isles are still afflicted, the burial of the Seigneurs of Sark must be held after sunset. In the light of the many torches and lanterns held by the villagers, the thing was done. The Bishop of Winchester, Father Ælfsige, recited the words from memory, without opening the great black book in his hands.

Hal could not help but wonder how differently things had been done in times gone by, or in old places where the old ways had not been forgotten. All the stones and monuments of the Hathaway family, and the Collings family before them, the Allaires, and the De Carterets, stood within eyesight of the great house, south and west of the chapel, almost at the low stone wall separating the lawns from the ancient wood. With the dead buried by each family in its own yard, or at the church at the center of the village, none would forget them, nor would they seem departed by so great a distance.

Hal stood there, sunk in utter misery. His best friend had died in a freak carriage accident. It was almost beyond imagining. The incident had taken place at speeds even the slowest lane on a modern highway would have found a snail's pace. The horse, startled by some sickly and thin drunk whom no one knew, had stumbled down a green slope, smashing the carriage to bits along rocky outcroppings. Hal's pangs of inner pain started not when he saw Laurel crawl unharmed from the upset carriage, for then his heart leaped for joy; but when Manfred did not follow her, and Hal knew his heart had not plunged down in grief as far as it should have done. Manfred had thrown his arms over the girl when the carriage flipped, and one jagged metal spar had disemboweled him, while another splinter pierced his back as he shielded her, penetrating his heart and ending his life as suddenly as a sword blow. That her mother had died in the same accident was merely one grief piled upon another.

As the days passed, Hal's misery grew. He was still tormented by his love and longing for the green-eyed girl. Her hair had been half-torn from her head in the accident, and now she sheared the rest of it off in grief. Years and years of growth had been clipped away and she almost seemed a different woman. The outpouring of love and support for her from the islanders, especially Mrs. Levrier and Mrs. Columbine, the housekeeper and the cook, affected Laurel in a way Hal had not known she could be affected.

Hal returned to Oxford and turned in his dissertation. When Dr. Vodonoy had leveled, merely for reasons of personal spite, accusations that Hal had plagiarized the work, the Dean of Graduates ordered the Ethics Committee to look into the matter. As it turned out, Hal had been so worried about the lapses of memory his loss of sleep and overwork had brought on, he had asked Mr. Drake, his landlord, to make photocopies of every single scrap of paper on his desk every day, in the stationery shop next door. But Mr. Drake never returned for his copies, and the clerk there, in a very tidy fashion, had filed them away chronologically, clipped to the receipts, which showed the dates. Hence his landlord could show the Dean a stack of papers as high as his chin showing the exact daily progress of the paper. Hal had seemed so lax only because nine-tenths of the dissertation had been done in the first month.

When the accusations turned out to be false, Vodonoy was shamed, and forced to resign.

Oddly, he also died shortly thereafter. After visiting the smoke shop of Mr. Drake, and berating and threatening the man whom he blamed for the ruin of his career, Dr. Vodonoy was found burned to death the next day, for he had fallen asleep while smoking in bed a rather fine cigar he had just purchased, and it had caught the mattress on fire.

The death was so freakish and odd, and Vodonoy so unloved among the students, that when Hal heard two underclassmen making a crude joke about the matter, Hal laughed, and then, a moment later, when his conscience fell on him like a sea wave, he felt truly horrible. Was he a monster, rejoicing in the death of everyone?

The guilt was unbearable. Manfred had died a hero's death. And yet that horrible and traitorous spark of hope and love and longing would not be quenched in Hal's heart. Was he glad his best friend was dead? The idea was so terrible, that he wished he lived in some world where a magic spell could sponge away all memory of his life, and leave him innocent again.

With such thoughts as these, he went and found an old church, and entered the booth and said his confession, even though it had been so long he had forgotten the formula. The voice from beyond the grille, blessing him with pardon and peace, also asked him a pointed question or two, and offered merely frank advice, but which, in this place, at that time, seemed almost supernatural. "Do not run away from this widow you love until she remembers her feelings, whatever they are, for you. Wait a year and a day."

His first impulse was to flee away from Sark and the strange house forever, and never lay eyes on it again. And yet, to Laurel, he was a firm and close friend, and she asked him to the funeral quite naturally, never imagining the storm of passion in his heart he hid from her so skillfully. And the priest's words convinced him not to obey this first impulse.

When he saw her by the light of the one candle held below her chin, now with her short pageboy bob of hair beneath her veil of mourning, he saw her face somehow wiser and sadder than he had ever seen it. Her saw her lips move, whispering prayers he had never heard her say before.

One by one, the mourners dropped their spent candles into the grave, and the diggers threw dirt atop the coffin.

And, afterward, he saw her blessing the villagers who loved her and whom she loved. Liam Levrier doffed his cap, and knelt, and kissed her hand, and Laurel looked as regal as a princess then, and nothing sly and ironic was in her looks, and there was no bitterness at the edges of her lips.

When the line of mourners started walking back toward the house, she stepped over to Hal then, and smiled at him, and took his hand. He was ashamed at how his hand seemed to tingle at her touch, trembling with joy.

Laurel walked slowly, letting the others get ahead, and out of earshot.

In the starry darkness of that unlit island, her voice seemed clear as music, and he was painfully aware of her nearness, her warmth, her scent. "I have a confession to make," she said softly. "For a time, I blamed you for his death."

Hal started to speak. She laid her silk-gloved fingers on his lips, silencing him. She said, "It is unfair, I know, but I found myself so full of doubts right before the wedding, and my mind was wandering. I think it was beginning to affect my memory. Do you remember the time we went golfing, just to have a day off, just to escape from the stress? I never did find out why you walked off in such a huff. But I so enjoyed that day. It was a time when I could truly be myself, say what I liked without calculating, just walk along with a friend. It is as if I remembered myself then. Well, I found myself thinking about you… a little too much, maybe. And that all came back in a rush when Manny died. So, unfair as it is, I blamed you. As if you had wished for him to die."

"I would hang myself before I would wish him harm," said Hal.

"No, don't do that. It is a sin. And besides, you would look ridiculous." She squeezed his arm. "But at the graveside now, when I was saying goodbye to Manny, I had this strange feeling. It was as if I were the damsel in some old story, about to be eaten by a vampire or a sea monster or something, and that you saved my life. As if you had helped Manfred win for me something very precious, something I had not known I'd lost."

Hal was bewildered. "What does that mean?"

"I mean, I felt grateful. While you never saved me from a monster, you did save me from my old life. It was just a little thing. A day on the golf course. But I decided to stop being an actress in my own life, to stop putting on airs and putting on acts. I want to be an honest woman. And who convinced me to do it? You did."

"I was not trying to."

"It is like a dance. If you try too hard, if you look at your feet, you stumble. So you look at your partner. You let him lead."

He shook his head, too choked by guilt to speak a word. But then the feeling that Manfred was standing behind him, just behind him, was so strong he stopped walking, and dropped the girl's hand and turned.

The night was darker now, and the pale stones of the graveyard seemed to float in the night. The cross above the grave of Manfred seemed like a somber face with level eyes, and a crease of a frown. It looked like Manfred's own expression. It seemed to be speaking to him, and offering a blessing. *You will love her and she will love you.*

All at once, Hal realized with undeniable clarity that Manfred and Laurel would have eventually come to hate each other, had he lived. Manfred, in a very real sense, had sacrificed his life to save his wife.

She stepped closer and looked up at his face, to see his expression in the starlight. "What are you thinking?"

"I just had a strange thought. What if the dead are still among us? What if they watch over how we live, and know what we make of the gifts they give us, and see what we make of the world they left to us?"

For it seemed to him then that Manfred did not want his young bride to live in friendless solitude all her life. Time would pass and life would continue. For now, Hal could be a friend and a stout support to Laurel in her grief, and help her however he could. Perhaps in a year and a day, perhaps longer, Hal could speak his feelings.

The girl took his arm in both her hands, and pressed her cheek against his shoulder. He put his arm around her. She walked with the grace of a dancer on a darkened stage, with no need to see her feet, and he marched like a soldier in a night march, who need not know his captain's hidden plans to love and trust and follow him. All the questions in his heart were calm.

Together, they walked down a dark path toward a strange house, not knowing what fate held, but, perhaps, beginning to know what was held in each other's hearts.

CASTALIA HOUSE

SCIENCE FICTION

Somewhither by John C. Wright
Awake in the Night Land by John C. Wright
City Beyond Time: Tales of the Fall of Metachronopolis by John C. Wright
Back From the Dead by Rolf Nelson
Victoria: A Novel of Fourth Generation War by Thomas Hobbes

MILITARY SCIENCE FICTION

There Will Be War Volumes I and II ed. Jerry Pournelle
There Will Be War Volumes IX and X ed. Jerry Pournelle (forthcoming)
There Will Be War Vol. VI ed. Jerry Pournelle
There Will Be War Vol. V ed. Jerry Pournelle
Riding the Red Horse Vol. 1 ed. Tom Kratman and Vox Day

FANTASY

Iron Chamber of Memory by John C. Wright
The Book of Feasts & Seasons by John C. Wright
A Throne of Bones by Vox Day
Summa Elvetica: A Casuistry of the Elvish Controversy by Vox Day
The Altar of Hate by Vox Day

SATIRE

The Missionaries by Owen Stanley

NON-FICTION

SJWs Always Lie by Vox Day
Cuckservative by John Red Eagle and Vox Day
Equality: The Impossible Quest by Martin van Creveld
A History of Strategy by Martin van Creveld
4th Generation Warfare Handbook
        by William S. Lind and LtCol Gregory A. Thiele, USMC
Transhuman and Subhuman by John C. Wright
Between Light and Shadow: The Fiction of Gene Wolfe, 1951 to 1986
        by Marc Aramini
On the Existence of Gods by Dominic Saltarelli and Vox Day
Compost Everything by David the Good
Grow or Die by David the Good
Astronomy and Astrophysics by Dr. Sarah Salviander

AUDIOBOOKS

A History of Strategy, narrated by Jon Mollison
Cuckservative, narrated by Thomas Landon
Four Generations of Modern War, narrated by William S. Lind
Grow or Die, narrated by David the Good
Extreme Composting, narrated by David the Good
A Magic Broken, narrated by Nick Afka Thomas

CPSIA information can be obtained
at www.ICGtesting.com
Printed in the USA
LVOW13*0046011216

515251LV00021B/345/P